"A well told tale of life as a missile crew member, with a good technical base and great fiction about the *Whiteman Scenario*."
Charlie Simpson, Colonel USAF (Ret), Executive
Director, Association of Air Force Missileers

"McCurdy captures all the humor of the crews and terror of some of those days. This is so what it was to be a Missileer during the hot parts of the Cold War. The pages come alive and I am right back there again."
Dale Manguno, Former Missile Launch Officer

"I thought I'd put this all in my past 30 years ago. I'm reminded that I should pray daily for the brave men and women who stand alert duty and bear this grave responsibility daily,"
Jerry Nielson, Former Missile Launch Officer.

"So exciting and accurate that I sometimes thought I was in the capsule or silo. It brought back memories of my missile maintenance days. I am a slow reader, but I set a new speed record with this book. It's electrifying."
Bob Kazian, 351st SMW Maintenance.

"McCurdy knows how to tell a story; one that is intriguing and horrifying all at the same time. Read it before your friends are telling you about it—because they will."
Sid Davis, Director of Fine Arts, St. Luke's UMC, Houston.

"I lost sleep because of this thing. I stayed up two nights running just to finish it. I could not put it down."
Bob Johnson, Executive Pastor Chapelwood UMC

"The book is TERRIFIC… it is entertaining, satisfying, and the quintessential 'page-turner.' "
Ken Bailey, Author, *I Flunked Sunday School*

# THE WHITEMAN SCENARIO

Thanks for the GREAT EAST TEXAS
Discussions! Fun!

Peace was our Profession —

2008 —

Steve McCurdy

A StoryMaster Press Novel

Published by
StoryMaster Press
14520 Memorial Drive
Suite M-141
Houston, Texas 77079
281-920-0442

Email: info@storymasterpress.com
www.storymasterpress.com

If you are unable to order this book from your local bookseller, you may order
directly from the publisher or the publisher's website.

ISBN: 978-0-9761179-1-9

10  9  8  7  6  5  4  3  2  1

# SOME HISTORY

WITH THE launch of Sputnik and the tension of the Cuban Missile Crisis fresh in the minds of all Americans, the Strategic Air Command (SAC) began construction in 1962 of six Minuteman missile bases. While most of the bases were in the extreme north—in Wyoming, Montana, and the Dakotas—one base was nestled in the heartland of America, in central Missouri—Whiteman AFB. Each base was home to a "wing." For purposes of clarity, we will detail only Whiteman.

Situated a mile south of Knob Noster, Missouri, about 60 miles east of Kansas City, Whiteman was home to the 351st Strategic Missile Wing (351st SMW). The wing comprised three Strategic Missile Squadrons (SMS): the 508th SMS, 509th SMS, and 510th SMS.

Each of those squadrons was composed of five flights: 508th SMS – Alpha, Bravo, Charlie, Delta, and Echo; 509th SMS – Golf, Hotel, Juliet, Kilo, and Lima; 510th SMS – Foxtrot, India, Mike, November, Oscar. Why they are not in logical order will be explored in a moment.

Each of the flights was composed of the Launch Control Capsule (LCC) buried 40–90 feet below the above-ground Launch Control Facility buildings, and ten remote Launch Facilities (LFs) located three to seven miles from the LCC. Using Kilo as an example, the capsule was named Kilo-01 and its ten primary missiles were Kilo-02 through Kilo-11.

When laid out initially, the base was to have squadrons with sequential identifying letters: A–E, F–J, and K–O. However, during construction, it became evident that the water table in southern Missouri was so high that several of those sites had to be abandoned and new sites—much closer to base—had to be built. As a result, the squadrons suffered some alphabet soup restructuring in order to keep all of a squadron's LCCs in close proximity.

Instead of the nearest missile or Launch Control Center being no less than twenty miles from the base, Oscar Capsule actually was built ON base and three of Oscar's ten missile launchers were within four miles of the front gate.

Though K-01 was responsible primarily for its own ten launchers, it could, by turning a dial, monitor any of the other flights' missiles, and vice-versa. Redundancy was the order of the day. In a nuclear war, the potential for huge, catastrophic loss had to be taken into account. As a result, a squadron could launch its missiles with only two surviving capsules.

Within each capsule, two highly trained officers stood "Alert Duty," watching over the missiles and a small red box secured with combination locks. Each officer had a lock, the combination to which only he (and much later *she*) knew. The procedure was that upon receipt of the "War Message," the officers would unlock the boxes and move the launch keys and authentication documents to their consoles. They then would open the prescribed authenticating document and compare its coded contents to those in the message. If the message authenticated, they would insert their keys in switches that were physically too far apart for one person to reach, and turn them according to timing specified in the message. The two officers' key-turns in one capsule made up ONE launch vote. Two capsules (four officers) acting at exactly the same moment constituted the necessary TWO votes to launch all of the squadron's missiles.

Naturally, there were contingencies by which the missiles could be launched by two sets of officers in remote command aircraft should all of the capsules be taken out or disabled.

It is within this context that the events of 1974, fictionalized in this telling, took place.

In 1995, Whiteman's missiles and LCCs were decommissioned and destroyed, according to SALT treaties. Only the on-base LCC "Oscar" remains as a static display and museum. Malmstrom, F. E. Warren, and Minot Air Force Bases have active wings that are on alert at this writing.

**Events**: Though set in a fictional context, the principal events of this story are drawn from a chain of circumstances that actually happened and that, until recently, were classified information.

**Command and Control**: The Command and Control checklists used by the Strategic Air Command then, and Space Command now, are highly classified documents and procedures. The checklists and procedures used here are, therefore, creations of the author.

This story is true in the sense that the precipitating events actually happened. Through months of research and intelligence gathering, the REASON for the precipitating event as it is detailed in the story also is the actual cause. The story is fiction in the sense that the actions and dialogue of the characters are pure invention.

# ACKNOWLEDGMENTS

IT TAKES a LOT of help to research a story that is wrapped not only in Top Secret classification but also in the lore of American history's darkest hour. Even forty years after the fact, these events are as fresh in my mind as if they happened yesterday. Some of the technical details and procedures are not. As a result, I am indebted to many. Here are some of them.

* Ruth McCurdy, my best friend and supporter – and first reader!
* Arnold Friedman, my editor and authorial left brain.
* Bob Kazian, 351st SMW Maintenance—a fount of technical expertise and good ideas.
* Lt. Col. (Ret.) Andrew Cole, Ph.D., a good commander, great teacher, friend, and a magnificent mind.
* Former Capt. Jerry Nielson, a lifesaver and one of God's truly special men.
* Former Capt. Dale Manguno, a smart, funny, insightful man you want by your side in a crisis.
* Former Capt. Bill Kallmeyer—mentor and friend.
* TSgt. Fleming and MSgt. Banks, Oscar Capsule historians, Whiteman AFB. Generous men with hearts for the Missileer.
* Colonel (Ret.) Charles G. Simpson, Association of Air Force Missileers—Keeping traditions alive.
* The Dirty Dozen—Training Class 105, Vandenberg AFB, June to August 1972.

Without the generous contributions and honorable service of these fine people, this story could not be told.

*Steve McCurdy*
*Houston*
*2007*

Schematic of a Launch Control Facility. The Launch Control Center which houses the crew and launch equipment is on the left at about 90 feet underground. The Launch Control Equipment Building is on the right across the Tunnel Junction. The hardened elevator shaft connects to the support building above.

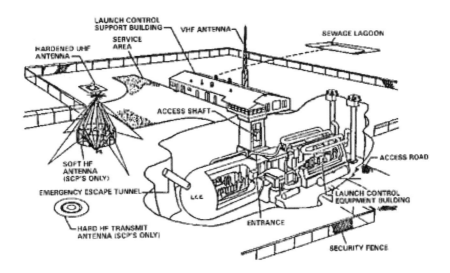

Aerial photo of an actual Missile Launch Control Facility.

Launch Control Capsule - normal operations status

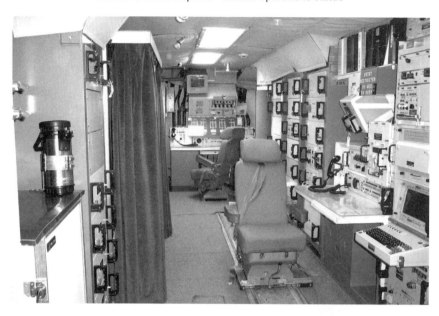

Same Capsule, same angle - under power failure.

Blast door entry to the Launch Control Center.

From the left. Blast door 4 ft thick with 8 inch steel pins that extend into frame.
Angled Pull handle above the seating latch
Two hydraulic pump handles, one for high volume and the other for fine control.
The entry – about 5 ft high.

Minuteman Launch Facility and Missile

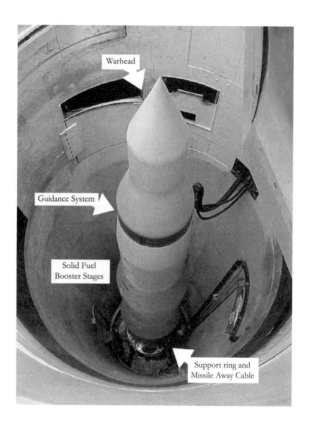

Label 1.     The warhead
Label 2:     Missile guidance system or "can."
Label 3:     Solid fuel booster stages.
Label 4:     Support ring and area of attachmen for the
             "Missile Away" indicator cable.

Minuteman Command Console at DELTA Capsule Museum

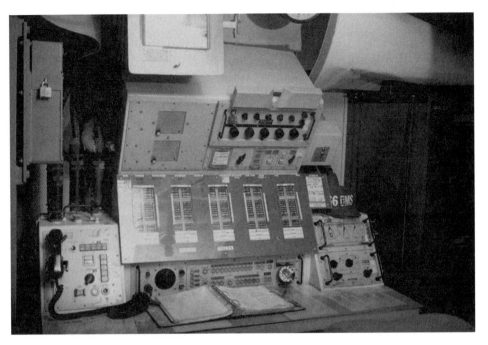

The large panel is the Plexiglas shield for making grease pencil notations on missile status. Each "window" in the overlay reveals two columns of indicators each of which represent status on one launcher. The entire panel represents all ten of the launchers for which this capsule (Delta) is responsible.

Above the indicators are two Primary Alert System speakers hardwired to SAC HQ in Nebraska. Beside it are HF radio Controls. Above is a mirror giving the commander and deputy eye contact. During the cold war a large clock hacked to Greenwich Mean Time and readable from anywhere in the capsule was where the mirror is and the mirror was in the space to the right. These locations are important when picturing events in the story.

Below the columns of missile status indicators is the com-console. The top row buttons are individual lines to each of Delta's ten launch facilities and buttons for outside phone lines. The bottom is in groups: the first three are various radios; the solo button connects to the Flight Security Controller topside, the next five are the individual direct lines to the other Launch Control Centers in the squadron (in this case Alpha, Bravo, Charlie, and Echo), and an ALL button that creates a conference line between all five; the last two are special function lines. Pushing any of these connects the handset (left) to that com-line.

To the right of the com-console are two critical panels. The top panel has three switches covered by a Plexiglas shield that folds down. The first switch has a key hole in its center and is the Missile Launch Switch. The second is a two position switch that selects War Plan A or B. The last is a CODE SET/USED switch.

The bottom panel on the left allows the commander to change which flight of missiles his command console represents. Commonly the switches will be set to the "home" flight – in this case Delta. However, the status of any of the 50 missiles in the squadron can be brought up on the columns of indicators by merely selecting that flight on the dials.

# BEFORE THE EVENT

# CHAPTER 1

*While all deception requires secrecy,*
*all secrecy is not meant to deceive.*
**Sissela Bok**

Whiteman AFB
15 March 1974
0601 Zulu
1201 Local

THE WARBLE tone sounded through the immutable Primary Alert System (PAS) speaker just above the Commander's chair. It happened six to ten times a day on Alert in Minuteman Launch Control Centers (LCCs), but First Lieutenant Gray Crawford usually was ten feet away in the Deputy's chair. Today, seated uncomfortably in the Commander's chair, he was only two feet away. He jumped when the speaker crackled to life.

"Skybird, copy coded SAC message."

"Deputy, copy coded message." Gray barked in his best SAC-standard command voice.

"Copy coded message. Confirm."

Both men grabbed their acetate-covered formats, which had a series of blanks that were grouped in paragraphs. The first group was four blanks into which they recorded the symbols...

"Bravo Sierra—Three Three." Gray grinned. Bravo Sierra was Air Force slang for 'bullshit.'

Then came six authenticators:

"Alpha Zulu Charlie—Whiskey Tango Juliet."

That was followed by the message body in two-letter groups. Groups of alphanumeric characters were recited as Gray and Dinkins carefully inscribed them with black grease marker onto the acetate-covered code formats.

The deputy, Lieutenant Manuel Dinkins, was 5-foot-8½-inches tall, maybe 145 pounds, and right now he was pale and drawn. He always had this unmistakable geeky–nerd look to him. Now, with no color in his face, Gray could add "wimpy" to the list.

"REPEATING—Skybird, copy-coded SAC message."

"Deputy, I have a complete message."

"Commander, I have a complete message."

"Decode without recopying—agree?"

"Decode without recopying—Aye… agreed."

The first four letters decoded to a red book checklist.

"Initial code Yellow," Dinkins muttered, mainly to himself.

"… Yeah. I see that."

Two more letters decoded and they found themselves on the Yellow/6 checklist. Evidently they were early in a war that might last only a few hours. Still, there was plenty of time for a dozen curves between here and Crimson/1.

The next six pairs of alphanumerics actually were in the clear and, when copied onto the code format, went directly into hour, minute, second, day, month, and year boxes…

| CODE FORMAT FLIMZY | | | | | | |
|---|---|---|---|---|---|---|
| Use grease pencil to enter alphanumeric codes | | | | | | |
| B 5 / 3 3 A Z C - W T J | | | | | | |
| Y / 0 6 | 1 9 | 2 7 | 1 5 | 0 3 | 1 5 | 7 4 |

They compared letters in the authentication box with the six characters on the AUTHENTICATION CODE SHEET for the time and date. They checked.

"Deputy, I have an authentic message."

"I have an authentic message. Agreed."

"Run Checklist Yellow Slash 6."

"Agreed..."

"Deputy, you call steps; Commander will acknowledge."

Some commanders insisted on calling the checklist while the deputy blithely acknowledged. Gray felt it was pure ego and not at all good management. Hell... the commander didn't get to vote. The Deputy couldn't improvise. Reading a checklist was the province of the Deputy and should, in Gray's opinion, be mandated by the "Book."

Actually, who called what was one of the few things a crew had discretion about. Gray felt having the Deputy read the checklist gave the Commander time to scan his missile status and look for problems in need of a command decision.

Dinkins was reading from the checklist, "Unlock Security Safe."

Gray already had checked the hash on the checklist and was moving out of his chair as he spoke: "Agreed."

They went to the 8 x 8 x 9-inch red steel box, which was welded to a 40-inch tall red steel pole which, in turn, was welded to the steel supports of the floor of the capsule. They deftly worked the combinations on their locks. Both locks spun open and both officers removed them and placed them on top of the steel box in almost choreographic unison.

They opened the safe hasps and folded the front door down, revealing two keychains and two neat stacks of plasti-locked documents. The very construction of the plasti-lock document was classified SECRET. Merely glancing at one required a TOP SECRET clearance.

Dinkins was reading again, "Strap in and lock chairs."

"Strapping, and... locked," Gray said.

Clicking the last of the four-point buckles into place, Dinkins noted the next step, "Alert Status Review."

Gray's eyes swept the Plexiglas-covered display before him: ten columns of indicators. Grease pencil exception notations on the Plexiglas in front of the panel gave him instant visual status of their 10 nuclear missiles.

"We have two missiles 'flagged' with faults. Both launchable."

Dinkins ticked the checklist and read the next line, "Ready all missiles, Commander."

"Roger. Kilo-03 is still marked as scheduled for maintenance but it is launchable."

"Check."

"Kilo-07 has maintenance in the hole. Get 'em out and get it back up."

"Ahead of you, sir." And he was. Dinkins already had rung the Launch Facility (LF) on the hard-line that ran from the capsule to each missile launcher.

"Kilo-07, Sergeant Dimwitty. Sir, I told you we'd call you when we got done. If you keep ringin' us up like this we'll..."

Dinkins cut him off. "Sergeant, are you the knowledgeable person in charge?"

"Well... yeah, I reckon I am, sir."

"Terminate all non-essential maintenance and restore the missile to launch status ASAP. Acknowledge."

"Damn! I mean... Yes, sir."

"How long?" Gray demanded as he took over the call and gestured for Dinkins to handle an incoming printout.

"We're replacing the Missile Away cable, sir. We can be out of here in half an hour, I think."

"And if you buttoned up now?"

"Um... Four minutes if you think we need to git, sir... but you'll never have confirmation of this missile being gone… if that is what is going on."

Dinkins now was handling three other problems and needed backup.

"Commander, I could use you."

"Proceed with reattachment but be ready to leave immediately. Keep someone within reach of this phone."

"But, sir, I…"

"Handle it. Kilo out."

And he hung up.

"Whatcha got, Dink?"

"Two minor missile faults showing on Kilo-02. Nothing mission critical—they'll launch if we get that far…"

Gray was blown away. Dinkins was COOKING on this stuff. The adrenaline had produced a lion where a mouse had walked. Just then, line one from the outside world rang.

"I'll take it, Dink. What was the fault code?"

Ring.

"Just coming in… SHIT. Gotta replace paper."

Gray whipped around to look at the printer. The computer paper was a moment to moment record of missile status. It was, in reality, a role of self-inking adding machine tape that turned purple on impact. Even a fingernail traced across it would result in a purple line four seconds later. The dot matrix printer inside the computer merely struck the paper and the image appeared in the pigment released by chemicals in the fibers of the paper that turned purple in the presence of air. VERY high-tech for a system designed in 1962.

It rolled out of the printer and down into a paper bag bearing the black grease pencil notation—TOP SECRET CRYPTOGRAPHIC WASTE. It was burned every shift—weather permitting.

The paper roll was difficult to thread into the machine and it seldom was achieved on the first try. If a printout was missed while there was no paper in the sleeve, it could mean a delay while you called your backup capsule for their copy of the readout. Gray knew of an unauthorized but foolproof way to change the paper and not miss a message. And he knew Dink knew it.

RING.

The approved by-the-book method was to remove ALL paper, slide in a new slip, and little-by-little, inch it into the lower feed slot. As the paper moved inward, the channel curved upward, made a u-turn and came back forward directly under the print heads to emerge back out in front of the deputy. The problem was that the paper often was too stiff to make the turn, or (if it had been exposed to humidity) too flimsy to be pushed, or (if so dry it had an electrostatic charge) it would stick to the metal guide channel.

A guaranteed successful (but not officially approved) method involved tearing off the trailing edge and taping the new leading edge to it, and then gently pulling it through or pushing the line advance button until the splice emerged. The distinct advantage to this unauthorized process was that NO MESSAGES ever were lost.

SAC, in its infinite wisdom, had decided that the risk of a piece of adhesive tape hanging up on the print heads—heads designed to be unreachable and untamperable—would render all of the messages thereafter compromised. So it was not authorized (but almost always done in the field).

RING!

"Use the tape method."

RING...

When on a "red book" checklist, even the way the phone was answered was specifically directed. Gray pulled up the Yellow/6 checklist, noted Step 2, and answered the phone, quoting directly from the page...

"At this time Kilo Capsule is not taking calls other than emergencies. Is this an emergency?"

"Uh... well... uh..."

Gray hung up just as the warble tone above him sounded again.

"Skybird, copy coded SAC message."

Quickly, they grabbed tissues and wiped the grease marks away from the last message to take the new one. It had the same time signature but a different checklist this time: Crimson/One—THE WAR MESSAGE. The directives indicated opening the authentication document marked 420.

"Deputy, I have a complete message."

"Commander, I have a complete message."

In absolute unison, both men said, "Authenticating with document Four Two Zero..."

Gray bent the plastic double and it cracked open, shooting a slip of paper into the air. He had to unlock his command chair and unstrap to retrieve it from behind the shock isolator where it had flown. Dinkins' code slip shot upward, hitting him in the nose, and landed on the console. They verified that the six letters on the message matched the six letters on the authentication document.

Strapping back in Gray read, "Romeo, Tango, India—Foxtrot, Oscar, Lima"

"Romeo, Tango, India—Foxtrot, Oscar, Lima. Agreed."

Together, "We have an authentic launch message." The very slightest of breaths and Gray continued, "Proceed to Crimson/1 Checklist."

Gray read as if the dozens of prior exercises during training had never happened and this was the very first time: "Insert launch keys... Compute launch."

Gray flipped down the plastic cover on his Launch Initiation Switch and inserted the chrome launch key as Dinkins swung open the much smaller cover on his Launch Verification Switch and inserted his chrome key.

"Key inserted. Computing launch."

Both men quickly added the minutes and hours to the original message time to arrive at the launch initiation time. It was seven minutes away. They picked up the hard line to the rest of the squadron and confirmed the message and launch time.

"Hotel Capsule acknowledges a valid launch message. Roll call. Go Golf."

"Golf Capsule acknowledges."

"Juliet acknowledges."

"Kilo acknowledges," Gray barked… a little too high in his vocal register to please him.

"Lima acknowledges."

"Proceed with checklist, Alternate Command Post at Hotel, out."

Hotel—and every other capsule in the 509th Strategic Missile Squadron—rang off.

"Unlock code—eight zeros, and I read Launch Option Code 83, Deputy."

"Copy. Eight zeros and LOC 83." Dinkins deftly rotated the computer's two thumbwheels to reveal 8 and 3 in their windows. 83 was the two-digit code specified in the message by the Joint Chiefs of Staff as relayed through SAC's Command and Control system. This two-digit code told each missile what the target was for this particular version of the end of the world.

Duplicates of the message would be arriving through four other communication systems over the next few minutes. SAC was nothing if not redundant. It simply wouldn't do for the war to be delayed because of lack of communication.

"Code inserted. And… initiating."

Dinkins held down the Initiate switch and watched as the light on his computer went on and off—indicating that their computer, one of five in the squadron, had been polled and their code had been entered. Now, ten missiles in their direct control and each of them three to ten miles distant from the capsule would receive the program—War Option Code 83.

Inertial guidance systems on each warhead would select target number 83 for that particular missile and pre-set a launch delay time for that target—and report completion of the reset back to the capsule.

Missiles had to launch on different targets at different times because any nuclear radiation field over a target contaminates incoming nuclear material causing it to deform—and not detonate. The delay built into each target, the launch matrix, ensured that bombers over a target would not be wiped out by "friendly nukes" or that sub-launched missiles would not be neutralized.

Within the squadron of fifty missiles, each would make this computation, adjust launch options, and report back—within two seconds. Each capsule would receive only 20 of the 50 reports—their ten primary missiles and those of the ten missiles they would launch if, for any reason, the capsule that was primary for them could not do it itself.

"Okay, let's get maintenance out of the hole."

Dinkins didn't answer immediately. He was momentarily mesmerized by the light blinking on and off every two seconds—computing the targeting for more than 150 million deaths by fewer than three thousand warheads, ten of which he would launch personally. The math worked out to about ten million people for his missiles—two hundred times the population of his home town.

Gray picked up the direct line to the Launch Facility (LF) and was prepared to clear them when he heard Dinkins unstrap. Looking up into the wide rearview mirror which gave him a complete view of the capsule behind him, he saw Dinkins move from the Deputy's chair toward the blast door.

"Dink, where are you going?"

The ringer from Flight Security upstairs started buzzing them on the direct line. Somebody up there wanted to communicate URGENTLY.

"Deputy, return to your station."

Dinkins half turned. "It's over... I'm going home. I'm going to find my family."

Gray drew his sidearm. It chilled him to hold a gun on another man. Dinkins heard it come out of the holster, but did not turn.

"Lieutenant Dinkins, we have six-and-a-half minutes to launch. We have three crewmen who will be toasted when Kilo-07 lifts off, unless *you* save 'em. You have to get them out of there."

Dinkins voiced what most Missileers thought but never said aloud, "I'm not turning keys, sir. I'm opening this blast door. You save 'em if you can."

"If you pump that thing one more time, you risk opening this capsule and I can't let that happen. The guys upstairs are buzzing us like nuts. They'll be down here trying to get to a safe spot if they see the sky light up..."

Gray, weapon drawn, had moved to the deputy's console, picked up the handset, and punched the key for Kilo-07.

"Shoot me. We're dead anyway. You'll save me the climb."

The hard line crackled to life, "Airman Glump."

At that moment, they lost all external power to the capsule. For two seconds they were operating solely on the powerful motor/generator mounted under the floor. This high-speed, heavy shaft generated the electric DC power that drove all of the operational equipment in the capsule. As long as that shaft turned, all combat systems would function. Illumination lighting was a crew comfort item, not a necessity, so without commercial power, only the red, yellow, and green indicator lights on the equipment were lit.

Loud reports sounded as blast valves slammed shut. Banging beneath them indicated the D/C brushes were dropping onto the drive shaft of the motor/generator, providing it continued power from the 11 refrigerator-sized batteries slung under the capsule.

Battery-powered emergency lights blinked on creating three distinct pools of light—one at the commander's console, one at the Launch Control Center (LCC) entry, and the middle one that lit Gray at the Deputy's console. Dinkins still stood in the blackness. He was beyond the LCC enclosure on the metal bridge that spanned the gap between it and the entry tunnel set in the concrete capsule from which the LCC was suspended. Dinkins could see Gray. But, Gray could not see him.

"Dink… we may both have to leave if we can't get air on. We'll melt in four minutes. Come get the Emergency Air Conditioning Unit working. Give me two minutes. DON'T MAKE ME SHOOT."

The handset was jabbering… "Sir! It just got bright as day out here at Kilo-07… SIR! SIR! I think we've got incoming. Tommy! Tommy, get out… we gotta get out!"

Gray screamed into the handset, "AIRMAN? AIRMAN! DINK. It's hot topside. You can't go up. Your only chance is down here."

The handset was a sea of static. "Sir, we're bookin' it. I think the war's started. Has it, sir? Are we dead? Will these monkey suits protect us?"

"Stay where you are until I instruct you. COPY?"

"Copy, sir… yes, sir. But… we gotta leave, sir. We're gonna die when this thing lights."

Dinkins appeared out of the gloom with his sidearm drawn and pointed at Gray.

"I'm not helpin' you do SHIT. I'm out of here."

"Lieutenant, we have about five minutes to get ready to launch, two minutes to get that EACU blowing cold air, or we have no choice… we'll have to leave.

"If we can't get air on, we'll book it. I'll get the door myself… but if I'm right, we have nothing to go up TO right now. The guys upstairs aren't ringing anymore… SEE?"

Dinkins considered it. For a second, his pattern of panic was replaced by the pattern of routine. "Two minutes… you've got two minutes."

"Great…"

Gray turned to the console and holstered his weapon. The green Missile Away light still glowed on Kilo-7. The cable had not been reattached yet. Dinkins was running restart on the EACU without a checklist. He wouldn't miss a step. Gray knew that.

"Dink, Kilo-7 took a near miss I think. Keep 'em on the phone until we can figure out how to know if we can get that missile launched and have confirmation."

The EACU growled to life, making evacuation unnecessary.

"You're down to one minute."

"Help me get these missiles gone and we'll leave together—if we can."

Whatever Gray had said, it was the right thing. Dinkins was now back—sort of.

In his genius-with-a-kid's-face style, Dinkins swung back into action. "Forget Kilo-07." He then rattled off the logic. "We don't know when she's scheduled to lift, Gray. If we hit Key-Turn on time, we can come back and plug her in when she comes up… find her next available launch window and send her off. For all we know, she might have enough delay built into her lift time that we'll still get her off on schedule."

The computer printer coughed and spit out a message. Dinkins bent over the tiny printout and swore. "Shit. Forget all that. Kilo-07 is a dirty missile."

Kilo-7 had reported in. It had a zero launch delay. That meant that when they turned the launch keys, Kilo-07 would immediately lift off.

The fact was that there were a lot of missiles with a zero launch delay. It also was a fact that SOME of those were missiles with special "dirty" warheads that were headed for the most sensitive military/political targets—Peking or Moscow. The payload was geared not only to destroy everything for miles—but also to heavily contaminate a wide area. It made Gray's stomach turn.

"The radiation suits...?" Gray groaned.

Dinkins remembered, "Initial briefing... 'Maintenance crew on-site to repair defective Missile Away cable and to check radiation levels. Hands-on Team radiation suited.' Gray, they're checking for leaking radiation. That's more of a risk with a dirty warhead."

There was a slim chance that they were wrong. But Gray knew they weren't. No one was supposed to know the targets of ANY missile. The whole idea behind separating the Deciders from the Doers was to keep hesitation and second-guessing out of the loop. The president decided to GO to war... the warriors WENT.

Once you know where a missile is going, it becomes entirely too real. Too many ghosts can haunt you from a specific target. "MOSCOW" meant "people." "RUSSIA" or "CHINA" seemed like just a vast zone of "enemy" that the subconscious could discount more easily. Kilo-07 took too much special handling to be ANYTHING other than a dirty missile.

Gray made a decision, "80 seconds to launch. Get them out of there."

"With due respect, sir, of all the missiles we need confirmation on, THIS certainly is the main one!"

"Complete the checklist and get the site commander on the line."

"Airman, Lieutenant Dinkins here. Get your CO on the phone and stand by."

"But, sir..."

"Airman, we are going to save your ass if we can. Follow orders."

"Yes, SIR!"

They completed the few steps left and had 55 seconds to Key Turn.

Gray got on the hard line, "Sergeant?"

"Sir, we can't get that cable on…and all hell is breaking loose out here…"

"Listen to me and do as I say. Do not button up. Get your men clear within the next 15 seconds—faster if you can. Acknowledge that you understand me."

"Jeez, sir, you're going to launch in 15 seconds. We're gonna…"

"Contact me by radio the INSTANT you get outside the gate. Do NOT offer me any argument or discussion. Acknowledge that you understand me."

"I understand, sir."

Line one began ringing… then line two.

Gray, "Let 'em go!"

The EACU stopped running.

Gray, "Let it go! We have time to launch before we have to shut down."

Dinkins started, "We never got back to fully cooled down. We don't know how long we have before this place superheats…"

"Doesn't matter, prepare to turn keys on my mark in ten, nine, eight …"

Banging began on the blast door. In his overhead mirror, Gray watched unbelieving as Dinkins got up and moved toward it.

"Four seconds, asshole. We can turn keys and be DONE…"

The UHF radio speaker crackled to life: "Maintenance three-seven calling Kilo Capsule; come in, Lieutenant. Over!"

Gray unsnapped and drew his .38. He was heading to get Dinkins when the computer began spitting out launch reports.

"We missed key turn. Damn, it! We missed it completely."

Dinkins was pumping the blast door pins, trying to retract them as fast as he could. The resistance was VERY high. At the Deputy's Console, Gray dropped his gun to the Plexiglas, dialed the radio frequency and keyed the mic.

"Sergeant, can you confirm launch?"

(Radio). "It's gone, it's gone… there was a huge light back over in the west and then the missile took off like…" A crackle and then silence from the radio.

Gray looked to the Command Console and saw five Missile Away lights already lit… including the one for Kilo-07… the one that had never been off. While he was watching, Kilo-08 went Missile Away.

Dinkins moved back into the capsule and past him toward the Command Console. In shock, he watched as Dinkins reached to open the Launch Inhibit panel cover. Gray grabbed his weapon and fired. Dinkins, having turned to draw his own weapon, was struck in the right chest and knocked clear of the Inhibit Switch.

Gray moved to his friend and removed his sidearm as a large red stain spread across Dinkins' chest and onto the linoleum-covered steel of the LCC floor. With both weapons drawn, he went toward the entry door—which began to open. Gray took up a firing position.

"Halt and identify yourself."

# CHAPTER 2

---

*... proving that the hand, is quicker than the eye.*
**~ Harry Houdini**

Minuteman Missile Procedures Trainer (MPT)
Whiteman AFB 15 March 1974
0857 Zulu
0257 Local

ALL SOUND stopped. No one moved. Lights came on in the Trainer and the unreality of the simulation gave way to a different kind of unreality. Gray's uniform was soaked through.

Dinkins rose from the floor and grabbed his shoulder at the wound. "Damn. I think that blood capsule cracked a rib."

His hands were shaking and he had to sit down in the Deputy's Command Chair. One of the evaluators walked to Gray and showed him a status card with filled-in blanks.

STATUS CARD:
* Deputy **_deceased_**.
* Personnel armed with assault rifles and weapons taken from the now deceased topside crew **_entered the capsule._**
* Commander **_repelled the initial attack with handgun fire._**
* A second wave of enemy entered the vestibule **_as the_**

_**Commander attempted to close the blast door .**_
\*   The Commander _**died in the resulting firefight.**_
\*   Exercise _**terminated.**_


Captain Dan Feil, Standboard crew commander, made a check mark on his clip board and announced, "Okay. We'll tally the results and let you know your score in about twenty minutes. Why don't you guys take a break and we'll meet you in the snack room."

Feil's cavalier tone made Gray want to punish him severely. Exercise or not, the adrenalin in his system was VERY real. He looked at Dinkins… a man he had just simulated killing… and wondered if Dink would ever speak to him again.

Hands shaking from his own body chemical overload, Dinkins said, "Let's get some coffee, Gray."

As part of SAC's policy of constant readiness evaluation, every crew went through random fitness review: three grueling hours in the simulation trainer with a pair of Standardization Board evaluators hovering over your every move. Then, that same pair of ghosts would shadow you into the field. Looking over your shoulder, they would watch and note every decision and action you took—or didn't take—during an entire tour of duty in the already cramped quarters of a Missile Launch Control Center.

Most crews got this nose-to-asshole pimple check every six to nine months. Gray's dumb luck, he had drawn evaluation almost every quarter since arriving at Whiteman Air Force Base.

Nine evaluations—nine HQs. Even the meanest Standboard Team on base had ranked him HQ: Highly Qualified—NO ERRORS… not so much as a misdialed phone number.

The highest HQ pin they made was 10. Dinkins wore a 7. Between them, they were among the best Deputy Combat Crew Commanders in the 351st Strategic Missile Wing, the Strategic Air Command's most decorated and celebrated Missile base.

"That was different." Dinkins's pallor was even more noticeable in the green fluorescent lighting of the trainer and against the red ascot of the 508th SMS (Strategic Missile Squadron).

At the Officer's Club, Lt. Gray Crawford could be heard to complain about the "sissy wear" ascots but, in truth, he was very proud of his royal blue 509th scarf, and of the 9-HQ pin centered in it. Donna had said that all that blue made his eyes irresistible. He was certain Dinkins hadn't noticed THAT particular effect.

In 1962, when the Strategic Air Command (SAC) had instituted the Minuteman Missile System, it knew it would be lonely, boring duty that, if done correctly, actually never would be "done" at all. Deterrence was the whole point. Putting the crews in heroic, manly uniforms came a bit later. The dark blue fatigues were practical. The ascots made them appear much more important and adventurous than they ever would get a chance to be. Unless, of course, all hell broke loose.

Gray and Dinkins were both 24 years old... and the top of their field. Both were under review for the coveted status of Instructor. Dinkins had insisted Gray Crawford take the Commander's seat.

As they moved out of the Trainer, the Operator stepped down out of the control booth. "I gotta hand it to you, Lieutenant. We have NEVER gotten that far in that scenario. No one EVER has shot their deputy before."

Gray's ears were turning red. How was a guy supposed to react under that kind of pressure?

Dinkins rose to Gray's defense. "Due respect, Captain... Shut the hell up. Gray did exactly what he should have done."

"No argument. I was impressed. Truly. And keeping the maintenance crew on-site for the launch confirmation... Boy. Talk about breaking three rules to accomplish a mission. They won't ever figure out how to score that."

"What do you mean?" Gray really was confused now.

"That was the 'Catch-22.' No way to win. Most OA scripts have a couple of parts that are designed to give you a Critical Error no matter which way you go. Look, Gray, you had to confirm launch. Dinkins was dead-on about that. No confirmation equals Critical Error. But if you'd forced them to go down under that missile and finish connecting the cable, the missile would miss initial liftoff and then the maintenance crew all would die at launch... DOUBLE Critical Error.

"If you'd delayed launch to the next available launch window to let them get clear... Critical Error. No one EVER thought about getting them out and then having THEM stay to confirm launch. Fuckin' brilliant."

"But we never turned keys. We didn't launch. Critical Error." Gray was so weary he barely could think.

"You didn't put in a Launch Vote... couldn't because your Deputy was trying to let the enemy in the door. And since he wasn't going to turn keys, your key turn would have been pointless. But all your OTHER actions ENABLED launch. Everything you did— EXCEPT TURN KEYS—put all the birds in the air on time. And by stopping Dinkins from putting in an Inhibit, you further avoided a subsequent launch delay. Great decisions."

"Yeah. I thought shooting me was a super decision, Gray."

"Sorry about that. It ought to get you a bid for Instructor."

Dink and the Trainer Operator exchanged glances...

"Gray... I was appointed to Instructor Shop yesterday. I start in a week."

"Come again?"

The Trainer Op was grinning like a jackal, "We so bagged your ass, Lieutenant."

"I have an apology to make, I think. This was a set-up, Gray." Dinkins was struggling with his part in the deception. "I'm already in. This was your test. Both the Instructor Shop and Standboard have been looking at you. They asked me to go along with this over-the-top scenario to cook you and see what kind of sauce you made."

The Trainer Op added, "I think they'll offer you Standboard, Gray."

That had not occurred to him. "I won't do that. That's not for me."

"I'm sorry, but I had to make it to Instructor Crew, Gray. We're trying to have a baby and Linda needs me there when her moon is in Virgo or some silly shit. I can't be gone two days out of six and hit her window of opportunity."

Gray was amazed that Dinkins could hit anything in that particular arena. He just never considered Dink as a sexual being. Gray and Donna had wanted to start a family, too. He had thought that the "Welcome-Home" reunions every six days would have upped the odds of a bingo... but, so far—no score.

Gray was stunned. A set-up. With DINKINS of all people. The guy could sure act; he'd give him that.

Dinkins pulled his fake-blood soaked shirt away from his chest, "I need a hot shower."

"I need a cup of coffee." And with that they all headed for the snack room.

Whiteman AFB
Emergency War Order (EWO) Building
15 March 1974
1130 Zulu
0530 Local

The Standboard crew debriefed every move Gray and Dinkins had made. There were a host of minor errors but that was to be expected in an Olympic Arena (OA) exercise. All crews were in the trainer for a minimum of three hours monthly for ongoing proficiency training, and another three hours if under crew evaluation. On top of that, though, any crew member could volunteer for an OA exercise.

Olympic Arena was usually nine to twelve hours of events and challenges packed into three hours of clock-time. All bets were off. While a normal "trainer ride" threw the occasional curve ball, Olympic Arena was nothing but curves. The purpose was to hone judgment and to cook leadership skills out of what might otherwise be men who were destined to be bean counters. It was the Air Force Missile equivalent of the "sheep from goats" division of King David's time.

Gray's regular crew commander, Captain Andrew Hardiman sat in on the debrief. He had watched the entire exercise. He had been in on the deception. He knew Gray was a natural and wanted that "golden boy" status to be known. It couldn't help but make him look better as a mentor and commander. Andy wanted Instructor Crew duty as much as any other missileer. If Gray impressed them, the two of them might even move up as a crew. Not unheard of… but not at all common. They had proven themselves a worthy team already, and maybe this would ice the cake.

The Strategic Air Command liked mind games. Its charter was mind games. The whole idea behind 1,100 ICBMs, 700 submarine-launchable missiles, and thousands of B-52-borne nuclear weapons was to scare the crap out of the enemy and intimidate them out of throwing the first punch. They might blacken our eye... but if the retaliation liquidated them... or liquefied them... the venture should seem unworthy.

# CHAPTER 3

*But cards are war…in guise of sport.*
**Charles Lamb**

Whiteman AFB Flight Line
11 January 1974
1854 Zulu
0154 Local

NINE MONTHS EARLIER

"WHY DID you have to pack your Mess Dress? You aren't going to a formal function without me, are you?" Donna grinned. She was very proud of Gray. Being selected as Whiteman's First Team delegate was quite an honor.

"There's some big dinner thing at the end and we're all supposed to be decked out in our finest."

Truth be told, Gray loved wearing his Mess Dress uniform, the Air Force equivalent of a tuxedo. Occasions to wear the Mess Dress were few and far between at operations bases. The monthly parties at the Officers Club were sponsored in rotation by each squadron on base, but only twice a year were they "formal." Gray was somewhat in the minority in his enjoyment of dressing up. It was usually pressure from the officer's wives… not the officers themselves… that ensured the two dress-up parties.

This occasion would be very different. No dance. No spouses. This would be all officers. Every year SAC had each base select two junior officers to attend the SAC First Team Briefing at Offutt Air Force Base in Omaha, Nebraska. The brightest and the best would gather and join their minds in an effort to poke holes in the defenses they only recently had been trained to use. Their "in the field" knowledge and "freshness," it was hoped, would unleash their creativity, and reveal any chinks in the armor that more seasoned veterans might not see—or feel safe pointing out to the brass. It would be capped with a full-dress dinner, possibly with CINCSAC himself in attendance.

Gray and Andy were picked up on the flight-line at Whiteman and flown the short 260 miles to Offutt Air Force Base in Nebraska. First Team Briefings were held at SAC headquarters. Gray tried to look cool, but being in the seat of the most sophisticated war center on the planet made his blood race. Everywhere he looked were officers— most of them lieutenant colonel and higher. It seemed they used majors for errand boys. And here he was, a lowly first lieutenant, being asked his opinion of how secure the missile system was—and what he would do to change it.

"'Ten HUT!"

Gray hadn't heard a command barked that sharply since he had done it himself during summer training at Tinker AFB, near Oklahoma City. On that occasion, he had been announcing the entrance of their teacher—Colonel Kraddaock. Gray's voice of command had been so effective that even the Colonel had stopped in his tracks and come to attention. That bit of embarrassing enthusiasm had cost him five demerits; five of the total 23 he earned during the entire summer. Average demerit total for his class was 325.

Thankfully, this time, it wasn't Gray. It was a full-bird colonel calling the room to its feet as the commander of SAC (CINCSAC)— Four Star General Wilson Killebrew—walked to the podium.

"As you were, gentlemen."

The general spoke to them as colleagues—contemporaries. He

"visited" with the young officers with a "peer-to-peer" familiarity and respect that elevated every man's ego, while convicting them of the depth of the responsibility his trust—and the trust placed in them by their commissions—called for.

"You know...we are chided and chastised for being a 'by-the-book' bunch. Apparently there are those who feel that there is something inherently un-American about the idea of following strict, professional guidelines instead of mounting up like a legendary hero, improvising with our wits, flying by the seat of our pants, and cutting down the enemy with our quick-draw expertise, and God-given, natural superiority.

"Admittedly, that is a much more romantic image. 'The book,' by comparison, must seem remarkably dry and unappealing up against such a scenario.

"But romance aside, gentlemen, the fact is that we are the guardians of the greatest country—moreover the greatest governmental *concept*—that humankind ever has dreamed into reality. That requires rigid adherence to proven procedures and practices. But, we also have a duty to leave no weakness unchallenged. There can be no sacred cows here. EVERYTHING we do—YOU must examine—and attack without mercy.

"You must expose the weaknesses that exist in our system... if there are any. SAC officers have to know the book... but we also have to WRITE the book... and REwrite the book. We must, all of us, test and prove the best ways to do our jobs. And we must be able to duplicate that ability right down to every plane, and every launch capsule, and every officer whose hand is empowered to release a nuclear weapon.

"From around the world, we have selected two of you from every base, and gathered you here to bring your minds to bear on one question.

"'If we are Trojans... what kind of horse could today's Greeks build to get inside our gates?'

"We rely on your diligence, creativity, and audacity to shine a light on any defense that we possess that won't hold under fire. Your parents, your president, and your posterity depend upon it."

Without another word, he rose and strode from the room. No one called attention... no one had to. Gray and his junior officer brethren were on their feet... jolted out of their jaded reverie, and humbled by the prospect of the weight they were being called upon to bear.

Then, for hours, they were "briefed" on how the system was designed to work. In the furthest from "brief" way possible, an endless procession of officers was paraded into the room to detail the status of various weapon systems and intricate intelligence-gathering methodologies—B-52 delivered bombs, Minuteman Missile systems, Titan Missile systems. They even trotted the Navy through to speak on sub-launched systems. Despite legendary rivalries, the respect shown between these services and departments when discussing their interdependence with respect to the "real thing" humbled Gray even further.

Gray watched and listened—and soaked it all in. He was exhilarated by the quality of leadership exhibited by the men at the top. And he was disgusted and wearied by the arrogant, promotion-seeking automatons who postured and droned on and on about their little departments' vital role—all the while missing the bigger picture.

Finally, they were asked to break into teams. Each team was sent to a conference room and tasked to identify every weakness in the process that they could, and to destroy or disable it if possible. No limits on men, information or resources... but any key resources needed were to be identified in detail. Teams were composed of a missile crew, bomber crew, and SAC's best maintenance and communications officers.

Around the conference table, the debate raged on for an entire day. Finally, a very frustrated captain wearing an Academy ring rose to his feet.

"Gentlemen, we have been debating this for hours. We're expected to propose a penetrating attack strategy *tonight*. From Alexander the Great, to Napoleon, to Patton, the mark of a great strategist has been simplicity. I think we need to make one round of this table with each man saying—in ONE SENTENCE—the core idea of what he thinks would do it. There are twelve of us. Twelve ideas. Twelve sentences. Among them, we may find a starting place of value."

The proposal was intimidating. It exposed every one of them PERSONALLY to the group mind. To his credit, the captain started it off himself. Gray, sitting immediately to his right, was praying that they would go clockwise and give him time to think up something… and to hear how other ideas were presented.

"My idea… so I'll go first. My plan would be to subvert at the crew level, place ringers in the capsules and cockpits, then order America to stand down; a bloodless coup d'etat."

Simple—it wasn't. At any given time, there were thirty-four hundred officers commanding crew capsules and B-52s. Whiteman's "crack" scheduling team couldn't schedule the same officers at the same Launch Control Center (LCC) with any dependable regularity for even three weeks in a row. That many undercover spies on duty at the same MOMENT—worldwide—would be impossible to achieve.

Around the table they went. A B-52 pilot from Anchorage said they were wasting time, and he wouldn't participate in such a patently sophomoric enterprise. Another suggested infiltrating the country and taking schools hostage until all officers walked away from all weapon systems.

The ideas ranged from intricately expensive and involved, to remarkably dumb. NONE addressed current weaknesses in the weapon systems or the Command and Control process. It became

Gray's turn. Eleven frustrated and competitive officers turned their eyes to the most junior officer in the room.

"Shoot them down with deer rifles," was what he heard himself say.

Andy looked at his deputy. Gray thought he was going to begin apologizing for his youth and idiocy… but instead, Andy's wheels began to turn.

The B-52 pilot who had refused to offer an idea now hit the boiling point. "THIS is what I mean! I think this room deserves more respect than that, lieutenant. This is a serious exercise."

"He is serious," Andy said. "Missile skin is less than the thickness of a dime. Any penetration or weakness in that skin could cause the solid fuel in the booster to deform, and cause the burn to move from a central, symmetrical consumption …"

"What are you saying, captain? That a guy with a deer rifle can bring down an American ICBM?"

"If he pokes a hole in it on launch… yes. The booster would disintegrate and explode shortly after that—long before achieving trajectory."

The B-52 pilot was incredulous. "You're suggesting that a sharpshooter—outside a launch facility—waits until launch, and then shoots it out of the sky?"

Another jumped in, "And maybe sharpshooters near every bomber base shoot out the tires of the leading planes steering gear? But, it would only cause a huge delay at best. I don't see how…"

"Launch blast would deflect a bullet…"

"But! If they blanketed the air sixty feet over the launcher, the blast would be minimal and the bird would have to rise through it…"

Gray soon lost track of who was talking. Someone asked, "How are you going to get twenty-six hundred sharpshooters into America with high-powered rifles and scopes?"

"Don't have to. This is America. They can buy the guns here. AND the damned ammo."

Within less than ten minutes, they had outlined what the Anchorage pilot demanded be code-named "The Whiteman Scenario."

They presented it to their senior officer for submission to CINCSAC. It was simple, achievable, and remarkably inexpensive.

The infiltrators charged with targeting missiles would not even be at risk. No one would be around to know where they had taken up shooting positions. Those trying to take out bombers would have to have CIA or suicide-mission mentality... but it was well known that the KGB had sufficient operatives with do-or-die mentality to staff the project. Possibly hundreds were already in the country.

The next morning, while the submissions were being reviewed, the attendees were divided into small groups to tour the SAC War Control Room deep underground. Three huge projection screens filled the far wall. Rows of desks and electronic equipment arrayed in front of it reminded Gray of the NASA Mission Control shots on television. These dozens of stations processed the calls and incoming messages that updated the room on every conceivable scrap of status. Since there were no staff officers in the room that day, the tour was able to watch the demonstration from the general's command station, high over the floor in a glass-encased booth.

Their guide ordered a demonstration. "Dave, could you get me a status poll, please?"

At a workstation near the front of the room, a major keyed his desk mic.

"Skybird, this is SAC with an interim status report request. Poll all stations and report status. REPEAT. Skybird, this is SAC with an interim status report request. Poll all stations and report status."

Gray had heard that voice over the capsule speaker hundreds of times. Glancing at the desk, he noted the name plate: Major Kennison. Gray knew that receipt of the message would cause missileers at more than 120 Launch Control Centers to call their Squadron Command post with the number of Green (ready to launch), Red (unable to launch) and Yellow (launchable but showing faults) sorties in their flights. That consolidated report would be typed into a "telegraph" type machine, and forwarded to the Wing Command Post at each base. Those reports would be consolidated, and reported to this room.

Major Kennison was watching a series of lights on a panel next to him. He keyed an intercom. "Where do you want it, sir?"

"Screen, two, please."

Major Dave Kennison, the man whom Gray had come to think of as "the voice of SAC," touched a key. Seconds later, all of the lights on his panel were suddenly projected on the second of the three 30 x 30-foot screens across the front wall.

The guide explained that every bomber, missile crew—in fact, every nuke in SAC, worldwide—had just reported status. The data was compiled and built into a dot graph showing every base with the number of Greens, Reds, and Yellows they had. That graph had been sent to a high density television monitor and a color transparency was photographed from it. That transparency then was processed, dried, mounted, and projected onto the screen.

From the moment the major issued the poll request to the moment the display of the status hit the screen had been only 43 seconds. The image was crisp and easy to read... even in the general's command booth fifty-five feet away. Gray was amazed. The hours he had spent in darkrooms trying to process one good black and white photo seemed Paleolithic compared to this technological miracle.

As they filed out of the observation room, Gray noted that, in stark contrast to the high-tech bells and whistles of the war room, Major Kennison now was busy trying to repair a triangular chip of laminate that had dislodged itself from his console where the arm of his chair apparently had snagged it and broken it off. It was a common Air Force paradox—a twenty million dollar room with cheap, laminated work stations.

The remainder of the tour was obscure and mundane. The SAC War Room had stolen the show. Gray never again would hear that speaker come to life without visualizing Major David Kennison, the mic, and that console at the leading edge of the War Room with the broken triangle of SAC grey/green laminate.

At the cocktail reception that night, the officers were treated to a glimpse of how generals live. The shrimp cocktail tables alone were staggering. Open bar, wine with dinner, remarkable Omaha Steaks, brandy, and cigars after. On a too-full stomach, the stench of cigars almost overwhelmed Gray, but Andy lit up with the rest of them. He really was enjoying this.

Gray noted that the seating arrangements placed him at a table with officers he hadn't met. As he glanced around the room, he noted that all the members of the Whiteman Scenario team were at different tables. He asked the officer next to him if that was a "mix and mingle" strategy.

"Two of the guys from my team are right here. I think it's just a coincidence, Lieutenant."

Coincidence? Maybe. Gray caught sight of an eagle-nosed colonel with an aide at his ear. Eagle-nose was staring at Andy. Gray quickly averted his eyes as the aide then pointed the colonel in his direction.

Gray and Andy were the focus of this colonel's attention. WHY? Were they in trouble? Had his comment about deer rifles been taken as too flippant? He hadn't meant it to be. It was a legitimate threat scenario. He was sure of it. Farfetched maybe, but far superior to many of the ideas forwarded.

Risking a glance, Gray found that the colonel and his aide now were gone. He was relieved—at first. The cloud of suspicion and paranoia began to form again.

There were two speakers that night. The first was General Dixett, the creator and organizer of SAC First Team operations. He congratulated the men on their selection and their efforts.

"We accept the expense of this exercise because we want our brightest and best to get a chance to think creatively. We need to be challenged. And, frankly, we want to seduce the best among you to stay in the Air Force. Nights like tonight are rare—but they happen."

After the chuckles subsided he continued, "Many good ideas were submitted and many of our minor weaknesses were pointed out. I would remind you that you were in secure War Rooms yesterday but you are not tonight. This ballroom is a part of SAC Headquarters but is not a free-speak zone. Until you hear otherwise, everything you discuss here—is classified." General Dixett delivered the last two words looking directly into Gray's eyes. This was not merely paranoia. Gray was being sent a message.

The general returned to his seat at the dais. On his left, Colonel "Eagle-nose" nodded to the general and then looked directly at Gray. He held the stare a long beat before turning to smile and respond to a question from the officer on his left. Gray's digestion stopped.

CINCSAC spoke, once again stirring the men's spirits. The next morning, they packed up and left their Visiting Officers' Quarters and boarded Air Force Blue school buses for the winding ride back to the flight line. They climbed back into the KC-135 tanker and strapped into the out-of-place looking web seats in its upper cargo bay. At 6-foot-4, Andy looked like he'd been folded up and had knees and legs left over. At barely 6', foot, Gray, too, found the seats a bit closer to the floor than he would have liked. In one move, they were transformed from dignified analysts of nuclear strategy, to humble kids being "carpooled" back to their various bases.

Nothing more was mentioned of the Whiteman Scenario—or any other ideas the groups had brought to the tables. Their job, apparently, was to bring the ideas—not to share in their development.

# CHAPTER 4

*What you see... is what you get.*
**Laugh-In**

Whiteman AFB
Emergency War Order (EWO) Building Parking Lot
15 March 1974
1130 Zulu
0530 Local

THAT WAS months ago. From First Team to the brink of Instructor duty, Gray's star had risen fast. He didn't feel like a star, though. The impact on his system from the stresses of the simulation and the psychological "reality" of having to shoot Dinkins had drained his energy almost completely.

The sun wasn't up yet, but the sky was lightening. Andy, Gray, and the Standboard team crunched through the gravel parking lot to their cars. Gray glanced toward the Squadron building next door and beyond it to the two-story building that housed Whiteman's extension campus of the University of Missouri.

Most of the Missileers were involved in the Minuteman Education Program to earn their MBAs. The "free" master's degree was the principal lure SAC used to seduce officers below ground for two days out of six to have their minds and spirits sucked dry. A few hours rest and then he'd have to hit the books. They had a test in Economics in a couple of days and...

Beyond the Education Building, Gray began to see missiles rising on columns of white smoke. It stopped him in his tracks. The Commander of the Standboard crew, Captain Feil, noted the look on Gray's face.

"You okay, Lieutenant?"

The distraction caused Gray to look toward Andy—with near panic in his face. Andy stepped into Feil's sight line, blocking his view of Gray, yawned and stretched.

"It has been a long night," Andy covered. "We have a major test in Eco coming up. Gray probably thought it was today. 'No, Gray, we have that test next week. Today is just review.' "

"Oh." Gray looked back at the Education Building to a brightening morning sky; with no missiles to be seen. "Good. I was ready to panic there."

"Yeah. Me, too," Andy said with just a touch of edge.

"Eco ate my lunch," Feil admitted. "I had to bone up for every one of Grant's quizzes. He really hates us, you know."

Andy was 6-foot-4½-inches tall. His Morris Minor topped out at four feet when the tires were fully inflated. As Feil walked past them to his own car, Andy looked across his comedic vehicle into Gray's intense blue eyes. "I don't want to know what you see when you look at the horizon, Lieutenant. I insist on not knowing. We have come a long way together. I know you to be a remarkably capable young officer and expect you will be a formidable instructor. But we have to GET THERE first. Now is a lousy time to have a cloud appear on your horizon."

The irony of Andy's choice of terms was not lost on Gray. A "cloud" on his horizon. How many other men saw missiles rising… missiles that weren't there? Why did he? "Don't let the cloud getcha," Simmons had said. Was this that cloud? What was he to do about it?

"Sleep." As if answering his question, Andy ordered him to "Go home and get some sleep. We're in Eco tomorrow… and there IS a test next week."

# CHAPTER 5

*Waddn't me, Lord... Musta been Eve.*

**—Adam**

103 North Carswell Circle
Officer's Housing, Whiteman AFB
18 November 1972
1520 Local

THE SECOND bedroom was principally Gray's study, where he could work on his MBA. Missile duty was so obnoxiously unglamorous and boring that the only way to recruit men into the concrete coffins for two days out of six—waiting for a war to start—was to give them something ELSE to occupy their minds. The Minuteman MBA Program had been the thing.

Missile duty rotations lasted three years and the MBA program took just over two years to wade through. Offering this academic diversion had moved the pendulum of unbearable boredom and tension successfully toward a more intellectual pursuit that promised to advance an officer's Air Force or civilian career. It also provided an excuse for turning one bedroom into a "study" where a man could stash things he didn't want his wife to worry about.

As much as she tried to stay out of the cluttered chaos of Gray's "study," Donna came across the bag in the second bedroom closet while trying to make space for her parents' Thanksgiving visit. "Gray, does this thing have to be in here... what's in it?"

He was ready. "Evac bag. Just some odds and ends. Old clothes we never wear. Stuff like that. If we get a squadron inspection, it's all set." The second best way to lie was to tell as much of the truth as possible... but only as much as you need to make your point.

"These assholes inspect our HOUSE?"

Damn. He'd gone one sentence too far.

"Listen, you tell those tin soldiers that I'm not in the goddamn Air Force and they can keep their white-gloved inspectors out of my goddamn house."

"Technically, Donna, it is not 'your goddamn house...' It is theirs. We just goddamn USE it."

Donna was rarely "colorful" in her language, and Gray's teasing of it often disarmed the situation. Often. Not always. Still... he had to get her mind off of the bag. If she bitched to her Officers' Wives Club cronies about a mandatory evac bag and in-home inspections, they would set her straight and his cover would be blown completely.

"Seriously, Donna, they won't inspect inside the house, but if I am asked about the readiness of my evac bag, I want to be able to say it is in place and ready with a straight face."

She was moving back toward the kitchen. As she went, she marked off items from her checklist and opened the front door for Noggin to go fertilize the front yard. Throughout the multitask exercise, she did not miss a beat chastising Gray for his incessant concern that everyone knew everything he was thinking, as well as things he didn't know... but should. "I wish you could learn to lie just a LITTLE, Gray. Most people don't even pay ATTENTION to you, let alone know or care what you're thinking. You need to give your paranoia a break."

She knew where his buttons were... even when she didn't know that she knew. "I moved the bag. Whole left side of the closet is clear for your parents' stuff," he capitulated.

The bag went under the day bed where it would run even less

chance of being messed with or asked about. It might go untouched long enough to even be forgotten.

"Gray, I know this is your first real job. Hell, seven months ago you were a part-time drive-thru teller at Lubbock National Bank… and now here you are defending the free world against the Red Menace. But I do wish you would let it go SOMEtime."

Gray dropped onto the chair at his desk, wishing he could. "We're never off duty, Donna. My records are tagged with a red triangle and so are yours. If we look or act suspicious, people put it in a folder. I don't know if I will be a career officer or get out in four—but I need to keep my options open."

Donna kissed him on the top of his head and started toward the kitchen again. "You're addicted to the power, cowboy. Don't try to kid me." She turned profile, presenting the picture he truly was addicted to: a 5-foot-2, green eyed redhead, with most of her hair tied up in a scarf, the rest escaping in several directions, freckles on her all the way down into cleavage, and a sultry grin that kingdoms have gone to war over.

Looking into his eyes, hers changed. "But, you have been paranoid ever since the first week at Vandenberg. I don't know what they did or said to you, Gray. But it's like all of SAC has a huge cloud on its judgment."

# CHAPTER 6

*You're in the Army now...*
**Irving Berlin**

Vandenberg AFB
Minuteman Missile Crew Training Center
28 June 1972
1813 Zulu
1013 Local

## FIVE MONTHS EARLIER

**M**UCH OF the footage had been on television since Gray was a kid—the flash of white and then the totally dark screen and then the emergence of the mushroom cloud. Fire in the sky. Buildings blown apart by the traveling blast and high winds, and then the sucking reversal as the fireball consumed all of the air and created a huge vacuum back toward Ground Zero.

The sing-song melody of "Duck and Cover" ran through his mind. But then came the footage that they hadn't shown the general public. Footage the average person hadn't even known existed. Footage of cadavers—men, women, and children—vaporizing in an instant. Protruding limbs being burned off clean while the rest of the body remained intact and unharmed behind a flimsy white shield. Flesh decaying from living beings as radiation sickness worked its way into them before allowing them to die. It was very hard to watch. It was horrific that the films had been made.

For almost two full days, ,the fifteen Minuteman Missile Launch Crew trainee candidates had been pummeled with image after image of nuclear destruction. If there was ever any doubt about the devastating power and finality of nuclear warfare—no such doubts remained for these men.

Gray had run into Dale Matteo in the parking lot on day one. They both were looking for the training center, both trying to look cool, both failing miserably. They immediately liked each other. They sat through the litany of carnage side by side—Notre Dame and Texas Tech graduates with a whole month of life experience behind them, now facing the intense reality of being hired killers for the U.S. Air Force.

"Watching this much total destruction is numbing," Gray whispered.

"Yeah. It's like stag films," Matteo agreed. When he became aware of Gray's raised eyebrow, he explained. "You know. You see a whole bunch of naked chicks and suddenly the one live naked chick you were just with seems somehow insufficient."

Gray might have made a response but the lights came on.

"Gentlemen, this concludes your two days of nuclear damage familiarization. Before we proceed any further, we have a paper for you to sign."

Dropped in front of each of them was a letter on SAC stationery, a formal business letter from the officer to whom it was given. It was addressed to CINCSAC, the Commander in Chief of the Strategic Air Command. It bore one sentence.

> **TO: Commander In Chief,**
> **Strategic Air Command (CINCSAC)**
>
> **Having been thoroughly briefed on the nature**
> **and consequence of nuclear weapon detonation,**
> **I pledge that, if given a lawful order from the**

> *President of the United States, I will turn my*
> *launch key at the proper time and launch the*
> *nuclear weapons for which I am directly and*
> *indirectly responsible on their assigned targets.*
> *Signed,*

They could take as long as they wanted. Gray decided immediately. He signed the page and handed it to the major, who indicated with his eyes that he could leave the room. "Need you back in twenty," was all he said.

Crawford had been seeking out the break room for a sugar fix when he first encountered Captain Dan Simmons. He was on his knees reaching up into the vending machine, trying to dislodge a Snickers that had hung up on a ledge.

"Be right with ya. What are the odds of a bar catching like that?"

"Use a pencil," Gray observed.

"A what?"

"A pencil, sir. Reach up inside from the delivery tray with the pencil. Sweep it off the ledge."

Simmons looked blankly at the candy bar. He could see the plan would work. Simmons didn't have a pencil. He knew that Crawford wouldn't have a pencil either. Officers do not clutter their uniform pockets with practical writing instruments, particularly the 1505s—the khaki summer uniform that was designed to be practical and lightweight, with unbroken, clean lines. It was a unique picture. Two leaders of the American military-industrial complex, one on his knees elbow deep in a vending machine and the other hands on hips... both staring at a Snickers bar hanging precariously between the frame of the vending machine's glass and the deflector designed to break the fall of a descending candy bar and guide it toward the delivery tray.

"I usually just shake the machine." Simmons seemed like an

innocent, geeky teenager who had not discovered that girls harbor interesting possibilities. Crawford saw the crisp white-on-blue name badge over Simmons' right breast pocket. Centered on the left breast pocket was the Missileer badge... the "pocket rocket" that Crawford would receive when his six weeks at Vandenberg concluded. So... Simmons was "one of them." Above the left pocket was a neat row of ribbons: service medals, but no wings.

Gray had only one ribbon above his pocket: the service medal every man on active duty wore. It impressed the uninformed but meant, principally, that you could reflect light, fog a mirror, and were on the government payroll in uniform. If you ceased to be able to fog the mirror, you were entitled to be buried wearing it.

"This guy was once in charge of launching nuclear weapons and is stymied by a stuck candy bar," thought Crawford, as he dropped his change into the machine and pushed E6... Snickers. It dropped, clipping the first one and together they fell into the receiving tray.

"Engineering?" Simmons asked, staring at the two bars.

"BBA—Management."

"Ah. A problem solver. Lieutenant Crawford, you would make a good trajectory engineer."

"Thank you, Captain Simmons."

"Dan." Simmons handed Crawford his candy bar. "You guys finishing up brainwashing day?"

Crawford took note of the irreverence and began to relax some. "Just signed our promises to destroy the world if Congress gets pissed enough."

Simmons' eyes flicked into Crawford's. For an instant Second Lieutenant Crawford felt his stomach tighten and his sphincter slam shut. Maybe he'd gone too far? Just as quickly, Simmons' eyes began searching for a place to put the Snickers wrapper. As he moved toward a waste can, Crawford noted that the man had an uneven gait; he was clumsy... his feet bumped together at one point. This captain was an unmade bed of awkwardness and lacked anything that could be perceived as "cool" or "sophisticated"—concepts that, for Crawford, went with the territory of Officer and Gentleman. Still, Gray found himself intimidated by the potential disapproval of this officer who might report him as unfit...

"Crawford? Grayson Crawford, Lieutenant?"

"Gray... yes, sir. How did you know, sir?"

"I'm your tech instructor. You get 96 hours with me next."

"Oh.... Well... great. Glad to meetcha."

"You know about record tags, Gray?" First name. Hadn't used his rank. This was a friendly guy...

"Record tags? Uhm... no, I don't recall them briefing us on..."

"You won't get a briefing on them. Anyone in your group not sign their pledge?"

"Sir?"

"Anyone say they couldn't do it? Just couldn't turn those keys and wipe out half or all the world just because it was their 'duty' to follow orders?"

"No, sir... well, I don't think so."

"They told you there would be no prejudice, right? You could keep your Top Secret clearance we've invested the last six months getting on you... and just transfer to some other duty, right? I mean, that is why you do the films, Gray—to cut out the men who know they can't do it. Better to do that NOW before we put another four hundred thousand dollars of training into you and send you to be in charge of enough nuclear warheads to split a continent in an instant... or worse, to contaminate an entire hemisphere and condemn millions or BILLIONS to a slow and agonizing death with almost no chance or desire for survival. You know we don't want guys down there who are gonna hesitate, or who decide at the last second that they maybe ought to think this over."

Was this geek with the goofy expressions serious or messing with him? His voice was calm and even and soothing—but the candy bar was a mashed mess in the captain's fingers. Gray desperately wanted to lighten this moment. There had been many serious moments in his life, and he had held job responsibility before. But, he was beginning to see that in the Air Force there would be days—maybe even weeks or months—with no light moments.

Crawford drew a calming breath. "I don't know whether anyone else backed out, Captain Simmons. I signed my paper and came in here for a sugar break."

"Three."

"Sir?"

"There are twelve of you left to go forward, lieutenant. Three decided to try something else... or maybe decided that they just couldn't do it... or they don't know if they could do it and their personal integrity won't let them just sign the paper now and figure it out later."

What did this guy want? Did he KNOW? Had Gray somehow telegraphed that he had no idea what he would do if push came to shove? Could Simmons see that he KNEW he didn't want to go to Vietnam? That he'd just face the consequences of a key-turn decision if it ever came up? Of COURSE. They must know! They did this all the time! They had psychologists. Gray had been profiled extensively. During his background check, they had talked with every teacher he'd had all the way back to junior high. Every employer... even the summer jobs...

*"Gray... what's up? The FBI came to see me today."*

*"I told them you were a good boy... never in trouble... always dependable."*

*"We are so proud the government is entrusting you with such an important responsibility."*

*"We always knew you'd go far, Gray..."*

"What happens to those three?"

"They know too much. Shit, they're dead men, lieutenant…"

Silence. Three seconds of it. Gray went white.

"Just screwin' with ya, lieutenant." The geek personality was back. "Hell, their careers might even survive. I'll see ya in class tomorrow. Don't let the 'cloud' getcha."

"Cloud?" Simmons had been moving out the door. He turned. Another of those weird eye-to-eye moments. Simmons' eyes narrowed a bit. Almost a wince. Almost a, "Shit. I shouldn't-a said that" feeling. As he looked at the mangled Snickers, his countenance relaxed completely.

"Geez, I made a mess here. Good to meet you, Lieutenant Crawford. Look forward to the class. See ya in the morning."

Simmons moved away, sucking chocolate off his fingers. Crawford stood alone in the break room staring at the empty door frame with a profound, "What the hell was THAT?" feeling in his gut. He headed toward the briefing room. At the door, for the first and only time in his life, he threw away an unopened Snickers bar.

Entering the briefing room, every eye snapped to him and it stopped him in his tracks. He had a conspicuous "is my fly open" sensation. Matteo caught his eye and nodded for Gray to sit in the empty chair beside him. As he crossed the three steps to the chair, he took a quick count… Eleven in the room. He made it an even dozen.

"I thought you'd bailed, man." Matteo was one of only three single officers in the group; all energy and nerve endings. It was why Gray had liked him immediately. He was quick to seek the laugh, the good time. Dale fully expected that the uniform, his dark-Italian-good-looks, and his Notre Dame class ring would get him laid on any given night in any given bar. He was unrealistically optimistic about other things as well. "Not everybody signed the fuckin' paper, man. I thought maybe you wouldn't be back."

"What? Am I wearing some kind of a sign?"

"No. No, man. Listen. This is NOT the place to talk, I'm discovering." Gray looked at Matteo, who was not looking at him but was glancing furtively in the direction of the film projector. "I think the Bell & Howell is bugged. Look at all the goddamn wires."

It was nuts. Who would bug a room by putting a mic in the only place that MADE noise? The supreme silliness of it relaxed Gray. Let Matteo be passionately paranoid. Gray would remain cool and detached. Wait. Watch. One step at a time.

"Relax, Dale. We did what we're supposed to do."

The flight line was more than a mile away but the louvered windows in the room rattled every time a heavy took off. They were rattling.

"That's those three guys now. Heading for Da Nang. The skinny second looie will be dead before Mass on Sunday." Matteo's eyes all but disappeared when he was grinning. Where was he when Gray was trying to lighten the moment in there with Simmons?

A major entered with a stack of paper and handed exactly twelve copies to the man on his left. "Gentlemen, your schedules for the next three weeks are being distributed now. You have the afternoon off. Questions before we dismiss you?"

Everyone wanted to ask about the three guys. It hung in the air as they glanced at one another. The major knew. He was daring them to bring it up. It was part of the test, maybe? No one had the balls.

"Major, what are record tags?" Gray was surprised to discover that HE had asked the question himself.

The major was one of those buzz-cut, should-a-been-a-Marine types. Apart from focusing on Gray, he didn't move or change expression. The passage of seconds seemed to point to a decision he was making about answering the question. At length... he spoke. "Officers in charge of nuclear weapons must be men in whom the ultimate trust of the country and the President can be placed. All of your records—medical, psych, efficiency reports—all of them are tagged with a red triangle." He shifted abruptly to a casual and non-threatening tone as he continued, "You don't want a certifiable nut case with a key in his hand, now, do you, Lieutenant?"

"No, sir." And then… "Why were we not briefed on the tagged records?"

"Need to know."

"We don't need to know that we're being watched like hawks for any little thing? Sorry, sir. I'm not trying to get out of line, here… but this is information that affects my life. I think I have a right to know."

"No offense taken, Lieutenant. I am glad to give you the information. You just don't have a NEED to know… or a right, actually. Nothing will change with your knowing. It is not information necessary to the performance of your job. Get used to not knowing, Lieutenant."

If he said one more independent-minded thing, Gray knew there would be a notation going in his tagged record. "I guess we'll get what we need to know to make decisions."

All of the new second lieutenants in the room were watching the exchange. All of the other officers were examining their shoe shines. "You did sign your pledge, didn't you, Lieutenant… Crawford?" He was checking for something on a note pad.

"Yes, major."

"Then, you've made your decision. Now you just need to know WHAT to do and HOW to do it. And that information… we WILL give you… starting tomorrow at 0800. Dismissed."

Gray Crawford was alone. There were eleven other officers in the same room with him—and all in the same boat with him. And each one of them was alone. Any doubt expressed, any concern voiced, any conduct "unbecoming an officer" would, he was sure, become part of the "tagged record." He could sense the paranoia and uncertainty closing in… like a cloud.

"I need a drink." All eyes cut to Matteo. "HEY… don't tag my record, fellas. I don't NEED a drink, but we should celebrate… you know? First hurdle jumped… on our way to glory for God and country. "O" Club for lunch—on me."

A confident, strong suggestion in a moment of indecision and uncertainty looks a lot like leadership. Actually it is salesmanship, but it looks like leadership.

The twelve, with an afternoon on their hands, travel pay in their pockets, and nothing much better to do, found themselves around a large table at the Vandenberg Officer's Club drinking their lunch. Someone toasted the Dirty Dozen and the name stuck. Everyone got chatty and tried to get to know one another. Gray Crawford, who never drank, had a bourbon and Coke. It tasted awful. Worse yet, it didn't help.

Lieutenant Dinkins, and the rest of the married officers, it turned out, lived in Lompoc, not far from the tiny efficiency apartment Gray and Donna had found.

Dinkins, "Dink" as he liked to be called, offered Gray a lift home, but Donna was expecting to pick him up at the Training Center at 4:40. And he needed to talk to Donna.

Gray was more open and sensitive than some men, more private than others. Part of why he had married at all was rooted in a deep need to connect—to belong. Dinkins dropped him back at the Training Center and he hardly had time to wonder how he would put it to Donna before his precious, emerald-green Cutlass swung into the gravel parking lot.

As he slid behind the driver's seat, she kissed his cheek. Redheads always had been a weakness for Gray. The green eyes had been a thoroughly unnecessary clincher. Though only married a year, they had been together for three. They knew one another very well. "So, soldier. Tell me about your day."

He loved her because she was beautiful, savvy, and intelligent. She also was a wide-eyed innocent who looked for the best in everyone she met. Lucky for Gray. It never would dawn on her that the superpowers might one day decide to launch missiles half a world away and, in less than thirty minutes, unleash destruction on an order not seen since The Flood. She never would ponder the notion that those not vaporized in the first blast would have to deal with a contaminated atmosphere and water table…or what a fetus conceived in a radiated environment would look like if it were unfortunate enough to come to term. She hadn't sat through thirteen hours of mind-numbing testimony to nuclear destructive power—and he didn't want her to. Ever. He and men like him were there to face that ugliness and to declare it unacceptable. The fact was, he realized, Donna didn't have a "need to know." Part of his job was to ensure that she never needed to know.

"Real training starts tomorrow. I met my teacher on break." And then, "Nice guy, I think." Secrets, half-truths, and subject changes would come easier with practice. It was the ability to tell the plain truth that he would lose.

# CHAPTER 7

*The best laid schemes o' mice and men gang aft agley;*
*An' leave us nought but grief an' pain, for promis'd joy!*
**Robert Burns**

Kilo-01, 509th SMS
6 miles southwest of Adrian
2 miles east of the Kansas line
24 March 1973
0251 Zulu
1141 Local

"THE VELOCITY of money has expanded steadily since the end of World War II. This is not NEWS," Andy barked into the squadron com-line.

"No. Not in general. But the expansion of the velocity of money as relates to spending in the Government Sector itself is the question I want to explore," Davidson responded. "And given that Patterson wrote a chapter in the text on it, I think it would be smart to include it."

"Only if we agree with his point of view and quote him profusely and with extreme precision," Andy countered.

The two men—and their deputies—were in the same Economics section in their on-base MBA program. Dr. Randolph Q. Patterson, their professor, had assigned a paper to the four men, knowing full well that Andy could not write a "team" paper if his very life depended upon it.

Even as a weather officer in Vietnam, he had NEVER initialed another man's weather report without first running the calculations himself and calling the man (out of the sack if necessary) to challenge any prediction that varied more than 5 percent from his.

Andy's psych profile made him a perfect missile officer. He knew the book, thought he was right, had no self-doubts, and—aggravatingly—WAS right almost always. If Andy prayed, it would be, "Lord, help me be open to the ideas of others—wrong though I know they are." Gray had every intention of letting him write the whole thing and doing whatever research Andy felt he needed to validate his positions.

"I'll write a draft and then we can talk about it," Andy concluded, and hung up. He didn't wait for a response. It hadn't been a question… merely a statement of what he would do. Period. To Andy, it had been information offered as a courtesy to smaller minds with no real "need to know."

Captain Andrew "Andy" Hardiman was 6-foot-4¾ inches tall. He claims he was 6–5 before he lost his hair. A starting center for the Texas Southern Tigers, Andy had kept himself physically fit. He was engaged in rubbing skin softener into a jagged white scar on an otherwise coal black knee when Gray first thought about broaching the issue.

"So… do you ever think about what we'd do if the real thing happened?"

Without looking up from his rapt attention to treating the now six-year-old war wound, he said, "What time is it?"

"A few minutes before midnight… You gonna answer my question?"

"I am answering your question."

"Oh. I seem to have missed it."

"I haven't finished. Within the next three to ninety minutes, we will have our regular "surprise" evening exercise. We will receive and record a verbal coded message, of which we will receive multiple copies over the next nine hours through the other forms of communication that surround us. We will dutifully decode the message EACH TIME. We will follow the orders in that message until such time that we confirm it is a repeat. If tonight is like the four thousand other nights that men have stood alert in this capsule, it will decode to the green exercise book and we will pretend to destroy the communist aggressors… and the world in the process."

"And if the first two letters decode to the red book?" Gray parried.

Again, without looking up, Andy paused in the administration of skin softener. The effect was not missed. "When you are done, I will continue."

"Sorry. Please proceed."

Andy rose to his full height. It was obvious that his ancestors had been Swahili giants. With a plastic bottle of skin softener in one hand and his pants gathered around his ankles, a different man would have looked comedic. Captain Andrew Hardiman did NOT look comedic. Somehow, he looked regal and imposing.

He looked squarely at his deputy. "If the first two letters decode to the red book—we will follow the orders on the rest of the message and on the pages of the checklists to which we are directed."

Their eyes locked for an uncomfortable several seconds until, "Lieutenant Crawford?"

"Yes, Captain Hardiman."

"Would you care for some skin softener?"

"No, sir. I don't believe I do."

"Abstinence will not make your hide tougher, Lieutenant.

Merely less flexible." Andy put the skin softener back into his "away bag" and began to pull on his pants.

In a much more conversational tone, he continued, "What we do down here is a slam dunk, Gray. Intelligence briefings aside, we cannot know the situation that motivates the men who command us through this speaker. They do not offer us options. Our fate is quite comfortably sealed for the five minutes to an hour or so that it will take to initiate the war and launch our missiles."

His tone had changed but the content had not. Andy was quoting the Operations Officer's Guide almost directly. Gray had not expected that. He had expected the intimacy of crewmembers and the frank, nobody-but-us-down-here honesty that he had shared with Andy when they had discussed the nightmares of Vietnam. The aching loneliness of missing someone who loved you. The relief of a massage girl looking into the sadness of your eyes and making an offer that your loyalty and guilt would not allow you to accept.

"It is what we would do if we were off duty that keeps me awake," Andy said, more to himself than to Gray.

Gray decided to gently press the point. "Well... that's really what I was asking."

"It was?"

"Yeah."

"You did it poorly."

"Probably. But really, Andy, c'mon. You've been in combat. Don't you have a plan?"

"The closest I came to combat was diving under a Jeep to save my black ass and losing a quarter inch of my kneecap to a mortar shell."

"Yeah, yeah. You're no hero. I got that... But, stay with me. I KNOW you have a plan. I know that if you were sitting in your government-issued, three bedroom base house and you thought there were inbound ICBM's twenty minutes from liquefying your living room, you'd have a plan for getting you and your wife and daughter as far away from Whiteman as you could."

It could go either way. Andy loved mental exercise. But he also had an unusually deep and hard-to-read sense of privacy. Gray's invitation might open him up or it might make for a cold, silent nine hours until the relief crew came down.

"What was that song you were singin' on the way out here?"

Lost him. Damn. "What song?"

"When we came past Clinton, you were singin' a song. Remember?"

"Oh, yeah. Muhlenberg County. I saw the Peabody Coal trucks strip-mining that section south of town and it reminded me of the chorus."

"How'd that go again?" Andy asked.

"You want me to… sing?"

"I do."

Figuring his commander wanted to change the subject, Gray, somewhat self-consciously, sang:

*"Oh, Daddy won't you take me back to Muhlenberg County,*
*down by the green river, where paradise lay…*
*Well, I'm sorry my son, but you're too late in askin',*
*Mr. Peabody's coal train done hauled it away."*

"All of Missouri is a coalfield, Gray."

"That's what makes it so sad. These beautiful hills are being raped."

"With alarming consistency—you miss my point."

"What point?"

"You asked a question. You hypothesized a series of events and asked my opinion."

"Yeah. And you changed the subject," Gray began, but Andy chopped him off.

"No. I did not. I urged your mind to function. It is, evidently, on sabbatical or possibly drummed to numbness by the infernal sounds of this cement bowel. The song reference, Gray. You even sang it—quite well I hesitate to add. That song reference was to have you think about what you saw today and hear the question you yourself asked, and attempt to make one and one arrive at two."

Gray knew Andy was driving at something, but it was completely opaque to him. "This has something to do with strip mining, I think."

"Yes. You have recognized the snow but you have missed the tip of the iceberg, let alone the mass of the thing below the surface."

"I have?"

"Coal, Gray. Missouri is made of coal. The whole state will be on fire with the third detonation. Not to mention that the base is in the CENTER of the launch footprint... and, therefore, the damage footprint. Fire—particularly that super-hot fire of nuclear detonation—consumes oxygen at chemical reaction speeds. Survivors of the blast and radiation will smother and perhaps even explode into the vacuum that consumes them.

"The fact is that, clearly, we're safer here on Alert. Even topside. We're in the westernmost launch center—on the outskirts—just a few miles from Kansas. Hell, we could launch the missiles, commandeer the crew vehicle, and be across the state line before folks on base could get past the gate."

"So if you're on base with your family, what do you do? Just sit and wait it out?"

Andy's professorial tone shifted abruptly, "Hell no. I die on the road trying to get my family the shit out of Dodge..."

"Which way would you go?" Gray knew Andy. He was on a roll now. He had warmed to the subject as Gray had suspected he might. Now he would unfold the thinking of a much more seasoned strategist—one who had been underestimated and racially dismissed for thirty years. Gray would make note of every nuance.

"Go East and you would have to drive through 130 miles of targeted area. If you DID get beyond the target footprint before the rain of missiles superheated the coal layer and set Missouri on fire, the winds from the west would blanket you in the smoke and radiation from the blast. If you didn't burn up, you soon would freeze in the resulting nuclear winter. Plus, you are driving into St. Louis and other densely populated areas of panicking civilians.

"If, on the other hand, you chose to head west, you have 45 miles of hot zone and then you're in relatively untargeted area with the wind in your face and the radiation and smoke and cataclysmic destruction behind you. Largely, it is a rural and unpopulated area."

"Still," Gray mused, "45 miles of hot zone with a half hour flight time... The math looks impossible."

"True. But what's your choice. The Soviets can't aim. No telling where their warheads will come down. You have to be alert and do your best. Denver, you'd have to avoid entirely. Cheyenne Mountain, just to the north, will be blown to hell and back; but, most of the rest of Colorado and down into New Mexico would be untargeted. The nearest targets west of there are near the coast, so radiation and winds would not be a problem—at least for a while.

"If you stayed on the eastern slopes of the Rockies, you'd be even more protected. Can't think of much in west Texas that would be targeted, either. There's oil, of course, but you'd have to target individual wells almost. Two hundred of them wouldn't impact the flow of oil out of that region—much too expensive a cost in warheads for Russia. Spend 2 percent of those warheads on the refineries east of Houston and you'd do much more damage. If you could stay fed and find gas, you could get to Mexico in a day and a half maybe."

"What if you flew?" Gray had noted with keen interest that just north of the base on Highway 50 was Skyhaven... a small private airport with about eight single-engine planes. Cessnas and Pipers, he'd thought. He was not a licensed pilot but his best high school buddy, and flight instructor at the age of 19, Paul McClintock, had seen to it that he knew how to fly… and land… anywhere.

"Flying would be a faster get away but very risky."

"Stealing the plane you mean?"

"Nah. That would be pretty easy if you were determined. The risk is what the winds will be doing if you're flying anywhere close to a blast wave. Two-hundred-mile-per-hour gusts would shred a small plane. But a private car in a gully might survive with little more than wear to the shocks. Either way, you'll have to find fuel eventually…"

"You could land on a highway and taxi right up to a pump I suppose."

"Gray… if the war starts raining mushroom clouds on heartland America, the upstanding white men of Kansas are going to shoot ANYTHING that comes down out of the sky. If you were in uniform, you might do better. But if you DID gas it up and get all the way to wherever you're going, you're still gonna need ground transportation eventually. You'd have to steal that, too… and be prepared to back it up. So weapons would be necessary. And ammo. Still, I think being in uniform might buy you enough hesitation on the other guy's part to talk your way through it."

"Andy, do you really think Americans would be shooting it out with each other?"

"If we launch these bastards, there won't be any more Americans—just a mob of individuals in survival mode. If you're in uniform, you might look like a survival asset long enough to surprise the SOB, take his car, and haul ass."

"So… stay on the ground you think?"

"I'd pack clothes for cold weather. Nuclear winter could be quick. The clouds will block the sun for weeks—even months perhaps. My big concern is that enough cloud and ash cover for a long enough period could trigger another ice age. Can't do much about that, so I'd pack all the water I could carry, food that would keep, and stuff I could trade. Daily doses of potassium iodide would ward off residual fallout poisoning. Money probably would be useless… Finding radiation badges might be useful—for a while."

"How far do you think your Morris Minor would carry you and your family?"

"That would become the supply vehicle. I'd put the wife, the daughter, and the cat in Eva's car and everything else in the Morris. Just like when we came here. It carries a lot, but is light and readily towed."

"Donna'd make me take the damned dog."

"You should."

"Why, Andy? Another mouth to feed, more water to carry."

"Someone to bark like hell when there's strangers about. Dogs don't eat much, Gray. A hungry one will eat stuff you won't touch. And if he won't eat something, you shouldn't, either. Plus, if it comes down to starvation time… two of you could survive for a month or so on that dog."

"EAT THE DOG? You don't know my wife."

"No. I've never seen her hungry. Have you?"

"She'd eat ME first, Andy. But I see your point."

They fleshed out, detailed, and challenged the plan until seven in the morning when Airman Davis called down for breakfast orders. They had worked up an appetite, but Andy insisted on cereal. The damage Davis could do to an egg rivaled the global carnage they had been discussing.

The line to the Flight Security desk topside rang. Gray glanced at their clock—always synchronized to Greenwich Mean Time. "Looks like our relief has had breakfast and is about to let us go up for a nap."

After moving through the steps of changeover, exchanging status information on all primary and secondary missile flights, and discussing the upcoming Eco quiz, Gray and Andy left the LCC and took the interminably slow elevator ride up to ground level.

In the ready room, the young Security Alert Team (SAT) was just finishing breakfast. In a few minutes, two of them would mount the SAT vehicle and visit each of Kilo Flight's ten missile launch facilities (LFs) on "the day check." Another tour would come tonight. The common joke was that they were called 'the SAT,' not because of their Security Alert Team duties but because mainly, they just 'sat' around waiting for a calamity.

The television was on and tuned to the Kansas City CBS affiliate. The President was speaking.

"Turn that up, please," Andy asked.

"…portions of the tapes are at variance with certain comments I made earlier."

A 20 year-old Security Police trooper huffed, "Meaning, the lies I told you THEN don't seem to agree with the lies I'm telling you NOW."

Another chimed in, "They ought to fry that crooked bastard."

Andy glanced his way and Gray felt certain he would unleash his intellect and his wrath on the impertinent enlisted man, but he did not.

His more informed buddy chimed up, "No, Rick. He won't let that happen. If he gets impeached and thrown out, he gets zip. NOTHING. But if he resigns, he gets $65,000 a year—FOR LIFE."

"Oh, great. He gets ten times what I make if he screws the country and then quits."

That pretty much did it. Not for Andy… but for the Site Manager. Sergeant Maxwell was a seasoned Air Force veteran with a sleeve full of chevrons and rockers. He quietly put down his milk carton and in a slow, measured cadence said, "May I remind you that you are referring to your boss? Our commander-in-chief? Like it or not, mister, if he says we go to war—we go. Eighteen-minute gap or not."

Airman Davis, the cook, whom NO ONE had ever heard utter a word, was listening intently to Nixon. He turned and walked toward the kitchen and said, almost inaudibly, "It would take a nuclear war to save his ass right now."

Before the Site Manager could make another comment, Andy said, "The madman sees more devils than all vast hell can hold," and moved toward the officers' bunk-room.

The Site Manager looked at Gray, who, guessing correctly, said, "Shakespeare."

"Which is he calling is the madman seeing devils: the President, or the cook?"

Gray decided not to field that one. "I'm sacking in. How's the hot water, Sarge?"

"Oh… not so good, sir. Give it a half hour to recover and you can steam yourself all you like."

"In half an hour I hope to be studying the inside of my eyelids. I'll shower when we get up."

"Want me to wake you, sir. Glad to do it."

"Yeah," Andy said, emerging from the bathroom with toothbrush in hand. "If we don't get up on our own, let us sleep until about six. Or suppertime. We'll go back down around seven."

"Roger that, sir."

On his way to the bunk room, Gray mused that anyone named Roger never should have to be in the military. The cheap jokes would be tedious.

Every missile wing ran its own schedule. Most used the two-crew rotation system. Crew briefing was at 8 AM, then everyone saddled up and rode out to their duty station in Chevrolet's most stripped-down version of the Suburban. Oscar Capsule (OSCAR—01) was three hundred yards from the briefing room. ON BASE! Hotel Capsule (HOTEL-01) was 123 miles south. It was almost ten-thirty before that crew could arrive to affect change-over and allow the crew that had been there for two days to start heading home. They'd arrive back on base shortly before two. Until the night crew arrived late that evening, the day crew were the only officers on station.

The evening crews arrived at the squadron HQ for their briefing at 8 PM and went through the same routine. By the time those crews got out to their sites, the day crews had been in the capsule approximately twelve hours. Night driving took a little longer (or was supposed to by regulations). The day crew then would go topside to get some rack-time on a more-or-less normal sleep schedule. They would get up at about 7 AM, have breakfast with the Site Manager, cook, and the six to eight security police who protected the site and its ten missiles, shower-shit-shave, and go down to relieve the night crew. The night crew then would go up for rack-time, arise at about six and go down to relieve the day crew—who then went HOME—again, leaving the site with only one set of launch officers until mid-morning the next day, when the new day crew arrived.

SAC advertised that two men were on duty and two on standby at all times. Technically, that is correct… because SAC wouldn't lie, and could not admit to being mistaken.

Every crew rotation had two crews assigned to each capsule; one set for the day shift, one for the night. But for each of those five capsules, there was an additional crew at the base on stand-by. They had to be within two rings of their phones and be able to get to the flight line within ten minutes should a relief be necessary.

Officers living off-base had to spend Standby Time somewhere on-base and sleep in the VOQ (Visiting Officer's Quarters). Flight time from the base to the most distant LCC (Launch Control Center) was just under one hour. But in Whiteman's antique choppers… it was a long, bumpy, stomach wrenching flight.

Gray contended that the choppers had no doors so as to facilitate throwing up without soiling the cabin.

An experiment had been done with three-man crews on thirty-six-hour alerts. With three officers in the capsule, one could sleep and there still would be two officers in control of the documents and keys. It hadn't worked out.

In any triangle, there are two who connect better, leaving the third to feel left out. In an already paranoid environment, it had led to enormous tensions in some cases. So, they were stuck at Whiteman with two-man crews and no "sleeping" in the capsule, even though it was furnished with a full-length bed, made up with fresh sheets every day by the Site Manager.

It was for "resting"—but "sleep," per se, was forbidden in the capsule. You could close your eyes—but you could not drift off... legally.

The problem for Gray was that he found it very difficult to sleep topside in the daytime. The bunkroom was blacked out and soundproofed marginally well. The problem was that his body knew better. Even in those months when they pulled only night alerts and NO day alerts, they still had four days between them on regular, work-day/sleep-night schedules. Their internal clocks couldn't reset that often. Night Alerts were the pits. It was like three days of jet-lag every week.

So, it was even worse that Gray had never been able to get more than four to six hours sleep during the topside "rest cycle." And once awake, he never was able to figure out what to do with himself until time to go back down.

The day room was open to everyone, but Gray felt it was enlisted man's territory. Not in a snobbish way, but out of respect. They needed a place to be themselves. They were 18 to 24 years old for the most part, and stuck out here for four to five days at a stretch. He felt they should be able to smoke and cuss and scratch (and do any of the other things they were forbidden to do with an officer present) in their own "home." He felt like an unwanted (or untrusted) visitor topside. He was there for barely a day and a half out of six. But if instructor crew did come through, he'd be out there... or some launch center... only a day and a half out of thirty!

The day they came in off that Alert, Gray began to pack the evac bag. It had contained thermal underwear, heavy socks, jeans, sweatshirts, and a case of dehydrated foods, which were a mystery since they had no labels. The Base Exchange supply officer had thought Gray was nuts, but on a lieutenant's wages, he had only enough cash to buy the case of surplus unlabeled packages. He knew that if he ever had to open one, he would not care what was in it.

He'd also stocked the tool shed with four cases of unmarked canned goods for the same reason. At a nickel a can, he bought out the supply and then hid them behind the rakes and lawnmower. He needn't have worried. Donna NEVER opened the door to that shed. Sweat was not in her repertoire and yard work meant sweat.

# CHAPTER 8

*Now that is a horse of a different color!*
**Gate Keeper, Oz**

North Eastern Russia
Near the Arctic Circle
24 March 1973
2045 Zulu
0445 Local

ENERAL VLADIMIR Sadok found these trips to the field invigorating. Seeing Mother Russia's resources applied with such great stealth and sophistication invigorated his peasant soul and made him feel very powerful, indeed.

Not that he needed the ego boost. As one of the most senior officers in the Russian nuclear weapons ministry, he wielded unprecedented power and discretion. This project was his baby. It was his crowning achievement. It would, without question, earn him the Hero of the Soviet Union as well as a parade in Red Square; a place in the history books; his picture on the Kremlin wall, and a bust in his hometown.

General Emir Gurov, by contrast, was more of an oxymoron. A diplomat by nature and a conservative by choice, Gurov was legendary for making the unworkable work by understanding the economics involved.

"You should have been a capitalist dog, Emir," Sadok would tease. "You have the soul of a Jewish merchant."

Still, Sadok had ensured that Guroval ways was on his staff, and always at a sufficient rank and grade to have the power to execute Sadok's will. They both were generals. Their arguments also were legend. Both knew that Sadok was the alpha dog. Both knew that his word was the final word. But both also knew that Gurov's instincts, his pads of calculations, and his words of warning always were to be heeded. He was the wise mind, Sadok the fist.

"It is a beautiful thing, is it not, Emir?"

General Gurov watched with frozen eyelashes as the tip of what could have been an ice mountain rotated aside. A large logging crane hoisted a missile into place and began to lower it into the launch tube disguised as a pile of timber. Even at this distance, one could be convinced it was a log. It took careful study of the silhouette to distinguish that this was man-made... and deadly.

"This project produces enormous misgivings within me, General Sadok."

"Your digestion does not interest me. Claiming a major victory over the Americans does. This will be their undoing. The party—history—will revere us as heroes."

"By 'us,' you mean, 'you,' of course."

Sadok smiled a sadistic grin. "I am trying to be generous, Emir. It is a rare enough occurrence that you should celebrate it, no?"

"The risks are formidable, General."

"Risks. Pha. General Gurov, don't be an old woman. Risks. No man rises to greatness without assuming and surmounting great risks. The only way we will ever know with absolute certainty that this system will work as designed is to execute this project with immediate dispatch," Sadok spat.

Gurov's head was shaking, "We have no data..."

"I am not interested, General Gurov, in scientific assurances. I am interested in demonstrable, incontrovertible truth. Demonstrations are what convince people. The Americans had their Hiroshima, their Nagasaki."

"And the world has never been the same. I, for one, do not think it any better off."

Sadok looked at his oldest friend with something short of contempt. "It may have been my gravest error to promote you beyond your stomach, General. You haven't the soul of a warrior."

"I never claimed to, General. My loyalty to my country, however, is no less than your own. We paint with different brushes… that is all."

A long moment passed. Sadok turned to watch as the missile's camouflage was completed.

Filling the uncomfortable silence, General Gurov said, "I will see to it that your plan functions and has no flaws, General. I am a loyal Soviet. I do not have to agree in order to comply with complete devotion."

General Gurov turned and walked down the hill. Sadok's eyes followed him with something between admiration, affection, and disdain. Half way down the hillside, his old friend reached out to push a low hanging branch aside as he paused for a moment to get a better view of the glorious missiles and their clever hiding places. A thing at which to marvel. A few seconds later, he moved on to the warmth of the staff car.

Such things were beyond Gurov's pedestrian imagination, Sadok concluded. There were no cautious men at the top. Gurov never would rise. Sadok's view of himself was another story. He would be Premier one day. He would see to it.

# CHAPTER 9

*Do something every day that you don't want to do;*
*this is the golden rule for acquiring the habit of doing*
*your duty without pain.*
**Mark Twain**

Kilo LCF (Launch Control Facility), 509th SMS
Deep in Mid-Missouri
5 March 1973
1751 Zulu
1151 Local

Just outside the gate at Kilo-01

"ONE, SEVEN, four… something. I can't figure out this last digit." Captain Bill Pratt was scrutinizing the inside of his left wrist just under his watchband, trying to discern the last of four digits written there in ballpoint ink. Perspiration and wet leather had rendered the last digit unreadable.

"Is that a 6 or an 8?" he asked, extending his arm toward Dinkins.

"Nine," Dinkins said, putting the crew vehicle into park just outside the entry gate to Kilo-01 LCF. Without looking at anything, he said, "One Seven Four Niner."

Peering once again at the glob of blue on his wrist, Pratt agreed, "Yeah… that's right. It is a nine." Then he leaned his head out of the window as if ordering fries: "Uh, Captain Pratt and Lieutenant Dinkins for changeover."

The Flight Security Controller knew Captain Pratt well after two years of ushering him in the gate every sixth day, almost like clockwork. He knew him by voice and he could see him very well from his glassed-in vantage point at the corner of the Launch Control Facility (LCF) building strategically located a crisp 45 degrees and 35 feet from the gate.

"Yes, sir. Your authentication day code, sir?"

"Roger. We authenticate One-Seven-Four-Nine. That you, Proctor?"

"Your authentication checks. Sergeant Proctor it is, sir. Welcome to Kilo, gentlemen."

With a klaxon-like buzz, the electromagnet released its three thousand-pound grip and the chain link gate began to slide open on its track.

Dinkins was glad he hadn't relied on his commander to remember day codes. Pratt was good at lots of things, but temporary numbers was not one of them. "Gray matter is too precious to waste recording numbers that will never be used again." Unfortunately, he didn't put them in short-term memory long enough to use them in most cases, either, rendering Dinkins his constant emergency 'chute.

Dinkins could tell you the day code for every alert he had ever pulled. Not that he wanted to. Actually he agreed, in principle, with Pratt's philosophy. However, the recording mechanisms of his brain did not care what his conscious mind thought. It blissfully recorded everything. That kind of trivia just stuck to his cortex like red to an apple. That same mechanism caused him to remember the exact Zulu time of every "nightly exercise" that he'd ever run. It was for that and a thousand other reasons that Dinkins preferred day alerts. His sleep cycle could stay intact and he didn't have to pretend to blow up the world nearly as often on the day shift.

With the gate finally clear, Dinkins dropped the truck into gear and pulled forward sixty feet past the security windows to the door of the support building. Waiting for them was Sergeant Will "Sarge" Maxwell, the Site Manager. Dinkins liked having "Sarge in charge." In the overlapping and unsynchronized schedules of launch crews, cooks, site managers, flight security controllers, and security police, it would be a miracle indeed for a launch crew to be on duty with all the same personnel twice. Even so, it happened.

Though SAC would be quick to take credit for the fact, and declare it a key component in security to ensure that no possibility for collusion occur, it was, in fact, just how stuff worked out. So having Sarge at the door was a welcome site in an otherwise dreary duty.

Sarge considered all the "regular Kilo crews" to be "his boys." He'd never allow anyone to hear him refer to these officers as "boys," but with a sleeve full of chevrons and twenty-four years in this man's Air Force, he had seen it all. Paternalistic pride was unavoidable. These young men, even the captains and majors among them, had a special place in his heart.

Sarge and his wife Sally had raised three daughters and two sons. Two of the girls were married, one of them now pregnant with twins. The youngest girl was at Texas Tech on a volleyball scholarship with her eye on veterinary school. The boys had followed the old man… but as officers—not enlisted.

Mike was at the Academy, with Uncle Sam footing the bill, and Jim had put himself through SMU with summer jobs doing construction, student loans up to his eyes, and all the help Pop could muster—which wasn't much.

When Jim washed out of Air Force flight school, he landed in a capsule in Minot, North Dakota. He had lost his chance at wings, but with a missile badge on his chest, Sarge hoped Jim still had a shot at command.

It was Jim becoming a Missileer that had made Sarge opt for missiles himself. He couldn't be on a crew, of course, but he could be a Site Manager and see to it that his flight was the cleanest, sharpest, best-mowed, best-run Launch Control Facility in SAC. He was a man of great pride even though, essentially, he was a janitor. It was a far cry from the policies of Sergeant Craddock, his counterpart.

Craddock and Maxwell alternated duty as Site Managers for Kilo. Dinkins felt certain that there had been alerts he had pulled at Kilo when he had not seen a Site Manger EVER… and those most certainly were Craddock tours. Craddock did the absolute minimum and managed to look like an unmade bed in the process. Pratt had written him up on more than one occasion, but Craddock was "short." He had less than three months to full retirement and his give-a-shit level was a negative number. What were they gonna do? Fire him?

One of Sarge's personal policies was to greet every launch crew at the door and unload their gear. While the crew received their holsters and sidearms from the Flight Security Controller, Sarge would remove their Tech Order and personal bags from the vehicle, arranging them neatly beside the elevator access door so that they could make an orderly entry.

The Tech Order bags housed the bulky three-ring binder—the three hundred plus pages of diagrams and checklists necessary to run an LCC and its missiles. Though trained to do every action from memory, policy was that the crew assessed a given situation, opened the attendant checklist, and step-by-step checked off each action on the acetate-covered page with a grease pencil. The T.O. bags were heavy, but the personal bags held not only overnight gear for each crew member but also his books. With almost no exception, every officer was studying for his MBA and had *lots* to pack to alert with him. Having Sarge wrangle it, even for a few feet was a luxury.

---

At 23, Dinkins was only a year and a half out of college. Deemed an Officer and a Gentleman by his commission, he had been catapulted from "grungy, broke college student" to "acknowledged military professional" almost overnight.

At his commissioning, the ROTC staff stood outside the ballroom to give each new officer his first salute… and receive, in turn, a shiny new silver dollar. They made quite a haul that day. Dink was proud… but having men twenty years his senior—his Dad and his uncle's age—defer to him made him very ill at ease. And now, he was uncomfortable having a man almost old enough to be his grandfather carrying his bags because one man had bars on his collar and the other had stripes on his sleeve. Oddly, he realized, he allowed it out of respect. The man's dignity was at stake. Dinkins also hated being armed.

One of the reasons Dinkins had selected USAF ROTC instead of Army was the notion that most of the shooting air officers did was from mounted armaments at distant targets. A sidearm implied closer conflict. The reason for the weapons in this setting was simple in principle but much more interesting in Air Force lore. Simmons had explained it.

"Ostensibly, the purpose for a Combat Launch Crew to be armed is to protect the contents of the 'safe.' This little eight-by-eight-by-nine red box contains twelve sealed coded documents and two sets of chrome keys. Between them, these items represent access to the fifty Minuteman Missiles in your direct squadron—and many millions of lives. As crewmembers, you are sworn to protect the documents and keys from unauthorized use at all costs. ALL costs. So you will be armed with .38 police specials."

Then his tone became very conspiratorial, "Now, the fact of the

matter is that you will be in a concrete capsule ninety feet underground behind two eight-ton blast doors the access to which will
be guarded by a Flight Security Controller armed with his own
.38, several M-16s and, depending on time of day, as many as six
other Security Police with equal or greater armament. No one is
going to get into that safe without a LOT of firepower."

At this point, he actually walked to the classroom door and
looked into the hall before proceeding: "On the other hand, there
may be a much more likely use for the crew's sidearms. After
USING the documents and keys, launching your missiles, and
being bombed by incoming nuclear weapons yourselves, the
greatest likelihood is that you are gonna find yourself trapped
in the capsule. In the event of a near miss, it is conceivable that
the elevator shaft will collapse—outside the external blast door,
blocking it from opening."

"Oh, shit," had been Matteo's response.

"No shit," Simmons snapped back. "In that case, you are to
open the "Emergency Egress Checklist" in the T. O. Let's all turn
to that, shall we? As you can see here, it details how a crewmember is to climb on top of the LCC and use that big-ass wrench to
open that huge iron door on the Commander's end of the capsule's sloped ceiling. As you will note from the diagram, the door
is attached to the ceiling with chains. Once loosened, it will swing
into the enclosure—most likely sweeping the man opening it off
of his perch."

Pausing for effect, Simmons added, "You will note that this is
a DEPUTY duty. If the impact of the half-ton door does not kill
him, falling off the LCC ten feet to the bottom of the capsule will
certainly make the next task a challenge."

They all turned the page to a new set of diagrams and steps as
Simmons continued, "Once opened, the door will reveal a corru-
gated steel tube filled with sand that rises to within three feet of
the surface at about a forty-five-degree angle. A shovel is provided

to dig the sand from the tube down into the capsule, allowing the crew—or what is left of it—to climb out. Provided, of course, that nearby nuclear detonation has not liquefied the sand, resulting in a tube now filled with molten or solid glass."

Waiting for the proper time to try to escape the capsule, he pointed out dryly, was totally a crew call. Understanding that a crew might have to survive in such isolation for some time, the planners of the capsule had provisioned it with food, water, and an air regeneration system. Yet another checklist in the T.O. detailed how to gain access. Though the provisions were given equal storage space, they were not consumable at the same rates. As a result, a crew had supplies sufficient for twenty-eight days of water fourteen days of food, and seven days of–air. With careful rationing, the water and food could be stretched. The air, of course, could not. This was when Simmons turned to them with a devilish look and said, "A review of this math will cause you to arrive at the awareness that quick use of the sidearm could effectively double all of those numbers."

Gray and Matteo had found it hilarious. Dinkins was not amused.

---

Standing at the loading barrel just outside the Support Building door, Dinkins again thought about how much he hated being armed. And, though he knew in his soul that none of those scenarios would ever happen, the idea that the greatest threat to him surviving his duty might be his commander unsettled him every time he holstered his weapon.

"Who are we relieving, Sarge?"

"Captain Farragut and Lieutenant Crawford."

I thought Farragut was crewed with Pickett," Pratt spat out "Pickett" as if the very name tasted bad. The effect was not lost on Sarge.

"Normally he is, sir. Seems Lieutenant Pickett has the flu and Lieutenant Crawford was on standby. Luck of the draw."

"The luck is with Farragut. A day without Pickett is a much better day."

Dinkins didn't say a word. Knocking another officer always was a bad idea, but in front of enlisted men who have to WORK with that officer, it was asking for trouble. Respect, Dinkins knew well, was either earned by character or demanded by rank. In Pickett's case, earning it was out of the question—but a comment like Pratt's could eliminate even the effect of rank. In the military, the respect structure was imperative.

Bringing focus quickly back to the matters at hand, Dinkins asked Proctor, "What's our status?"

"SAT is out on the day run. Roads, as you are aware, are clear and dry. The guys are halfway through LF checks as of last report which was… eight minutes ago… and we have no incident reports. They are scheduled to gas up at Waverly, finish the route, and be back by three or so."

---

The SAT was a blue pickup truck containing two 19 to 23-year-old security policemen, whatever the cook had packed for their lunch, two M-16s, an obscene amount of ammunition, and a radio. Their job was to ensure the security of the actual Launch Facilities—the LFs.

Located in a wide circle roughly three to ten miles from the LCC, the missile site LFs were 100 by 100-feet-square and surrounded by a twelve-foot chain link fence topped with razor wire. Leading up to them from the nearest road was a gravel drive that continued through the gate to a concrete pad, and below that pad, the missile launcher itself. Around the pad were three posts containing movement-sensing radar aimed in an overlapping pattern to cover the area above the enclosure. Anything moving in that "outer zone" would trigger an "OZ" alert on the commander's console—and, potentially, a Situation 6 (SIT 6) security alert.

This Outer Zone Alarm easily could be triggered innocently by birds, rabbits, or even snow falling off the radar stanchion. Once the OZ Alarm went off it was given time to reset—five minutes—and if it reset... no harm, no foul. However, if it did NOT reset, a SIT 6 was declared and the SAT was dispatched to find out who was there and what were they doing, and report it to the FSC by radio.

Similarly, sensors placed beneath the surface could detect vibrations underground, to keep a savvy enemy from tunneling into the site. Inner Zone alerts were much more serious. But, an IZ by itself could be nearby thunder or a herd of buffalo stampeding by... no kidding. If an IZ Alert light appeared on the commander's console, it, too, was given the five-minute reset opportunity. If it did not reset, the SAT made a trip.

If both the IZ and OZ alarms were triggered at the same time, then the SAT was dispatched the instant it came on. Even if they reset in five minutes, the SAT was to examine the site thoroughly for signs of foul play.

Alarms notwithstanding, the SAT went to inspect every LF twice every day, just to see if everything looked "okay." It also gave them something to do. For six days out of eight, up to six of these young men hung around the support building waiting for barbed wire-encircled concrete pads to come under attack from communist aggressors. It was damned dull work. In fact, the sheer improbability of an attack on American soil was so ludicrous it never made it past the "possibility" filters of the brain. Most of them looked forward to the route. It took them off site. Broke the boredom. And if the crew was "cool," it could mean an ice cream run. Totally unauthorized and totally against regs. And—totally worth the risk.

But today... nothing like that would be happening.

---

"That it?" Pratt asked.

Proctor checked his day sheet and added, "Not quite, sir. I show us scheduled for power failure simulation today…"

An enormously child-like groan emanated from Pratt. In his best unhappy-five-year-old voice he said, "Noooooo. I don't wanna do a power failure simulation…"

With a totally straight face, Dinkins looked at Pratt: "Now, Billy, if you're a good boy and kill the power like a big, strong captain, Sergeant Maxwell will see to it you get two desserts tonight."

Pratt looked from Dinkins to Maxwell, raised one eyebrow and waited.

"Well, see how it goes, Captain," Sarge said.

Stifling a grin, Pratt looked at his shoes, sighed and said, "Okay, let's do it."

Sarge stepped out of the room for a moment as Dinkins and Pratt gave Proctor the code word they would use for access. Control of the electromagnetically sealed access door to the elevator was held by the crew below in the LCC. Proctor stepped to the door, lifted the handset, and pressed the call button.

Ninety feet below him, a buzzer sounded. Deputy Commander Gray Crawford grabbed the hard-line and began to walk to the back of the capsule, where the entry door access panel was mounted.

"Kilo completely ready for relief. Whaddaya say, Sheriff?"

Ignoring Gray's casual tone, Sgt. Proctor said, "Relief crew plus Site Manager to enter, sir."

"Say the magic words…" Gray grinned.

"Seventeen-seventy-six, Sir," Proctor responded.

"Words of freedom. Y'all, come on down."

With access authentication verified, Gray pushed the button on the panel in the capsule and ninety feet above him, the access lock topside buzzed. Proctor snapped the door open and Sgt. Maxwell entered with the crew's personal bags. Dinkins and Pratt carried their own Tech Order bags and entered the elevator for the long, slow decent.

"I hate power loss simulation. When the diesel cuts in, it is deafening," Pratt whined as he screwed in his earplugs.

"Let a storm come up and we won't have to simulate loss," Dinkins said.

Pratt had been a radio announcer in college and now he assumed his best radio voice, "Welcome to central Missouri; the intergalactic headquarters of unstable power."

Not wanting to be left out, Sarge chimed in, "I think the thunder frightens the squirrels in the little cages, sir."

"Roger that," even Dink was into it now.

As they thumped into place at the bottom of the shaft, Sarge swung the elevator's grating open and Dinkins went to open the outer ten-by-ten-foot blast door. Captain Pratt, 25 years old and ready to doff his blues for a cushy corporate job with some real pay, held court over his two subordinates. "Gentlemen, even if we were in the midst of a raging thunderstorm resulting in an authentic, complete power failure—on the first Monday of the month, we'd simulate power failure anyway. That's the book. And SAC is a by-the-goddamn-book organization."

"Roger that," Dinkins agreed. He and Sarge were putting in their earplugs against the anticipated din of the LCEB—the underground Launch Control Equipment Building.

## Kilo-01 Capsule

In the capsule, Gray stood at the entrance to the capsule watching a panel that tracked the status of various access doors between topside and his capsule. He already had watched the ELEVATOR ACCESS DOOR light illuminate and go out as the crew entered. Now the OUTER BLAST DOOR OPEN light illuminated, indicating that the pins of the outer blast door had been withdrawn and the relief crew was entering the Tunnel Junction, a small vestibule between the capsule and the Launch Control Equipment Building (LCEB). Gray had donned the headset connecting him to the LCEB headset and was moving back to the deputy's console to open his T.O.

"Time to put my shoes and weapon back on, I guess…" Farragut said, beginning to reach for his holster and gun belt, which hung from the equipment rack handle behind his right shoulder.

"Not unless you're in a big hurry. They'll be killing power in a second," Gray replied. His gun belt hung on the equipment rack nearest the combination toilet/sink near the entry to the capsule.

"Oh, yeah. It is first Monday, isn't it?" Farragut realized.

Gray opened the T. O. and thumbed down a long series of dymo-tape labels attached to the acetate-bound checklists until he reached one marked PwrLoss.

### Kilo-01 Tunnel Junction

Once past the blast door, Maxwell and the relief crew stepped into the small vestibule—the tunnel junction. To the immediate right was the closed blast door to the capsule. To the left was the opening to the LCEB. Deputy Dinkins took out his Tech Order and thumbed down his tabs to one marked PwrLossSim. Opening to that checklist, he began to read very loudly to be heard over the massive air chiller and through the ear protection each man wore.

"1. Site Manager to Power Panel."

Maxwell replied, "Check."

"2. Crewmember standing by with insulated hook."

Pratt took a wooden walking cane hanging from a handrail and stood prepared to pull the Site Manager from the electrical panel should he somehow come in contact with live electricity and need to be dragged from the source, "Check."

"3. Throw the main commercial power breaker."

Maxwell probably had said, "Check." But the instant he opened the main power breaker, all lights went out in the massive underground building, the air chiller made a deafening groan of protest, and both blast valves on the thirty-six-inch external air intake and outtake tubes slammed shut, creating an instant over-pressure. Without ear protection, they might all have ruptured eardrums. All of it was perfectly normal power loss simulation activity.

## Kilo-01 Capsule

Inside Kilo Capsule, the overhead lighting suddenly went out and both of the capsule's twenty-four-inch intake and outtake blast valves slammed shut. A shudder ran through the enclosure as the battery-powered DC brushes dropped onto the motor generator shaft to keep all equipment in the capsule fed with stable power.

With only three pairs of small, DC-powered emergency lamps for primary illumination, the capsule took on a very dramatic look with three "pools of light" surrounded by vast lakes of darkness lit only by equipment indicators.

"What a shock," Farragut mocked in his best super-hero voice, "Loss of primary power! Deputy, note the time."

Dinkins glanced at the huge clock over the commander's console, "1803 and thirty seconds Zulu... Loss of Power checklist open. Verifying all systems running on DC power."

"Check."

"Ensure startup of Emergency Air Conditioning Unit."

Taking things a bit more seriously, Farragut cut Gray off, "You get EACU startup steps and I'll run the Command and Control steps independently."

"Sure."

Gray moved to the enclosure entrance and stood beside the Air Force blue, double refrigerator-sized Emergency Air Conditioning Unit (EACU) and noted the first step: WAIT 60 SECONDS FOR EACU TO AUTOSTART. He took a look at the capsule clock mounted above the commander; one of the key areas lit by the limited emergency lighting. Simulation was one thing, but if they didn't have cold air over those racks in two minutes, they would have less than two more minutes to evacuate the capsule alive.

### Kilo-01 LCEB

The crew and Sarge awaited auto-startup of the stand-by diesel generator. This massive Allis-Chalmers engine was designed to cut in within thirty seconds of a sustained power loss. It would return AC power to the Air Chiller and to the capsule. Flashlight in hand, Dinkins watched as the second hand approached the thirty-second mark.

Starting the diesel manually was the next set of contingency steps on the checklist. Dinkins' right hand was poised over the Manual Start switch while the other hand attempted to hold the flashlight on the T. O. and cover his left ear at the same time. Everyone HATED being in the Equipment Building when a diesel started up or was running. What had been loud before became a chest-crushing din. Dinkins watched his second hand pass the thirty-second mark. It wasn't starting automatically.

When the designers at Boeing initially wrote the specifications for a stand-by power system, they were operating under a larger set of specifications outlined by SAC. With the Cuban Missile Crisis fresh in their memories, the generals had required back-up systems to the back-up systems. "What good would it be," they reasoned, "if you built a big war machine that ground to a halt if the plug got kicked out of the wall?" Independent, redundant systems would act as a series of safety nets to ensure that the thirty-minute war would not be interrupted by something as trivial as a storm over mid-Missouri… or, much more likely, an ice storm across the Canadian border, where the other five missile bases and the bulk of the missiles would be. In that spirit, the auto-start system for the diesel had one battery-powered electric starter motor and timer for auto-start, and the manual-start motor was separate and independent.

Just as Dinkins depressed the Manual Start switch, the internal clock of the diesel sent a start signal of its own. Like grinding the starter when turning the ignition key of a running engine, the resulting commands arrived just enough out of sync to create a conflict unforeseen by the design group at Allis-Chalmers. An arc of electricity created a small shower of sparks, and the room fell completely silent.

"What the hell was that?" Pratt asked.

"I don't know. But it wasn't good," Dinkins replied. He had wanted to say 'I didn't do it!' but his hand still was on the starter switch.

## Kilo-01 Capsule

Gray had checked off the EACU START on the Power Loss checklist. The monster had growled to life right on cue. Gray had taken only three steps when the EACU stopped.

"EACU failure. Attempting restart."

Going through the motions of the exercise, Farragut was startled by this news. Most of the exercise checklist steps were for practice—just in case. This actually was a problem.

"Stay on the checklist. We'll probably have good air in another couple of seconds when the diesel kicks in," he said.

"That seems late, too," said Gray, turning the restart key.

### Kilo-01 LCEB

Pratt had become all business and was taking command: "Sarge, reset that circuit breaker."

"Yes, sir."

"What's our time, Dink?"

"We're two minutes into the five-minute lockout, Bill. We won't have commercial power for another three minutes."

"Roger, that. Try the diesel again."

"Have been. We have a total failure on standby power. I think they've shorted each other out." Dinkins was glad it was dark so no one could see just how pale he probably was becoming. This wasn't supposed to happen. The paperwork on this would be horrific. It might create some cloud of doubt about his Instructor status. He already was wording his report in his mind and wondering if the wording on Pratt's and Sarge's reports would back him up.

"Dink, get on the horn to the capsule and let them know what's going on."

"No juice," Dinkins reminded him. The capsule and equipment building were connected by a hard-line headset and buzzer system. Unfortunately, it was AC powered. For the next couple of minutes, they were blind, deaf, and dumb.

Pratt resigned himself: "So. We wait on commercial power. Everybody take a breather, I guess."

### Kilo-01 Capsule

Things were heating up—emotionally, and physically. The many thousands of miles of electrical wiring in the capsule still had power from the motor generator and were creating resistance. With no cooling air moving across them to carry the heat away, the temperature was rising at the rate of a degree per second. What had been a cool and constant sixty-five degrees was already ninety and moving up.

Procedure called for shutting down all non-essential systems, transferring control of the missiles to the back-up LCC, and evacuating immediately. It was a survivability move to preserve the equipment and life of the crew—and in that order. SAC was very unforgiving about messing up its equipment. SAC also was notoriously unforgiving about transferring launch authority unless the emergency was dire and authentic.

The sweat was starting to roll into Farragut's eyes as he read and reread the checklist line that they had come to: Go to Shutdown checklist.

"GOING TO SHUTDOWN. I'll run everything and you get that damned blast door open."

Gray wanted to argue. Farragut was an unknown. It had been a very relaxed Alert and Gray had liked him... but he'd never trained with him and didn't know Farragut's capability under pressure. If Gray wasn't with him on the checklist... wasn't backing him up on each line... he would have no idea if Farragut had run the list completely or properly. Whatever SAC felt about this shutdown wouldn't touch Farragut. He wasn't staying in the Air Force. This could hammer Gray, though. Never mind retaining instructor status, his career would be damaged if not ended if wasn't completely justified—and if it ever was discovered that he hadn't even run the damned checklist!

With the heat crossing a hundred degrees, Gray headed for the blast door. His career would be even shorter if he died in a flash fire in the capsule. Estimates were that it took "about" four minutes without cooling air for the capsule to superheat to levels beyond human tolerance. They now were coming up on three.

The blast door had two manual hydraulic pumps. To open the door, the operator stooped down, entered the five-foot high, four-foot wide access tunnel and swung a bracket into place that held the door in perfect alignment so that the eight-inch diameter steel pins would not drag against their housings as they were extended or retracted. The operator then selected the pin's direction of travel—OUT to seal the door, or IN to withdraw the pins for exit— and manually began pumping the hydraulic fluid that moved the pins from one end of their travel to the other. As the pins neared the end of travel, the resistance on the pump increased and the operator had to move to the second handle, which offered finer, more sensitive control and greater mechanical advantage. When both were pumped as far as they would go, the operator would release the bracket and push on the door to begin its opening.

On his best day, Gray could pump the manual hydraulic pins of the blast door in, release the alignment bracket, and push the door open in thirty-five seconds. With the adrenaline in his system, he was betting on twenty-five. He would be wrong by nearly two minutes.

Kilo-01 LCEB

Dinkins decided to try the diesel again. Pushing the start button produced a loud CLICK-CLICK-CLICK-CLICK-CLICK and another small shower of sparks.

"What the hell are you doing, Dink?"

"Just giving it another shot."

"Damn, it, Dink. We know it's busted. Does that reset the five-minute timer?"

The question jarred him. Trainer after trainer had drilled him with the axiom that the checklist was "GOD." Taking an action that delayed return to normal status was a major error. He knew better; yet here in the reality of the moment, he found himself acting independently and thinking instead of blindly following the instructions on his flash-lit page. And... he'd screwed up. He knew this wasn't being scored, but the sense that he was "*always being watched*" never left him. Would Pratt put this in the report? Would Sarge?

"We'll, sir, you know, the circuit breaker don't know nuthin' about the generator," Sarge offered from the darkness. "It'll reset in a coupla minutes here. I wuz gonna ask the Deputy to take another shot at it myself. Didn't think about the checklist. Sorry 'bout that."

Bless him, Sarge was right. The circuit breaker didn't "know nuthin' about the generator." If Dink had been thinking clearer, he'd have come to that conclusion himself. At least he knew now that Sarge wouldn't rat him out. As a bit of insurance against Pratt doing so, he said, "Yeah, Captain. *everybody* knows that the circuit breaker timer is independent."

Sarge was glad the darkness hid his grin. The little lieutenant was covering his narrow ass nicely. But, no one was grinning in the capsule.

Kilo-01 Capsule

"Hotel Capsule, this is Kilo we have commercial power failure and EACU failure. We're in shutdown, and are transferring control of our missiles to you. I have nine clean and green with KILO-08 showing a fault. It is launchable. We're approaching three minutes without cooling air…" Farragut's voice was controlled, but panic was leaking around the edges.

Hotel-01 Capsule

Hotel was not only Kilo's back-up capsule, it was the Squadron Command Post, and, as luck would have it, the Wing Alternate Command Post as well.

"Transfer accepted, Stan. Get your ass out of there." The commander on duty at Hotel-01 was Major Lawrence Collins, Whiteman's second most senior active Crew Commander.

"C-Major," as his men called him, claimed to have seen and

done it all. When a smart-ass second lieutenant with one too many Scotches in him had challenged the Major's generalization and asked if he'd turned keys, the Major pointed to a picture over the bar. A glorious color shot of a twin Minuteman launch from Vandenburg was labeled, "Whiteman crew turns keys on test birds."

Collins wasn't running the Alternate Command Post for nothing. "Deputy, I'll report Kilo capsule unmanned and missiles transferred. You get on the horn to the Command Post and have the hospital alerted, then call Kilo's FSC and let him know his crew's in trouble."

"I'm on it."

## Kilo-01 Capsule

The temperature inside Kilo was passing 145 degrees. Both men were soaked with perspiration and finding breathing difficult. With the equipment shut down, Farragut hoped it wouldn't get much hotter before the blast door was open. Gray had pumped both levers until they would go no farther, dropped the seating bracket, and was pushing with all his energy… but the door would not move. In his stocking feet, he was slipping and sliding, unable to get any traction on the painted concrete floor of the access tube.

"OPEN THE GODDAMN DOOR, GRAY! WE'RE GONNA DIE IN HERE," Farragut screamed.

"I can't get it to move. It's stuck!"

"Oh, God. Overpressure in the LCEB."

Farragut was right.

## Kilo-01 LCEB

With all of the blast valves shut, the air pressure had built up to a point that it had become painful, even with ear protection.

"Let's pump the exterior blast valves open," Pratt suggested. "At least we can get rid of this damned overpressure while we wait."

Pratt hardly had finished speaking when commercial power returned. Lights came on, the blast valves cycled open, and the air chiller charged to life with a roar. Though the temperature in the equipment building hardly seemed to change, it became immediately cooler.

Dinkins took the headset to call the capsule and advise them that they were ready to enter.

## Kilo-01 Capsule

As AC power was restored to the capsule, powerful electromagnets in the motor/generator engaged, drawing the DC brushes back up and off of the power drive shaft. Turns of the motor/generator did not vary as it switched from battery power to commercial power. Temperature in the capsule was 165 degrees and still climbing, though slower. The headset buzzer from the LCEB was sounding— as was the FSC's direct line.

"We gotta open the blast valves. Gotta let in the cool air. Farragut?"

Exhausted from the ordeal of trying to pump the door open, the commander was barely conscious. Not enough to understand what he was hearing. Gray mustered every ounce of remaining strength to walk back toward the capsule—now hot to the touch— to try to cycle the internal blast valves open.

### Kilo-01 LCEB

"Bill, I'm not getting an answer."

Pratt had moved into the vestibule to await opening of the capsule blast door. He turned, curious. "Really? Wonder if they're in an exercise or something?"

"In the fifty-three day alerts I have pulled, we have never had an exercise between 0945 and 1415 Central," Dink said.

"You're shitting me, right? How the hell would you remember exercise times?"

"No, I'm not kidding. I... well... I DO remember stuff like that."

Pratt looked skeptical and impressed. "Yeah, well. It would be just like SAC to pull an exercise just when they know that every LCC in the country is simulating a power loss. Besides... what can we do? The book says we wait."

Still. Dinkins had a bad feeling. If he could communicate, Gray would have found a way.

### Kilo-01 Capsule

Gray hadn't opened blast valves manually since initial training. He found that, even half-conscious, it was like riding a bike—his hands knew what to do.

Overcoming external pressure was the job of a blast valve. In fact, once in place, external pressure kept them seated. Placing the hot T-handle into the pump, Gray pushed. Nothing. He pushed harder. Nothing. Finally, he lay on it with his whole body. The magical physics of uncompressible fluids in the tiny hydraulic cylinder overcame the pressure. The blast valve seal broke. Even though the valve was opened only partially, the cool air began rushing in.

Heat within the capsule had risen to almost intolerable levels.

Pressure changes caused a weak linkage in the number four shock isolator to rupture and bleed out, but surface tension between the internal piston and the cylinder walls combined with the perfect balance of the capsule floor caused no noticeable changes.

Two more pumps on the handle were all he could manage. The hot metal had burned both his hands unmercifully. Gray abandoned the pump and, stepping across his Commander, he leaned into the blast door, hoping and praying.

The door began to move.

## Kilo-01 Tunnel Junction

Pratt heard the blast door seal hiss and disengage. He moved aside, expecting it to open.

"Here we go."

In an instant, the super-heated air from the capsule rushed into the super-chilled air of the vestibule. Within seconds Pratt, Dinkins and Sarge were surrounded by a hot, swirling fog as moisture in the air condensed rapidly, making the USAF regulation painted concrete floor and walls slick as ice.

With the blast door open only a few feet, Gray slid into the tunnel junction—barefoot, shirtless, and soaked from head to toe. He gestured toward the capsule, "Get him. He's out."

Before either officer could move, Sarge grabbed Gray and slung him across the slick floor into the cooler air, away from the capsule. Then he began pushing the blast door open with the apparent intent of going in after Farragut. The heat pouring out of the capsule was like a blast furnace.

"Don't go in there!" Dinkins shouted.

Sarge looked at him in disbelief. He was about to protest when Farragut, who seemed to be vomited out of the capsule, knocked Sarge from his feet. The exhausted commander collapsed beside his deputy with a wet slap. One sock and his briefs remained on his body. He had stripped off everything else in the oven that the capsule had become.

Something inside Dinkins clicked. Quickly, he dragged Sarge to the external blast door. "Get this open and go topside. Call the Command Post and get medical help out here, now."

"Got it," Sarge snapped, and turned to the task of opening the external blast door.

Pratt was staring into the capsule, trying to decide the next move. Dinkins urged him to check Farragut, which caused Pratt to leave the capsule blast door and move toward the now reviving Commander.

"Get on this side and help him up, Bill," Dinkins urged.

As Sarge pushed the main blast door open, Dinkins said, "Sarge."

"Sir?"

"The crew has suffered an overheat condition and needs assistance. That is 100 percent of everything you say. Everything else you may or may not have seen down here is classified. And you'll have to run your reports on today past us before filing them."

For a second, Sarge was truly hurt. How dare this little pipsqueak tell him what he could and couldn't say. He'd been inside the capsule hundreds of times. He often brought chow and came in to clean up and run maintenance. He was cleared to be there. His reports were NOT theirs to censor. He had a duty. He didn't need to be told...

"Move, Sarge."

"On my way" is all Sarge said. What he didn't say was, "Sir."

"Classified?" Pratt asked. "What the hell about this is classified?"

Both men were beginning to stir.

"EACU failed," Gray started. "We were cooking in there. Blast door wouldn't open..."

"We transferred launch command to Hotel and shut down. God,

it got hot in there," Farragut added. The blisters on Gray's hands were oozing and his face was cherry red.

"We'll have to do a slow restart and assess damage," Pratt mused aloud.

"Right, but FIRST we need to get back into the equipment building and tag-out the diesel, Bill." Dinkins looked at him with an intensity that was as confusing to Pratt as the "classified" comment had been.

"Ok, Dink. Tag the diesel and I'll help these guys..."

Dinkins cut him off, "You have to sign the tag-out with me, Bill. You *know* that."

As this pissy little exchange continued, Farragut took stock and realized several things: Dinkins was one by-the-book guy; he, himself, was lucky to be alive; and, wearing only one sock and a pair of very wet briefs, he was seriously out of uniform. So was his deputy. He also was getting damned cold.

Reentering the capsule was not something Gray relished, but his clothes were in there and his commander certainly couldn't go topside in skivvies. Farragut already was moving back into the capsule so Gray fell in behind him.

The soaked uniforms that had been shucked like wet suits had baked almost dry in the blast furnace the capsule had become. Gray welcomed the toasty warmth of the cotton against his now very cold, wet skin.

"I never thought I'd want to be warm." Faragut was buttoning his shirt and tucking it in. Grabbing a towel out of his personal gear bag, he began to dry off his head, "It was getting cold out there."

"We'll probably get pneumonia from the cold-hot-cold changes," Gray said, looking for his own towel.

Coming out from under the terry cloth hair dryer, Farragut's eye line brought him up short.

"Holy shit! Look at that."

Farragut was pointing at his gun belt, hanging on the equipment rack. The leather of the holster had cracked and peeled in the heat.

A few seconds later the realization hit both men at pretty much the same instant. Their guns had never left the capsule.

# CHAPTER 10

*Remember men, we're fighting for this woman's honor;*
*which is probably more than she ever did.*
**Groucho Marx**

"**H**E WANTS to see you in the Oval."

White House Press Secretary Jeb Klein pulled on his jacket and headed toward the Chief Executive's office. The firestorm that had been his life for the last several months was becoming even hotter. With blood in the water, the sharks were circling closer every day. As he turned the corner, a phalanx of reporters spotted him and surged into his path. The assault became a barrage.

"Do you think the 18-minute gap was intentionally erased…"

"Will he resign?"

"Is he considering resignation?"

"Mr. Klein, there is talk of imminent impeachment, what do you…"

"Will he be impeached, sir? Or do you think he'll resign?"

"Is Vice President Ford preparing to take office?"

Klein made it as far as the access corridor to the Oval Office.

This was off limits to reporters and was like sailing into a sheltered port after weathering a killer storm. The waters here were smoother but he could still hear it raging behind him. One more doorway and he would be out of their sight and they would quit barking—silence the clamor.

Then came the one piercing question that caught him off balance. It pierced the din of voices as if amplified—as if giving voice to his own questions.

"What will it take to save this presidency, sir?"

Stunned, he turned to the flashing bulbs and glaring film camera lights. Wide-eyed he uttered the only sentence forbidden to a White House Press Secretary.

"No comment!"

The question and its response led every news report that evening. The banners over *The Washington Post* and *The New York Times* were identical.

"NO COMMENT"

# CHAPTER 11

*They are all my sons...*
**Arthur Miller**

ARGE REMAINED hurt and pissed as he exited the elevator alcove into the FSC Ready Room. The FSC, Sgt. Proctor, was on the phone and turned in shock as the door opened.

"Sarge! We got a call from Hotel saying there was trouble downstairs. I've got the hospital on the phone right now. The Flight Surgeon wants to know what is going on." He quickly extended the phone, "Talk to him."

"Sergeant Maxwell here, sir."

"This is the Flight Surgeon, Colonel Samuels. What's the situation? Anyone hurt out there?"

Sarge thought about Dinkins and spat out the words carefully, "The crew has suffered an overheat condition and may need assistance."

"What the hell does that mean? Were you there? Tell me what happened, Sergeant."

Sarge was trying to figure out how to explain it. He was

113

visualizing the little snot, Dinkins, on the floor beside the all but naked Captain Farragut, and Captain Pratt all bent over helping Lieutenant Crawford when the totality of the picture he had seen began to crystallize.

"*Holy crap,*" he thought. The little lieutenant, that Dinkins... he had choreographed the whole thing! He'd arranged it so that the on-duty crew was physically between the relief and the capsule entrance. Dinkins had positioned the half-conscious crew so that they were protecting their capsule. Or, at least it was defendable that way. Except—Dinkins and Pratt were armed. The on-duty crew was NOT.

"SERGEANT! Answer me," the Flight Surgeon insisted.

THAT was why Dinkins had been so adamant.

"Uhm... I can't say much beyond that, sir."

"Was the crew coherent? Were they injured? Do we need to send a chopper? I need details, man. Get me some information."

The last sounded like an order—and a way out. "I'll check and get right back to you, sir."

Sarge handed the phone back to Proctor and headed for the squawk box.

"Are you out of your MIND?" Proctor hissed. Then, into the phone, "No, Sir. No, Colonel, I was NOT speaking to you just then, sir."

### Kilo-01 LCEB

"Okay. Tag-out signed. I hope you are happy now, Deputy." Pratt was not amused.

"Bill, we have a situation here. We need to talk before we go in."

"Those guys have been through enough, Dink. They've been in there close to seventeen hours now and were almost cooked alive. They need rest. Hell, they probably should to go to the hospital.

We have to sort this whole thing out in reports that will take us the rest of the tour just to organize…"

Dinkins cut him off. "That is my point. Bill. They were outside the capsule—unarmed."

It took a second for the implications to hit Pratt. "Oh, my God. They'll go to jail."

## Kilo-01 Topside

Maxwell starred at the squawk box—the direct line to the capsule—for several seconds. He KNEW that it was not his place to make the call. He knew that if he did, he might blow whatever plan Dinkins might be up to in order to save those boys from Leavenworth. Hell. All they had done was get caught in a war game gone bad. Nothing they did was wrong until the door opened and they were not armed. Even if they'd been buck-naked, they'd be smelling like a rose if they'd had their guns on to protect that damned safe.

He turned to the FSC and said, "You'll need to contact the capsule crew and see what help they need, Proctor. They just shooed me out of there and… and…"

Sgt. Hank Proctor had been a sky cop running LF duty for four years at Minot and a Flight Security Controller for going on three-and-a-half years at Whiteman. During which time, exactly NOTHING had ever happened. Now there was some kind of action and he was totally in the dark.

"And WHAT? Sarge… what happened?"

Sarge met Proctor's eyes for just a second. Dinkins had been right. There was nothing more he could say, "Do your job, Hank. I gotta go move the crew vehicle. We might need a chopper to land out there."

Proctor barely breathed it, "Sonofabitch."

Whatever it was, he wasn't getting it out of Sarge today.

"Permission to enter?" Pratt called out.

## Kilo-01 Tunnel Junction

"We're in restart. Come on in," Gray shouted.

Now, both fully dressed—and armed—Farragut and Gray were calling out steps on the restart checklist. Dinkins and Pratt tried to act naturally but had no idea how to do that unselfconsciously.

"We'd like to hold changeover off until we get her back up," Farragut shot over his shoulder. "Wouldn't want to give you a dead capsule attached to no missiles."

"I'd sure as hell take it," Pratt quipped.

The topside direct line was buzzing.

"I'll get it." Dink offered. With both men up to their eyes in checklists, it gave him something to do, "Whatcha got, Sergeant?"

"Lieutenant Dinkins? Sergeant Proctor topside, Sir. The Flight Surgeon is clamoring for details. He wants to know should he send a chopper."

Proctor then heard the two words he least wanted to hear.

"Standby one."

Pretense aside, it was now time for some truth-telling. Dinkins didn't know any other way to handle it.

"Guys, the Flight Surgeon wants to know some status."

Farragut was stuck. He didn't want to screw up Gray's career, but he also didn't want to be caught in any kind of a lie. Gray knew it was the commander's call; a commander he hadn't even met until thirty hours ago when "Picky" Pickett was too ill to report for duty. The question hung for a second. It was Pratt who broke the tension.

"Tell the Flight Surgeon to dispatch a helicopter. The deputy has blisters to his hands. Tell him the crew wishes to remain on duty but probably needs for him to certify them as duty-worthy. That is the situation, isn't it, guys?"

There was a moment of stunned silence as each man realized he couldn't argue with Pratt's logic. The unspoken message was

that Pratt expected them to come down to relieve him that night…
not to get carted off to jail.

Dinkins relayed the message precisely, with his my-mind-is-
a-recording-device accuracy. Moments later, Hotel restored the
missiles to Kilo's command and congratulated them on managing
the crisis.

A few seconds after that, all the men in Kilo Capsule, and the
entire wing for that matter, heard C-Major over the PAS advise
the Wing Command Post and SAC Headquarters in Omaha that
Whiteman's Kilo-01 was back up and combat ready, with full
reports to follow.

After completing changeover, Dinkins was moving to open the
blast door and let the crew go up to meet the inbound helicopter,
and a pretty jazzed flight surgeon, when Pratt said, "Hang on a
second, guys. I think we all need to visit a minute."

## Kilo-01 Topside

Changeover often lasted up to 45 minutes. On power-loss simulation days, it could go to an hour and a half. This changeover was
moving toward its third hour and no sign of the night crew coming
up. Proctor was getting itchy. His radio crackled to life.

"Kilo-01, this is chopper November 179er inbound. Please
advise landing status, over."

Proctor waited for the crew below to respond, hoping he could
recognize the speaker and get a clue as to which crew was at the
consoles. That, in turn, would give him a hint as to where they
were in the changeover process.

"November 179er, this is Kilo-01…" Proctor recognized Pratt's
voice. "Stand-by one for landing status."

If Pratt were in the command chair handling the radio, maybe
changeover was complete?

He heard the elevator motor engage just as the squawk-box

started buzzing. Proctor smiled. The capsule was in command of the Launch Control Facility but at ninety feet below ground, they needed a "forward controller" with eyes-on topside to guide a helicopter landing. Most crews clung to that status like a dog with a new sock. The smart ones handed off everything they could to the person most able to monitor and make decisions.

Security police caught a lot of disrespect, as did any law enforcement group, and it never helped when someone lived up to the low expectations. Proctor was not about to foster that stereotype. He knew what they would be calling for and was way ahead of them.

He was crisp and professional: "FSC Proctor here. Sir, the landing pad is clear and the windsock indicates a light breeze directly out of the west."

"Thanks, Proctor. Take over direct communications with inbound chopper November 179er if you have a spare hand or two," Dinkins said.

"I got this, sir," Proctor smiled. He hung up the handset to the capsule and was already keying the radio, "November 179er, this is Kilo-01 FSC, Sergeant Proctor. You have clearance to land with a light westerly breeze. Welcome to Kilo."

"10-4, Kilo. We're two minutes out."

The elevator access door opened and for the first time in almost eighteen hours, Proctor saw Captain Farragut and Lieutenant Crawford emerge. They looked okay except for flushed faces and their shoes and their gun belts had cracked and split leather. Lieutenant Crawford had his hands wrapped with gauze.

"Good to see you, sirs. You guys okay?"

"Glad to be seen, Sergeant." Farragut said. "I think we're fine, but Flight Surgeons are in the 'NO' business. I gotta get him to pass my deputy's hands."

"I'd be happy to unload your weapon for you, sir," Crawford offered.

"Thanks, Sarge," Gray said. Then, glancing toward the landing pad, "I think I'd better not show any limitations here for a few minutes."

"Oh, yeah. Roger, that, sir."

Around the corner, just out of sight in the Day Room, Sarge listened to the exchange. What was the story to be? Only two men can truly keep a secret. More than that and the word will leak out, and no one will ever be able to determine with certainty where that leak came from. There had been five men down there. The only story that could survive would be the truth. But the truth could do so much damage.

Farragut walked straight to the loading barrel to unload his weapon. Turning back to hand the empty weapon and cartridges to the FSC, he saw Sarge standing there, mop in hand.

"Sir…" Sarge offered.

"Sarge…" Farragut responded. Sarge was the wild card now.

Gray carefully unloaded his own weapon, proving that his hands worked. He ducked back into the LCF just as the prop wash from the copter raised a mini-tornado of dust and grass clippings outside the door.

Farragut looked at Sarge and quietly said, "We were damned lucky, Sarge."

For a long moment, the three men let it hang there.

"You'll be needing this, sir. Lieutenant Dinkins said my log had to be in an officer's custody on this one," Sarge said, handing his log pages to Farragut as he went out to greet the chopper.

Glancing over the page, the two men saw a very simple report on a diesel failure and an overheat condition in the capsule requiring the Facility Manager to go topside to coordinate a call for assistance. There was nothing on the page that wasn't completely true—nothing on the page that would raise a follow-up question other than status of the diesel.

The Flight Surgeon entered saying, "Okay… let's see how you guys are. What happened exactly?"

"The EACU failed. We got hot," Gray said. It was his intention to leave it pretty much at that.

### Kilo-01 Capsule

Much later, Dinkins had the draft of the report completed. It was in triplicate—naturally—and it focused mainly on the failure of the diesel to come online. There were notes about the capsule suffering an overheat condition. But nothing—not a word—about the crew, how they looked, what they wore… or what they didn't wear.

Dinkins had never told an untruth in his life. His Catholic mother and almost-a-priest father had ensured that he was honest to a fault. The conspiracy about the reports troubled him. The pressure was not lost on any of the other three, either.

Pratt had aged ten years in the last hour. "Dink… Lieutenant Dinkins. I wouldn't blame you if you wanted to make a full and detailed report. I don't think they'd send us to Leavenworth… but Lieutenant Crawford's career would be over—his instructor status at the very least. I'm getting out in a couple of months anyway, Farragut even sooner. But I think Gray Crawford is a very good officer with a bright future ahead of him. I think he is an asset to the Air Force. I know I'd be a more confident civilian with men like you and him defending this country."

Then Pratt made the point that turned the tide.

"Who would be HURT by a brief report, Dink? Who would a more 'detailed report' *serve*? The answer both times, I believe, is NO ONE. There are enough witch hunts in SAC without writing a report about your buddy's 'broom.'"

Ironically, it had been Gray Crawford who had once said, "The second best way to lie is to tell only enough of the truth to make your point."

What Dinkins had written was true... as far as it went. He hadn't done or said anything wrong. But his soul kept telling him that "not wrong" just wasn't the same as "right."

# CHAPTER 12

*Men fear death as children fear to go in the dark;*
*and as that natural fear in children is increased*
*with tales, so is the other.*
**Francis Bacon**

Juliet Capsule, 509<sup>th</sup> SMS
Mid-Western Missouri
13 March 1973
1801 Zulu
1201 Local

PULLING THE ill-fated overheat Alert at Kilo fulfilled Gray's requirement for March, but not Andy's. Gray and Andy were in the elevator at Juliet heading topside after a typically "nuthin' happ'nin'" night Alert. The night before, Andy had watched with interest as his deputy had meticulously run his changeover checklists with particular attention to the power and diesel control panels. He also noted that, once in the capsule, Gray had seemed to hesitate before sealing the blast door shut. "once bitten…" Andy thought.

A capsule going to shutdown and transferring control of her ten missiles was the closest thing to real "action" of any kind that had occurred at Whiteman in some time. Everyone wanted to talk about it. Everyone except Gray and Farragut. Andy was caught in the squeeze between his curiosity, which would normally have been quiet, but in the face of Gray's uncharacteristic silence, was now operating on all jets; and his determination to maintain his aloof and indifferent image with its inherent disdain for gossip.

Riding in the elevator with them were three grocery-like bags that were stapled shut and bore the grease pencil labels, "Top Secret Cryptographic Waste." As sexy as it sounded, it was nothing more than garbage. But it was garbage that must be destroyed so thoroughly that no evidence of its existence could be found. Due to recent rains interrupting the normal execution of this duty, it was a substantial pile; and that destruction had to be executed and witnessed by two officers of the line. Gray and Andy were taking out the trash.

It had been Caesar who first decided to hide his messages in codes. Or at least it was he who first devised a system that was complex enough to baffle the average reader, but simple enough for decoding to be taught to his generals. It was important that the bearer of the message did not also have knowledge of the code key. If so, sufficient persuasion could be brought to bear to compromise the message. Though the messengers rarely ever had the key, proving it tended to consume messengers in any event.

The coat-of-arms for the Strategic Air Command was an armored fist clutching red lightning bolts and green olive branches in a clouded sky. The implication was plain: "We bear destruction through the air—destruction so powerful that we, ourselves, must be protected from it. Our goal is peace."

The mission of the Strategic Air Command was deterrence. Its motto was, "Peace is our profession." Scare the other guy so thoroughly that the idea of misbehaving carried penalties too painful to contemplate.

Since Sputnik, it had been decided that bluffing wouldn't do. There needed to be genuine, deliverable power. And if the power were that terrible, then there must be absolutely secure lines of communication so we didn't do ourselves damage while intimidating the other side. That gave birth to an explosion in cryptographic science. And that gave birth to an explosion of paper that had to be disposed of with remarkable care. Hence, the three grocery bags.

Getting off the elevator became a scene out of a Jerry Lewis movie. The challenge was to remove both their T. O. bags and their personal bags along with all three bags of paper, open the elevator grate, leave the elevator, close the grate, exit the elevator alcove, never have any of the bags out of both officers' sight, and still maintain the grace of an officer in the eyes of the security police who would watch them exit.

Andy had determined that there needed to be a procedure. Gray had thought maybe they could just make more than one trip. Or maybe one guy could handle all the bags and the other handle all the crypto? Or maybe they just could leave their personal gear in the elevator until they handled the crypto? Or maybe the Site Manager could help with the gear?

None of those plans fulfilled the image Andy had been shooting for. It was decided, by Andy, that he would stand with his T. O. in one hand and his personal bag in the other. Gray then would put one bag of crypto under each of Andy's arms. Then Gray would pick up his T. O. with his left hand, put the remaining bag of crypto under his left arm, and then operate the elevator grate with his right, use his right to move his personal bag out of the elevator, put it down, close the grate, open the elevator vestibule door, and, as Andy walked into the FSC room—all the while staying in sight— Gray would pick up his personal bag again and join him. Once in the FSC room, they could put their bags down and take the trash out to the burn barrel behind Juliet's topside support building.

"I went to college... for this." was Gray's dominant thought.

The professionalism of the FSC rescued Gray from the most dignity-damaging part of the dance. Once the elevator hit the top, the FSC already was on the horn to the capsule and had the vestibule door open. Gray and Andy entered the FSC room and dropped their bags, and now Andy had two bags but his Deputy only one. Gray wondered if this unanticipated breach of etiquette needed correcting. Then Andy handed him one of the bags. Breach averted. The two defenders of democracy then left the building and headed for the crypto barrel.

It was cold. Not windy, of course, because they had checked that detail with the FSC before agreeing to do the burn. But it was in the twenties, cold, and a crystal clear mid-Missouri afternoon.

Juliet capsule was only twenty-three miles from the Kansas line and a bit farther than that south of Kansas City. Juliet wasn't the farthest, but was among the most difficult to get to. The nearest town was Appleton City, population around three hundred, and between Juliet and town were some of the hilliest, roughest, most primitive roads in the state. Remote. Beautiful. But remote.

The driveway into Juliet turned off of County Road 12. Across the road and about four hundred feet north was a farmhouse; white clapboard with green shutters and a full porch all across the front. Gray always wondered who lived there. When they would arrive at Juliet on night alerts, it often was well after 10 PM. The house would be dark. Farmers rise early. Every once in a while, though, a faint glow of what must've been a television could be seen flickering at a window.

Once, when they'd been heading back to base on a Sunday afternoon, there had been people on the porch. A man sat on the steps in a pressed dress shirt and jeans. An older man in a straw Stetson and bib overhauls was in the rocker. There was an old woman on the porch swing, leaning forward attentively as a little girl of four or so explained something to her that must have been very important. Two teenagers were peering under the raised hood of a pickup in the yard as a woman came out of the screen door with two glasses of something cool. Gray bet it was for the two men. The menfolk waved as the crew vehicle passed. Glancing back,

Gray caught a glimpse of the woman watching them drive away, halted in the process of delivering the drinks. Gray wondered about their lives. Did they have any idea what that government building was across the road? Did they have a clue that they lived less than a quarter of a mile from ground-zero?

They wouldn't be on the porch today. Gray wished that the Air Force provided heavier jackets. Crews got nylon flight jackets. They were warm but never were meant to be real cold-weather gear. The SAT troops had parkas. Now, those were warm. Of course, the SAT troopers were in their vehicle for hours at a time and could be called upon to sit at an LF for an entire shift... even days on end living in a camper if, for some reason, security was in question. So maybe they needed parkas more than their officers did.

The burn barrel was a fifty-two gallon aluminum trashcan perforated with one-inch holes every eight inches or so. It looked like it had been hit with a fifty-caliber machine gun with remarkable precision. The can was mounted about a foot and a half above ground on a metal pole. The lid was attached to the pole with a wire to ensure that the set stayed together.

Andy and Gray tore open the first bag and fluffed the contents to ensure adequate air supply around all the paper for a clean burn. The bag contained the self-inking paper from the computer. It looked like a bag of adding machine tape. On it were short one to four line reports from the computer. "LF-08 2048938" was one entry Gray saw. It had something to do with Juliet-08 but Gray had no idea what the code number was. He had no need to know.

The second bag had more of the computer tape and many pages of expended codebooks. SAC never sent a message to the field in the clear when it could put the same message in code of some kind. There were no less than three types of codes the Missileers had to be able to decipher. Two of those code systems changed constantly. To decode the message, you noted the time received and the time on the message. The time on the message told you what page in the crypto-book to use in decoding it. One system changed code pages every six hours! A code page was worthless after its "shift," so you threw it away… properly. In SAC, that meant the burn bag.

These types of cryptographic waste were flat and had to be crumpled so they would burn. A stack of pages *easily* could cling to one another, burning only the edges of the outermost leaves. If ash and fragments remained, they could be read. Even a sheet of ash from a burned page still could be read. Of course, it wasn't easy, but the spy business didn't recruit in the Help Wanted section of the *Moscow Star*. These guys were pros and many were touched for service directly out of college, to be plunged into intense covert training in things like "Burnt Trash Reading 101." Or, so SAC would have you believe.

If waste was burned and the ashes not stirred, some slick agent could come to that part of Missouri, hide out at the farm house—perhaps posing as a hired hand or Jenny Lou's new beau—and make a midnight raid on the burn barrel to secure the two-by-three-inch scrap of ash bearing a code like "LF-08 2048938." Armed with that critical information he could, it was argued, topple the government of the United States and we'd all be eating borscht by Christmas.

The third bag was some of both. They fluffed it up and prepared to light the paper. It was then that Gray realized that he had nothing with which to light the paper. Neither he nor Andy smoked, so a lighter was not likely. Andy picked up the three-foot long piece of rebar that was used to stir ashes and took up his position upwind of the barrel. Both men were standing back waiting for the other to ignite the secrets of the United States. Unfortunately, neither of them had a match.

"Andy, I don't have a lighter or anything."

"You don't?"

"No."

"Why not?"

Andy had the capacity for questions that defied answering. The best Gray could muster was, "What?"

"What kind of Deputy are you?"

"An ill-prepared one?"

It was at this point that Andy's customary mental journey took a detour. Normally this would be an excellent opportunity to get Gray to squirm. It was not sadistic pleasure on Andy's part, but rather, a key tactical component of what Andy considered his duty in honing Gray into a competent officer, capable of handling any situation; capable because he had *anticipated* the situation and been *prepared*. Andy felt the same way about the raising of his children (which caused no small amount of tension between him and his more nurturing spouse) but then, it occurred to him that there might have been a reason; a painful one.

"Does this have anything to do with the overheat condition at Kilo?" Andy asked, much more tenderly than he had planned to.

Gray was still patting pockets that had never contained either matches or a lighter. Again, the most insightful response he could muster was, "What?"

Which was all Andy needed to know that his deputy was not suffering unsurvivable trauma. He reverted instantly to his prior mode.

"From now on, when we depart for Alert, I will be asking you if you have your lighter." With that, Andy produced a disposable lighter from his pocket and handed it to Gray.

Relieved, and only a little ticked off that Andy had put him through the ringer for nothing, Gray moved to the barrel and began flicking. After several attempts he said, "I am not familiar with lighters. I may be doing this wrong."

The contempt with which Andy looked upon his Deputy would have withered a lesser man, or at least one who noticed and cared.

Gray just chalked it up to one more way in which he had failed to live up to the expectations of an Air Force ultra-overachiever.

"Give me that." Andy extended the stir-rod to Gray while holding his palm up to receive the lighter. That exchange completed, Andy bent over the burn barrel, "You release this little safety and…"

Flick.

Flick.

Flick.

FLICK FLICK FLICK FLICK FLICK.

Andy was much too black to blush. How useful Gray would have found that from time to time. He would have enjoyed the moment, but now they had a real problem. The lighter was "inop." The crypto was loose and filling the barrel. Until destroyed completely, that paper had to be under the watchful eye of two U.S. Air Force officers bearing Top Secret Cryptographic clearances. They were behind the support building. Eventually, they supposed, the Site Manager or the FSC would send a search party. Hopefully, one of *them* would have a match.

"What do you think we should do?" Gray asked.

"I think we should ensure that our deputy possesses the means to make fire," Andy responded. "Weren't you a Boy Scout? Don't you guys make fire with sticks or something?"

Gray hoped it was just frustration talking, and that Andy didn't expect him to make fire with a twig or take Andy's eyeglasses and use the sun to spark a flame… But with Andy, one never knew.

A klaxon-like horn sounded, giving both men a start.

"That'll be the 3901$^{st}$ evaluators from DOV come to certify us beyond incompetent and escort us to jail." Andy observed dryly.

It was, it turned out, the SAT back from daily LF checks being cleared through the gate.

"Hey. We can have the SAT get the Site Manager and have him bring us a match or something," Gray suggested.

Andy did not look happy. As the two young security police parked the SAT pickup only twenty feet from them, Andy gazed in their direction.

"Stay with the crypto," he snapped.

Never knowing what hit them, the two young SAT troops dismounted the cab of the pickup loudly and came face to face with Captain Hardiman. Reflexes and basic training brought both of them to attention in a flurry of arms and rifles and hat squaring and cigarette jettisoning and parka zipping. They saluted.

Andy stared at them for a long moment, and then very slowly returned the salute. Gray and Andy were facing one another at a gap of about thirty feet. Both officers still could see the can containing the crypto. Between them, and much closer to Andy, were SAT troops, standing and awaiting their fate, wondering what it was they might have screwed up. Though Gray couldn't see their faces, he could see Andy's. Even without the benefit of their facial expressions, it was obvious the two young men were intimidated. Gray would bet that they hadn't stood attention before an officer since training.

Andy hooked a thumb indicating the elevated gasoline tank over his shoulder (and a good eighty feet across the compound). He then gestured in the direction of a cigarette butt still smoldering on the ground where the driver had cast it upon seeing the giant officer standing there. The airman quickly stomped out the cigarette and returned to attention. Andy said... something. The young man fished in his pocket, withdrew something and handed it to Andy. Andy seemed to examine it for some time. He then dismissed them and they "left the area" with some haste.

Once they were safely around the corner of the building, Andy walked to Gray and handed him a lighter. "Let's hope this one works."

Computer paper caught on the first flick. In a few seconds, the barrel was a tiny vortex of flame. Using the stir-rod to extend his reach safely, Andy settled the perforated lid on the barrel.

"What did you say to them to get him to give you the lighter?"

"Nothing."

"Nothing?" Gray asked.

"When I pointed out the danger of the smoldering cigarette and the emergency gas supply, he turned into a flood of confession. Part of that, I suppose, involved him surrendering his lighter voluntarily," Andy explained. "When we go inside, I shall return it to him."

"What are you gonna tell him?"

"Nothing."

"You're just gonna give it back."

"Yes. With a resolute sadness. Then I'm hitting the hay."

Mind games. Gray supposed that it was necessary. The stakes were so very high. It was part of what energized him about his role. There was a certain romance to it. But it also was alone-making. Andy had just performed a complete mind-screw on a nineteen-year-old just so he wouldn't have to ask for something and possibly appear imperfect.

Gray wondered if the day would come when he would make such choices. Even now, he wondered if Andy found it fun and ego-building, or was it something he did just to protect himself?

The smell of the fire reminded him of childhood campouts. Gray never had been the outdoorsy type, but every summer he would spend some time with his cousins at the lake. Dinner was an open-fire operation. His thoughts drifted to the family across the road.

The house wasn't visible from where he stood, but he glanced past the barrel toward the north anyway... and saw them rising. Juliet-02 must have been the furthest plume. The one to the west of it a ways must have been Juliet-11 and the one to the left of both of them might be Kilo-3. Missiles were on their way to Russia.

From the plume nearest him, something fluttered and moved toward him. It was a scrap of paper. It got closer and closer to him until he could see it was a scrap of computer tape. It was burning. He could read "Launch Code: P..." and the rest was charred and unreadable.

"Gray! Catch that paper. We lose a slip of this shit and we go to Leavenworth."

Gray looked up to see two tiny scraps of paper floating on the column of hot rising air. By the time the smaller piece floated near him, it was merely curled ash. He batted it from the air and ground it under his shoe, reducing it to a gray stain on the gravel. Nothing intelligible was left. The other, a scrap of crypto book page, he snatched deftly from the breeze and handed back into the flames.

Glancing back in the direction of the farm house, he noted that the skies were clear. No missiles were rising.

He needed some sleep.

# CHAPTER 13

*It is when power is wedded to chronic fear
that it becomes formidable.*
**Eric Hoffer**

Office of the Press Secretary
The White House
15 April 1973
1322 Zulu
0822 Local

"CLEAN IT up and make it go away."

"I'd love to, Mr. Haldeman, but I'm not a magician." White House Press Secretary Jeb Klein normally tried to speak in more respectful and deferent tones around White House chief of staff, H. R. Haldeman. He was not a man possessed of a sense of humor. Nor patience.

"This is the President. The office of the President."

"I'm aware of that, sir."

"We're talking about the PRESIDENT of the goddamn United States, Mr. Klein, and these jackals are NOT to print anything about my President without my approval."

When he was like this, pointing out the history of the American free press was pointless, if not suicidal. Pointing out any truth that might be contrary to Haldeman's will could prove even worse.

Klein could not believe these things about his President. Mr.

Nixon had denied it. Flat out. He had looked Jeb right in the eye and denied any complicity. Haldeman and Ehrlichman were another matter. Nothing they were capable of would surprise Jeb Klein.

"If Agnew had kept his nose clean, we wouldn't be under this insipid microscope. Since his resignation it's like RN... it's like the President is walking around with a target painted on his back. We all are. Damn it, the man almost single-handedly got us the hell out of Vietnam. If he could, he'd of flown the fricking choppers himself. I want the IRS all over this Woodward and Bernstein. I want their information flow STOPPED."

"Is it true?" Klein, by necessity often was left out of some information loops. It was necessary for him to maintain his credibility with the press. It was important to ensure that he didn't know things he would have to lie to the press about. But this was not one of those kinds of things.

"Is what true? What the hell difference does that make now?"

"What happened to the eighteen minutes on that tape? I watched Rose Mary spin that yarn about what she would have had to do to 'accidentally' erase that tape and, Bob, that woman wouldn't SURVIVE being in that position." Klein was running a huge risk but his integrity was pushing his judgment aside.

"Just contain this thing, Jeb. Do your job. Dam up this river."

"Woodward and Bernstein are an expletive we aren't going to be able to delete, Bob. Sometimes you have to give up on dams and start building an ark."

# CHAPTER 14

*While pensive poets' painful vigils keep,*
*Sleepless themselves, To give their readers sleep.*
**Alexander Pope**

103 North Carswell Circle
Whiteman Air Force Base
09 April 1973
1245 Zulu
0645 Local

**D**ONNA CRAWFORD shot up in bed and clapped her hands over her ears. The windows were rattling. Her grandmother's framed needlepoint fell from the bedroom wall, cracking the frame that her grandfather had carved for her by hand. Noggin, too frightened even to bark, huddled under the bed, cowering in a nest of purloined shoes.

Turning to Gray, she found the right side of the bed empty. Since he had become an Instructor, she had grown accustomed to him being home more and out on Alert only once every three to four weeks. She remembered now, though. He had gone out last night. Where was he this time? The schedule was on the fridge.

## Kilo Capsule – 509th Squadron

Line one blinked on the Comm-Console. Gray depressed the blinking button and said, "Kilo Capsule, Lt. Crawf…"

"Gray, what the hell is THAT?!" Donna held the phone toward the windows, beyond which was the source of the roar.

Without question, it was Donna. What Gray needed to know was: what was she doing up at 6:45, and what was the roar in the background?

"Hold on a second, Donna. What's the problem? What's going on?"

Andy could only hear Gray's side of the discussion. Privacy in the capsule was difficult enough. Hell, the toilet was in the same room and the little curtain around it was a joke. So, when one of them was in a private conversation, the other tried not to hear. It wasn't always easy. But one could always pretend he did not hear.

"What kind of explosions?" Gray was asking. "On base somewhere?

"Donna, I can't understand you if you don't take a second to breathe and compose yourself."

That, Andy could not ignore.

Wheeling in his command chair, Andy could see sincere concern on Gray's face. One of the things Andy found impressive about Gray was his ability to track more than one thing at a time. While genuinely concerned and focused on his wife, Gray also had the presence of mind and quickness to put his hand over the speaker and say, "Some kind of huge roar on base. Buildings are shaking. She wants to know if the war has started."

Andy's console was clean and green, as was the entire squadron as far as he knew. While Gray dealt with Donna, Andy commandeered line 2 and quickly dialed the weather station.

Though pilots were doubtless the kings of the Air Force, it was the weather-weenies who told them whether or not they could go out and play with their multi-million dollar toys in the sky today. Stationed at airfields around the world were weather officers who constantly tracked and updated status. They also were privy to almost all the scoop and gossip.

Andy didn't know many of the base weather officers, but he did know several of the enlisted men. A couple had been Vietnam vets and, though they'd not served with Andy, they always welcomed his visits to the weather station to swap lies and get him a weather update.

"WHITEMAN WEATHER STATION, SERGEANT BASS SPEAKING. TALK LOUD, PLEASE."

Andy could hear the roar through the phone.

"Bass, this is Captain Hardiman. What's that noise?"

"WE HAVE THREE FIFTY-TWOs INBOUND FOR ROTATION DUTY AT THE NEW SCRAMBLE BARRACKS AT THE NORTH END OF THE RUNWAY, SIR."

Andy had watched that renovation with some interest. Barely five hundred yards from the back gate and his bank—the Credit Union—the Scramble Barracks had been getting fresh paint and a variety of other activities. Still, it was news.

"B-52s? At Whiteman?" Andy challenged.

Suddenly, the racket abated dramatically. Either that or the line had gone dead.

"Whoa! FINALLY... Sorry, sir. Sounds like they're shutting down now," Bass said.

In Donna's kitchen, the noise had stopped abruptly. It had been so loud that it still rang in Donna's ears.

"It... quit," she said.

"Just like that? It just quit?" Gray asked.

Andy snapped his fingers and Gray looked his way. "We have B-52s on base now. I'm getting the skinny. No crisis."

"Donna. I'm learning that what you heard are B-52s that are on base now for some reason. No crisis that we know of. I'll get the info and call you back," he said.

"We have nuclear warhead-bearing airplanes parked out our back window, but you don't see that as a crisis? Great. Gray... they're loud. Are you sure there isn't some earth-shattering problem?"

"Andy is getting the details from one of his sources. Sit tight." And then much softer, "I love you. Go back to bed."

"Hell, I'm up now. I'm going to ask Gena Kovacs about this."

"The Wing Adjutant's wife? Donna... don't get me in trouble."

"We ladies have a code, Gray. You guys are not part of it. Relax."

With that, she was gone. Gray turned to Andy, who was hunched over the console in deep conversation with one of his "contacts," as Gray liked to call them.

An only child, and for much of his life a loner, Gray had come to appreciate the network of individuals Andy knew personally in a wide range of fields and disciplines. No matter what he wanted to know about, he seemed to have an insider's phone number in his little index. It would be a hard habit for someone like Gray to acquire, but the benefits were self-evident.

"Why would they be uploading bombs here? '52's fly loaded," Andy insisted.

Sergeant Bass became much more conspiratorial. "Not if they can't take off or land without tearing up the runway."

"Are you saying Whiteman's runway can't support a loaded B-52?"

"Never designed for it," Bass said. "So they fly in empty, load up, wait around a week for the war to start. When it doesn't, and Monday rolls around, the bombs are off-loaded, and the Air Reserve pilots fly the birds home to Barksdale. Another batch comes in later that day and the dance begins again."

"So you are saying that in order to spread our bombers across a wider area, we have stationed three at a base where they can't take off loaded without destroying the runway?" Andy had said it more as a matter of fact than with any surprise.

"Oh, they could launch but nothing else could take off or land for a while," Bass agreed. "Missouri's congressman got them assigned here in some shrewd trade-off to get more federal bucks into the state. Now he's trying to make campaign mileage out of his lobbying powers with the DOD."

"I see. You've been a big help, Sergeant Bass."

"No problem, sir. We look forward to your next visit to us."

"Thank you, Sergeant."

"Noisy beasts, sir. Don't plan to be sleeping in on Mondays." And with that, Bass rang off.

Andy swiveled toward Gray in his command chair, "Nothing earth-shattering; window shattering, perhaps. Hmm. Sorry about that. It would seem that Whiteman is now host to B-52s piloted by Reservists. They'll be flying in and out every Tuesday."

"That racket is going to become a regular occurrence? The mayor of Knob Noster will protest."

Knob Noster was the Missouri hamlet just north of the base on US Highway 50, population about 840. The mayor ran the combination gas station and bus depot just down the road from Gray's favorite (and only) fast-food establishment – the Dog 'N' Suds.

"Yes. I'm sure the congressman will dread that call."

"Donna is calling Mrs. Kovacs. I hope there won't be fallout from that."

Andy paused a moment. "Yes. The Officers'Officers' Wives Club connection. Kovacs' wife is interesting. She receives wifely protests with enormous sympathy and promises to straighten David out about these issues. She then promptly wipes it from her status board when the phone call is over."

"How do you know?"

"I am the husband of a 'wipe-ee.' When we were first married,

Sandra used to puff up her feathers and buzz around with the senior officers' wives." Andy rarely spoke of his wife or her practices.

"I take it she doesn't anymore."

"No. Or only rarely."

"She got 'wiped,' you say?"

"Actually, she had to be the 'wipe-er' and realized that whether she has rank or not, she is in the Air Force by connection. What happens to me happens to US. Petty complaints most often are just a need to voice displeasure with unchangeable conditions." He went on, "Men sometimes see that as tilting at windmills. Sandra sees it as boundary-setting. It's as if she is saying, 'Okay, I can't change this, but I've noticed it and I'm not happy, and I'm serving notice on your ass. So don't push me or no tellin' what I just might do.' "

"So, what do you recommend I tell Donna?"

"Tell her she lives on an Air Force Base," Andy tossed off, turning back to the console. "It can get noisy. Deal with it."

"Thanks. I'll review that for survivability and get back to you."

# CHAPTER 15

*It is impossible to be at the*
*wrong place – at the right time.*
**Rick Stephens**

Charlie-04
10 April 1973
1245 Zulu
0645 Local

G RAY FOUND it endlessly amusing that, given an almost limitless
budget, defense contractors had unleashed the little boy
in themselves when designing the components of the weapon
system. In an effort to spread the missiles over as wide an area as
possible, while creating the smallest individual footprint possible,
the designers of the Minuteman Missile System had landed upon
the idea of one-acre plots of land with a small steel and concrete
tube in which the missile would reside, possibly for years on end
awaiting launch – or disarmament.

To affect this grand scheme, hardware had to be designed
and created to put the missiles into these tiny holes. Enter the
Transporter Erector – the T/E. Basically it was an eighteen-
wheeler trailer containing a complete missile assembly and with
the remarkable capability of being tipped up on its end 100 percent vertically to lower the entire thing into the launcher. Sort of
a high-tech dump truck.

A very powerful crane at the top would support the weight of the missile and its cables as it was ever so gently lowered into the launcher. Once near the bottom, it was carefully balanced on the steel support ring that suspended the booster's launch funnels a few feet above the concrete floor of the launcher tube.

On this particular day, Gray was standing "codes" duty. There was a little plug—hardly bigger than a hairspray can lid—that fit into the bottom of the missile's guidance system. Wired and programmed into this silicon Pandora's Box were all the targets and war options for that particular weapon. It could not be exposed, moved, removed, or installed without a certified Operations Officer present. Gray was so certified.

Now, he had no idea which of the shiny things on the bottom of that circuit board was THE codes plug... nor did he know whether the maintenance crew had removed it, installed it, pocketed it, or wrecked it with a screwdriver. He just knew that he was there when they exposed it and was there until they buttoned it up. He felt like the worthless first lieutenant that most of the maintenance crew probably held him to be.

Just before they moved to reseat the warhead, the maintenance sergeant popped his head in and immediately went ballistic.

"Johnson! Secure that driver!"

All attention shifted to the nut driver on the platform beside Johnson's hip. Its handle dangled precariously over the edge of the platform.

"Long drop to the bottom," Gray observed.

"And lots of banging around opportunity between here and the support ring," snapped the sergeant. "The skin of this puppy is less than a dime thick. Wouldn't take much of a ding to have to declare it inop. That's a booster and a career trashed, sir. If this was a Titan booster, it would be even worse. Toxic liquid fuel and paper thin airframes on those antiques."

"Yeah," Gray agreed. "Heck, a couple of thousand sharpshooters with deer rifles could shoot America's nuclear missile system out of the air."

He had expected good natured laughs and a spirit of camaraderie. Gray turned to see the entire maintenance crew staring at him in stony silence.

"The Whiteman Scenario. I thought we weren't supposed to…"

"Quiet, Johnson." The young maintenance troop was cut off by his sergeant. Everyone quickly—and silently—returned to reseating the warhead.

"We kid about a lot, sir. But some things are better not discussed… at all."

It slowly dawned on Gray that these maintenance guys had been briefed and a protocol had been established regarding "The Whiteman Scenario." HIS scenario.

Gray had kept his word. He had not spoken of it since First Team. Evidently, CINCSAC was spreading the word himself. He had to talk to Andy about this. First he had to face another three hours with this crew. This mood would not do.

"So… Johnson. Or any of you… Help me out here. If the booster were to blow… if I dropped a pair of pliers on it and dinged the skin or something… the warhead wouldn't detonate…"

"No, sir. It doesn't arm until it is past apogee and well into reentry." Johnson was grateful for the change of topic and a chance to display his knowledge of unclassified details.

"But, if the booster did blow up," his assistant added, "it could fracture and scatter the warhead. This might be a very nasty environment for a few hundred years, I imagine."

# CHAPTER 16

*Some books be lies from end to end.*
**Robert Burns**

Briefing Room Corridor, West Wing
The White House
1 May 1973
1300 Zulu
0800 Local

WOODWARD AND Bernstein were, no doubt, the leaders of the charge, but now they were abundantly aware that every reporter with an Executive Office beat was hot on the trail. Every day seemed to reveal yet another chink in the presidential armor and ANY break in the story was the lead that night. Even innuendo was becoming plausible enough to air without even a hint of confirmation.

Now with the prospect of Haldeman, Ehrlichman, and Dean possibly resigning, it wouldn't be long before there was no one left to hang. Well, almost no one.

Robert Geoffrey had never been what one would think of as an aggressive researcher. Though having had his turn with the tabloids in London, he had never had the killer instinct... no taste for the jugular. He was curious, however. He had an appetite for news but not a hunger for headlines. He would not be the man to break the story of the century. But he could provide background for the network's ravenous need for details to fill in where it lacked facts.

It had been Geoffrey's curiosity question, voiced as he moved through the hallway toward the West Wing Briefing Room, that had prompted a more aggressive reporter to unearth the entire Oval Office taping debacle. Investigative reporting became much fuller when the targets offered you records of their conversations!

Never in its history had the ship of state been so publicly riddled with accusations, personnel problems... and evidence. There had been points, one could argue, when the character of the chief executive and the conduct of his administration had been far worse and, perhaps even more provable... but the *Washington Post* hadn't had access to those stories. They certainly had access to this one—plus an audience that was now global.

If news sold papers and bad news sold even more, scandal had to be the star salesman. The sharks of humankind always had a taste for a big man floundering in the water. There was blood in the water now and the feeding frenzy was just getting started. The shock was that Nixon expected the public to believe him. Hell. He believed himself innocent—or the very worst—justified. The man operated as if it would all blow over and he had much bigger fish to fry.

Agnew's resignation had broken the façade, though. How could so public a figure truly be guilty—and even worse, PROVABLY guilty? Unheard of. But with Agnew's fall, the fall of the President became much more plausible... to everyone, that is, except the President. No matter how much Nixon tried to distance himself from Spiro, the stain stuck.

The reporters were awaiting the emergence of Press Secretary Jeb Klein. There was so much they needed to know. He wouldn't help them, of course. He would read a statement, spout the cover story, play the pawn—a role for which he was losing the taste.

No one expected him to become flustered to the point that he actually SAID anything.

Apart from his early denials, when he actually had NOT known anything, Klein had been very careful to control what he did and did not SAY. What they were hoping for was a stumble, a look of recognition—or fear—that would serve as confirmation. Not sufficient confirmation, of course, to print or go to air with--but sufficient to focus subsequent queries.

Jeb Klein, the press corps believed, was an honest and honorable man. His boss's peccadilloes notwithstanding, Jeb himself was loyal. He believed it when he said, "I serve at the pleasure of the President."

He had painted himself into quite a corner saying that the Watergate break-in was a third-rate burglary. He was right. But it became very un-tasty crow he now had to eat. If he never heard the words Woodward and Bernstein again, he would not grieve.

"Good morning. Today we're going to touch on the staffing changes precipitated by the resignations of John Dean, John Ehrlichman, and H. R. Haldeman. I have a brief statement to read; then I'll take a few questions."

Air Force Chief of Staff Office
The Pentagon

Two men watched the briefing on a closed circuit system. The smaller, wirier of the two brushed his hand across his crew-cut and spoke.

"We may have some decisions to face in the very near future, sir."

"I know," the balding senior man replied.

"I'm wondering, sir, if we need to give some thought to how we might handle things if he becomes unstable."

The senior man didn't speak. It was very like him to not respond when he didn't have a clear response to offer. He allowed the question to live in the air for a while.

On the monitor Klein's statement had concluded and the barrage of questions was rising. The word "resign" was penetrating, and Klein was unmoved. The idea of the power trio resigning had prompted the questions, but no one believed Nixon would even consider resignation.

"Turn that off."

Crew-cut was persistent. "It won't make the problem go away."

This brought the smallest of smiles from the corners of the great man's face.

"I believe we have some contingencies to explore, sir. Further, I believe it to be our duty. This is precisely the kind of volatile and uncertain environment in which the Whiteman Scenario becomes a real possibility."

Their eyes met for the briefest of moments. "Preaching to me about duty is unwise... and unnecessary."

"Oh... I'm aware of that, General. My main concern here is General Paxton."

"Men don't make it to the level of Chief of Staff of the Army without considerable judgment. Don't let his volume throw you."

"I'm not worried about ME. I'm concerned about the sway he might have on others," crew-cut spat. "If Nixon..."

A sharp look from the General caused crew-cut to moderate his tone.

"If President Nixon leaves—or is removed from office—the country will be in a highly vulnerable position. Doubtless, the Soviets have been watching with deep interest... and glee. The gap left by a bulldog like Richard Nixon will have to be filled by a strong, DECISIVE leader. I doubt the JCS will see Gerry Ford as that man."

Their eyes locked in a disturbing silence for some time. Then, softly, the General looked at his adjutant and said, "There will be no military coup in the United States, Colonel."

"Well, perhaps not by the Air Force, sir."

In the windowless room, the weary leader studied the awards and photos arrayed around him. He had led a life of distinction and service, a life that had brought him to the position of Air Force Chief of Staff.

He never had run from a problem and he'd never taken an action to forward himself at the expense of his duty or country. Nor had he ever been tempted at this level.

"Goddammit," he breathed.

# CHAPTER 17

*Let the fear of danger be a spur to prevent it;*
*he that fears not, gives advantage to the danger.*
**Francis Quarles**

Emergency War Order (EWO) Building
Whiteman AFB
19 April 1973
1400 Zulu
0800 Local

"**I** NEEDN'T REMIND you that we both make one hundreds on this test or we both go through retraining."

Andy had a standard speech on EWO day. For eight hours on one day in each month, every launch officer went through a detailed intelligence briefing, was brought up to date on the current status of SAC and political and economic conditions that might affect that status... and given a series of tests. Anything less than 100 percent on any of those tests would bust not only the crew member who made the error—but his partner as well. Even so, collaborative test-taking was not allowed. Each man took his test alone, but both failed if one of them did. It was a peer pressure technique used to ensure that each crewman held his partner accountable for the two of them. SAC's basic strategy was to be liberal with punishment—as a deterrent to unwanted behavior. It was psychological torture.

"Andy, I heard something while on codes duty that I need to speak to you about."

"Until we get past the test, I don't want to hear about anything else."

Gray was agreeable, but before the fun and games came the briefing.

Gray always had been amazed at the slides that were shown. SAC had determined that he did not have a "need to know" what all the codes he programmed into missiles represented, so he didn't get that information. And yet, on briefing day, he would get bombarded with a hundred slides of Russian positions, movements, and speculation on Chinese activities that he CERTAINLY had no need to know. Unless. Unless knowing them kept it "real." With SAC, applying reason often was a wasted effort.

The Captain was running them through the weather conditions in Siberia and the probable impact of an air burst in that area over the next ninety days when the scene on the screen became much more interesting.

"Yesterday, we received these slides. As you can see, this looks like a normal logging operation in the Northeastern regions. We blew up this area of the shot and you can read the driver's watch. If it is correct, this was taken at about three in the afternoon local time. The next slide, however, tells another story about this logging operation."

As the slide changed, Gray marveled at the resolution of the pictures. An amateur photographer himself, he had tried to blow up 35mm shots before, and at that ratio the grain overtook the image and it became an unintelligible mass of dots. The film they were using must be amazing. Normally, the briefing featured uncanny satellite shots, but these photos were from ground level. Very unusual.

"As you can see here, these are canvas covers painted to look like logs. And in this slide, you can see that they are camouflaging SS-9 missiles."

"Holy shit." Gray was glad the room was dark and no one could pick out which officer had voiced what they all were feeling.

The Captain turned toward the room, but instead of chastising, he grinned and continued, "Exactly. These are SS-9 launch tubes disguised as a logging operation. The missiles are transported on these disguised logging trucks and then loaded into the tubes at night when our spy-in-the-sky satellites are less effective."

The next slide was almost black and white. It was a high contrast shot of the missiles being removed from the phony logs with what appeared to be a logging crane. Even the missile itself was painted to look like a log. In the next shot it was being lowered into what appeared to be a pile of logs. In the upper left corner of the shot, Gray could just make out a gloved hand holding back a branch. Suddenly the picture fell into place. Someone on the ground with a hand-held camera was risking his life for a slide show—a slide show Gray could do nothing about.

"Our operative was able to get these amazing shots out last week. We had long known the Russians were masking their launchers. Now we have this confirmation."

"What use can we put that to? There must be hundreds of logging operations up there."

"Correct. Intel puts the number at about seven hundred actually. But the interesting thing about THESE logging operations is that they are laid out EXACTLY the same way. Typical logging camps are creatures of opportunity... you drop the logs wherever you find a clear spot. All of these sites have the same configuration. We have teams of cartographers combing the aerial photos of the region, and so far ten such sites have been identified. We expect to find a hundred or so more. The satellite night photos help, too."

"Sir, I thought you said they were less effective at night."

"They are. All they pick up are logging operations with unusually bright lights on."

The effect was unmistakable. Seeing the lengths to which they went made the targets real. It made the threat real. It made his job real... and it made the damned tests he was about to take real and very necessary.

"Okay. Before we get to our tests today..." Groans all around. "Yeah, yeah. Before we get to the tests, we have a new series of threat awareness exercises we need to do. Since SAC does not hide its missiles..."

"Hide 'em. Hell, there's signs on the road directing you to them." Laughter all around.

"Right. Exactly. Since finding our launchers isn't a big challenge, SAC has identified several vulnerabilities to our system that we'll be covering from now on. It's a briefing package called 'The Whiteman Scenario.'"

Gray's blood stopped flowing for a second. Andy had turned to stone. As Gray began to speak, Andy all but imperceptibly shook his head and quashed the intention.

"No one in EWO is sure why Whiteman got the distinction. I guess SAC thinks since we're the banana belt of Missiles that we are the most vulnerable to simple incursion. Whatever the reason, we are not to discuss this outside of fully secure environments. Not even the call sign. It seems someone at SAC thinks that we need to be on the lookout for deer rifles."

The laughter in the room covered the exchange of looks between Andy and Gray. Their "wild hair" was being taught. Their "what if" notion had attracted enough attention that now every SAC base was being briefed on countermeasures.

In the hubbub that emerged, Andy turned to Gray, "This is what you were going to mention?"

"Maintenance crews are getting this info, too," Gray responded.

Andy was not happy. "I wonder who is getting 'credit' for this?"

The trainer joined the joviality, "So now when you stop for pie on the way to alert, be sure to check those pickup trucks out front for gun racks." More laughter.

# CHAPTER 18

*Children from humble families must be taught*
*how to command just as other children*
*must be taught how to obey.*
**Nietzsche**

Blue Inn Café
Appleton City, Missouri
21 April 1973
0245 Zulu (22 April)
2045 Local

PERHAPS THE sole joy of duty at Juliet Capsule was the opportunity to buy a pie at the Blue Inn Café in Appleton City. Like a thousand other rural communities across the country, Appleton City had one major street flanked by adjoining buildings. A hardware/feed and grain, an appliance store, a pharmacy, a bank... but the only building of interest to crew members was the Blue Inn. It had identical sisters in every town in America.

A counter, a cluster of tables, and across the north wall, a string of booths with cracked and worn vinyl seats. The tables had held more coffee than everything else combined – except, maybe, for pie.

Andy was a stickler for rules. Gray couldn't point to a time when Andy had acted out of his own mind without first considering what the rules had to say about a situation. So it was with more than a little surprise that he found himself instructed: "Pull over at the café and let's get some pie."

When he had been crewed with his first commander, they stopped for pie on every alert. Stopping was not specifically forbidden, but if challenged, there needed to be a defense that involved a USAF agenda. Gray wondered what Andy's would be.

Two Air Force officers in combat blues with ascots had become a fairly common picture in the Blue Inn. Still, when a six-foot-six black man entered their territory, the locals took notice. A group of six farmers, none of them under fifty, halted their discussion to watch Gray and Andy approach the waitress at the counter.

"We'd like some pie," Andy stated. When Gray noticed that Andy had not sat down, he decided to get off the stool he had just dropped onto. How to do that without looking like an idiot was going to be a challenge. "And we'd like it to go," Andy added.

For the first time, Gray noticed the sign over the cash register. "We reserve the right to refuse service to anybody." The silence in the café was palpable. Gray decided to stay on that stool until the pie arrived.

"Y'all want a piece of pie or a whole pie?" the waitress—or owner—asked. She was about five feet tall—and wide. Her hair was not exactly red... closer to orange... and from the height and size and number of intricate folds in and out, Grey wondered if she'd ever cut it in her life.

"A whole pie, please. Apple, Gray?"

"Uhm. Yeah. Good idea. The apple pie is great here."

"Shore is, boy. But we ain't got none. Sold out." Here it comes. A subtle and non-confrontational way to not serve them. Though the 'boy' was sure to raise hackles on Andy, Gray decided to play it as if it were for him.

"Well, I guess we're out of luck, then..."

He was up and ready to head out the door. Just then the waitress added, "Yeah. Alls we got is fowuh pieces of rhubarb and a peach pie that just come out o' the oven. Sherry habm't cut it yet."

"The peach sounds good." Andy was making a statement, much more than asking Gray for his opinion. A moment's hesitation, then Andy added, "We'll take that, please. To go."

"Y'all want it cut, or just a couple of fowuks?"

Gray was astounded that this actually brought a smile to Andy's face. "No. We don't need any forks. But we'd appreciate it if you'd cut the pie."

The waitress headed for the kitchen, "Sherry, the Ayuh Fowuce wants yo peach pie. Cut."

Gray noticed that the sextet of farmers hadn't moved or spoken during the entire exchange. They began to murmur among themselves and cast furtive glances toward the crew. Glancing out the front of the café, Gray noted that almost every pickup had a gun rack… with a deer rifle.

The waitress dropped the order at the window to the kitchen and snagged a fresh pot of coffee in one move as she rounded the end of the counter and headed for the table. "You boys need some heatin' up? Earl, whut's wrong with you? You look white as a sheet."

Earl was soft spoken, "I'm okay, Juanita." She patted his shoulder as she finished topping off his cup and started around the table. Earl looked back toward Gray and Andy with a flat, expressionless face.

Gray's mind was running wild. His previous commander was a rowdy, freckled redhead whom the waitress had immediately taken a shine to. "Juanita" didn't seem to recognize Gray in Andy's company, though. Everyone always had seemed cordial and friendly before. Now he was imagining them with hoods and burning crosses. Was this why Andy had decided to stop? To assert his RIGHT to pie?

"You a big peach pie fan, Andy?" Gray asked, almost under his breath.

Keeping his voice low, Andy said, "I don't eat pie. I knew you liked to stop here, so we're here."

Gray decided it was a bad time to tell him that he didn't care much for peach pie.

"That's gunna be thuhree sebmde fahve," the waitress drawled as she dropped the ticket and headed for the cash register. Gray wondered how many cans of hair spray it took to keep that impressive Gordon Knot aloft. Certainly none of it moved, no matter how much she did.

As Gray started digging in his pockets for what he knew was not much more than $3.75, Andy said, "I got this." They stood, preparing to leave.

The scraping of chairs from the table behind him sent a chill down Gray's back. He felt Andy stiffen but not turn. Instead he remained focused on paying for the pie. Gray felt more than saw Earl behind them. Andy's eye flicked toward Gray and then he casually turned, as if to speak. In the process he "noticed" Earl standing there. This gave Gray the opportunity to look toward Earl as well.

Earl was in his sixties. If there was any fat on him, Gray couldn't see it. He was about five-foot-three, with wiry, taut arms. His tanned and deeply weathered face yielded to a snow white bald scalp that was revealed as he adjusted his Caterpillar cap. He was nervous and stalling before speaking. His ancient blue eyes were crystal clear and bore a kind of innocence mixed with wisdom. His mouth was a lipless straight line.

Ultimately he looked up at Andy and said, "I know about them pads." His voice was soft but not timid. Behind him, the other five watched with deep interest.

Andy turned to retrieve the pie. "Keep the change, ma'am." And he walked out of the diner to the crew vehicle.

"No kidding?" Juanita exclaimed. She turned and jogged toward the kitchen, waving the change in her hand. "I just got a buck and a quarter tip, Sherry."

Earl and the boys watched Andy go. Gray was stuck, with Earl between him and the door. No longer intimidated, Gray noticed a looming sadness about this old farmer... this old American.

"I sold the gov'ment that little patch out by the road 'cuz they said I had to. But I don't like them pads. None of us do."

The boys at the table slowly shook their heads in tacit agreement.

Gray searched for a response. With nothing coming to mind, he resorted to the truth. "Neither do I, sir."

And with that he moved toward the door.

"What's under there?" Earl called out.

Gray stopped. Earl DIDN'T know about 'them pads' after all. It wasn't classified. Gray thought EVERYONE knew what was under those concrete pads. Andy was in the truck staring straight at him...from the driver's seat.

"Let it go, Earl." It was one of the guys from the table. "He's just a kid, hisself. He cain't talk about that stuff."

Another added, "He's just doin' his job, Earl. You go on now, soldier. Have some pie."

"They ain't soldiers in the Air Force, Gene."

Andy started the crew vehicle and the boys at the table began to engage in a debate over the proper way to address various members of the armed services. Gray took that as his cue to walk out without adding anything to the "mystery of the Blue Inn."

As Gray and Andy were backing out, they could see Earl at the register. He watched them leave as his buddies continued to split hairs and Sherry emerged from the kitchen to catch a glimpse of the rich Air Force boys who had given her sister such a huge tip.

Swinging almost off the road to avoid an oncoming tractor pulling a wide set of implements down the middle of main street, the crew crossed the railroad tracks and were officially "out of town."

"This is why there are rules about stopping in the community," Andy stated flatly.

"I didn't ask to stop, commander."

"You are angry."

"You noticed?"

"You believe I left you to the wolves?"

"You walked out on that man without a word."

"Debating nuclear deterrent strategy and the principle of eminent domain did not seem prudent, Lieutenant."

"They are scared, CAPTAIN. They are simple, country people who don't even watch the NEWS. They are unsophisticated."

"What did you say to him?"

Deciding to be petulant, Gray answered him literally, "Neither do I, sir."

Andy immediately knew this was not one he would win. Still, it was not in his nature to leave it alone. "Obviously I do not have the complete context. What was said that provoked that response from you?"

"He said he didn't like the 'pads,' Andy. Said, none of them liked the 'pads.' Not feeling a debate of nuclear deterrent strategy and the principle of eminent domain was prudent, I decided to simply honor the man's dignity and agree with him."

It would take another thrity-five minutes to get to Juliet. For fifteen of those minutes, there was no other sound uttered. Gray did wish, however,that they had accepted the offer of forks. Hot peach pie smells amazing.

Passing a farm house rekindled the image of Earl standing at the cash register... helpless to protect his land from the 'pads' and whatever horror they covered. Gray broke the silence.

"Most of the time this job seems like make-believe to me."

It hung there for a while. Then Andy responded softly, "It is designed to be that way, Gray."

"But tonight I felt like a thief. I felt like I'd stolen something from those men. When I think of the impact of what we're here to do... When I think of what would happen if we..."

"Lieutenant, it is very late at night and we'll be arriving at Juliet Capsule shortly. It has been a night of some drama in a parade of otherwise dreary and eventless nights. You conducted yourself well this evening, Gray. Your conduct honored both those men in the café and the uniform you wear. Let that be sufficient drama for this night."

"Andy, I'm not sure that I can..."

"Do not make the mistake of confessing things to me as a man—as a patriot—as a husband—as a warrior—that will affect my ability to support you as an officer and a gentleman in need of good efficiency reports."

Gray let that sink in for a bit. The secrets of this business were lonely-making. Gray could not tell his wife his deepest fears. Nor, it seemed, could he talk about them with the man beside whom he might be called upon to die. Gray wasn't sure he had what it took to walk this road much longer.

"Gray, hand me a piece of that damned pie."

It turned out that Sherry had packed paper plates, forks, and napkins in the box. Evidently she knew things about the power of peach pie that Gray and Andy had yet to learn.

# CHAPTER 19

*In every adult human there still lives*
*a helpless child who is afraid of aloneness.*
**Louise J. Kaplan**

Whiteman AFB
Jogging Track
29 April 1974
1900 Zulu
1400 Local

WITH THE exception of racquetball, Gray detested physical exertion—during the exertion. Afterwards, he felt great. Usually, it was only with supreme mental effort that he could put himself into that future state long enough to anticipate that pleasure sufficiently to induce himself to endure the pain of jogging. Today, however, he could not wait to get to the track.

The loneliness that had engulfed him over the last weeks was beginning to affect his judgment. He could feel the cloud of paranoia beginning to obscure his reason.

At his core, Gray was a softie; a tender, gentle spirit with a creative and whimsical streak. As a child, he had been a sparklingly delightful little boy—until he was five. Hearing his parents argue was something he had learned to tune out. He hated conflict. He hated the tone his mother got when his dad would ask her questions about addition and subtraction.

He could not know at the time that his mom had married in a rush and, in her opinion, much too far beneath her. His dad was a welder, his mom a bank teller. He couldn't do math. Numbers were her life. One night, when he was five, he entered their bedroom after dinner. His dad was packing. His mother sat on a small stool beside the bed, her face tight and expressionless.

"Where you goin', Daddy?"

"Away."

"When will you be back?"

His welder father looked at his banker mother and said, "I won't be back."

Though only five, little Gray's mind began to turn. It rejected the idea of his father not returning. He looked to his mother.

"Don't cry," she said. "I can get through this if you just don't cry."

Years later, he would relive that moment over and over again. The moment he shut down. His dad was leaving and his mom said if he cried she couldn't get through it.

That left it up to him. Very calmly, little Gray walked to the linen closet in the hall and began sorting through towels and hand cloths.

"We have more than two of these. You can have one, Daddy."

A five-year-old's unconditional love and courage was more than his dad could take. He slammed the bag shut, left, and Gray never saw or heard from him again.

Gray's grandmother told him much later that she had come over and packed the rest of her son-in-law's things. Neither he nor Gray's mom could do it themselves, certainly not with Gray's help. He didn't understand. He was just trying to minimize the conflict, trying to be a peacemaker. No five year-old is equipped for that job. Few fifty-year-olds are.

Later, school would teach him that the attention he so desperately needed came in several forms. "Sympathy for the poor little boy with no father" was easy to pull off, but there was something dissatisfying about it. And people tired of it quickly. Some kids got lots of "attention for bad behavior," but Gray never found satisfaction in mere attention... what he craved was "approval." So he became funny.

As an only child, he had learned to play alone. As a loner, he had learned to watch and observe. His keen observation skills gave him an ability to identify opportunities for humor and his quick mind was very useful in the spontaneous generation of material "in the moment." And, though he got approval, being that fast required enormous focus, energy, and effort—effort that others didn't seem to have to exert to be accepted and approved of. And energy that, though it kept him involved, demanded too much to allow him to be fully engaged. So the clown on the outside became a sea of resentment on the inside, alone in the midst of the gathering, and no amount of laughs seemed to fill the void which that night had created. It did, however, create a world-class analytical mind.

It was only in real friendships that Gray found what he so desperately longed for. It was an intimacy born of informed respect. People he knew who knew him—and liked him anyway—and people he loved because they were just who they were. Where some people had dozens of "friends and acquaintances," Gray only had a handful of relationships. But they were deep. Usually, they were fringe types: other outcasts in need of understanding. But they usually were brilliant as well.

Gray had expected the Air Force officer corps to be a much larger pool of such people. Turns out they were pretty much like the normal population—but with the added agenda of covering their butts. That is why Major Wilson seemed like the perfect person on whom to unload. Wilson was a chaplain. Maintaining a personal confidence was his job. For once, the secret-keeping power of an Air Force officer might work in Gray's favor.

Though not an ideally secure environment, the outdoor running track at the base gym was, in its own way, private. After the first lap, both men were warmed up enough for the adrenalin and endorphins to begin working their way into the bloodstream. Wilson broke from the steady jog into a brisk walk. Gray matched him.

"What's on your mind, Gray?"

"What makes you think…"

"Can we cut through this dance and you just tell me what's going on? Are you and Donna okay?"

"What? Sure. Of course. Why? Why do you ask that? Has she come to you about… anything?"

"If she had, I wouldn't tell you, would I? If it isn't your marriage, then is it your work?"

This made Gray think. He hesitated a moment and then admitted, "In a way it is my marriage. It's work… it's my life. Damn, this is harder than I thought it would be."

"My logic professor used to say that if you could not express an idea in two minutes you didn't understand it."

"Maybe I don't," Gray admitted.

"We could do this in my office, Gray. It is very private…"

"Tagged records, Walt. I don't want to raise any issues—questions about my fitness."

"Should they be raised?"

"No. I'm fit. I'll do my… job. Oh, God."

"What?"

"Maybe I'm not fit. Maybe that's it."

"Why would someone find you unfit?"

"I signed a document… a pledge… to follow orders and turn keys. To unleash those missiles if…"

"And now you're having doubts about that."

"I've had a lot of opportunity come my way. First Team, Olympic Arena training… I guess that…" Not knowing how to approach the matter with any subtlety, Gray decided to speak more plainly, "I have come to see that when I was a rookie in training I signed that document because I knew it was expected, and that I'd never get ANY opportunity if I didn't sign it. Even with days of those horrible films, it wasn't real to me."

"Something is making it real to you now?"

"Secrets. My life is non-stop secret management. I can't talk to my wife about things that are ripping at my gut."

"Could she help?"

"… Probably not. That's the thing… it would just start ripping at her gut, too. Knowing less than me, she'd have even more opportunity to second guess and 'what if' herself into insanity."

"You think you're becoming insane?"

"Don't make me shut down, Walt. I don't think I'm becoming insane. But I no longer am confident that I can turn that key if given an order to do so. I love the Air Force and I hate my job. I love the relationship with other officers and their families, and I hate the secrets and the duplicity. It is tearing at me. I resent Donna's freedom to criticize every idiotic Air Force reg. I resent her peacefulness and her joy. I'm angry at her for not seeing what is going on around her."

"Around YOU, you mean."

"What?"

"None of this is going on around HER. It's going on around YOU. You are resenting her for not seeing you are in pain. For trusting that when you say you're 'okay' that you mean it. You are upset with her for being so stupid she can't see that you're lying."

"Donna is not stupid."

"I certainly don't think so, Gray."

"And I don't lie to my wife."

"Bearing false witness is one of those things people like to take literally. They think that if they don't SAY anything that is specifically untrue then they haven't lied. What if bearing false witness is defined as communication with an intent to withhold or deceive?"

"I'm sworn to withhold certain things."

"About how you feel?"

"No. But it's a... that would be hard to put a lid back on if I started."

"If you don't start with her, you'll be divorced or living in an empty marriage in two years."

"I don't want her life to become the constant looking-over-her-shoulder that mine is."

"Probably won't, Gray. Donna doesn't need much approval. If she doesn't like something, she'll say so. If that craters your career, she'll look at it as 'meant to be' and you two will move on to the next thing."

"I'd like to control my options better than that."

"Then you have a problem."

"No shit. Why do you think we're having a conversation on a frickin' jogging track? I detest jogging."

"Me, too. Listen, Gray. Let me get off my high horse a minute and let's level with each other. There is no place for a man of God in a nuclear attack group... but here I am. There is no justification for supporting worldwide holocaust... but here I am. Why do you think that is?"

Gray stopped for a minute to give this some real thought. It hadn't occurred to him that Walt would be facing very similar conflicts. Somehow it comforted him.

"This is a dark and ominous business..."

"Yes, it is, Gray. Go on..."

"In such a business, it's vital to have men of deep conscience and restraint."

"Okay. What else?"

"Your job is not to talk me out of turning keys; your job is... What? What IS your job?"

"My job is to keep men like you close to their God, Gray. So that when they are faced with the most difficult of life's decisions, they do whatever it is they choose to do with fear and trembling and humility... not brash arrogance or indifference.

"I believe in your deep intention to do honor to yourself and your family and your country... and, yes, your God, Gray. And I also believe that there is not a man alive—from the President to the newest rookie from Vandenberg—who actually KNOWS what he will do when that moment comes. I don't."

---

The hot shower felt so good that Gray never wanted to leave. He wanted to dissolve into the steaming warmth and have it hold him while time just stopped. But... Walt had asked for a ride so he toweled off and slipped into his jeans and sweatshirt.

Walt was in uniform. The same man who had borne the burden of Gray's soul minutes before now stood in Class A blues with a Major's gold oak leaves on his shoulders and a silver cross on his chest... nearest his heart. The symbolism of all of that imprinted itself on Gray.

Walt constantly bore the burden that Gray only recently had become aware of. Walt's life choice had been to bear that burden for himself and others.

"We heading for the chapel, I guess?"

"No. I need to go over to Wing HQ today. Just drop me at the awning."

As he pulled away from the 351st SMW Command Post and Head Quarters building, Gray felt the paranoia urging him to check the rear view mirror. Walt stood there watching him leave before turning to enter the building. Was that compassion? Or—was he trying to decide whether or not to enter this discussion into Gray's "tagged records" jacket?

Immediately Gray's "second guesser" began wondering if he

should have confessed to Walt. Then he imagined Donna sitting in the seat next to him. What would she say? That's when Gray laughed out loud. He knew exactly what she would say.

"Screw it."

# CHAPTER 20

―――

*"Ethel, I've searched for hours and I can't find it."*
*"And this was the last place you had it?"*
*"Oh, no. I lost it on Fifth street but the light's better here."*
**Lucy and Ethel**

Mike-01, 510<sup>th</sup> SMS
2 May 1974
1945 Zulu
1345 Local

A S THE alarm sounded on the Command Console, a report spat out of the Deputy's printer. The commander looked up from his novel and jabbed the alarm silence button. "What the hell?"

The red Outer Zone violation light glared orange-red near the bottom of the Mike-11 launch facility status column.

"I have an OZ on Mike-11," his deputy reported.

"Well. It sure isn't snow falling off the radar stanchion. It's got to be 74 degrees and sunny out there."

"Probably a bird looking for nesting stuff."

The commander flipped open his checklist; "OZ alarm noted."

Deputy: "Check."

"Sending reset command. Now. We get to wait five minutes for a reset report."

"Time of alarm on the printout 1944 Zulu," the deputy read.

Then marking in grease pencil on the tape, he wrote the reset time, "Reset report due at 1949."

"Check."

Mike-11 Launch Facility
Highway 50, 18 miles East of Kansas City
1945 Zulu
1345 Local

With the strains of "Let the Sunshine In" blasting from an orange and cream Volkswagen bus, four exuberant youths began the artful addition of a phosphorescent green peace sign to the top of the launch enclosure of Mike-11. Their straggly hair and sparse beards notwithstanding, the artists had a certain flair.

Two of the girls were adding an orange phosphorescent edging to the right side of the guy's design, giving it a psychedelic drop shadow that would be almost three dimensional from the air.

"A peace sign on a nuke. Dude, this is so far out."

"Is there really an atomic bomb under here? Could we get, like, sterile or something?" one of the girls asked.

"No, man. They've got shielding and shit all around here, man."

The blue eyed girl in the almost-not-covering-everything-it-should halter was having second thoughts. "Danny, I don't think you should-a cut that chain."

"So how would we get in? Fly over the fuckin' barb wire? It is sixty feet off the fuckin' highway. If they wanted to make this place secure, they shouldn't've put it here where us malcontents could screw with it. Hey. If you're afraid your eggs are getting fried, go turn up the tunes and hang in the van."

This set off a series of giggles and jeers at Blue Eyes.

"Fine. Asshole."

Mike-11 Launch Facility
Highway 50, 9 miles East of Kansas City
1945 Zulu
1345 Local

"So do they have a sign on them that says, "Welcome to Bubba Three, Nuclear Launch Site?"

"B is Bravo… not Bubba." Though Gray knew it was just Donna's way of being funny, he always felt a little embarrassed when she treated Air Force protocols that made complete sense and helped everyone understand exactly what was being discussed as if they were little boys playing *spy*. "But yes…yes, there are signs saying Charlie-07… but that's it. Just a designation."

"The signs say 'Charlie Seven'?"

"No. It says 'C dash zero seven'… Charlie is…"

"I know. So. Do these people around here KNOW that they have nuclear weapons on their property?"

Gray had thought that they did. Now, he wasn't so sure. "I'm not sure what they were told when they sold their land to the government. Lots of things had to be cleared though 'cuz there are miles and miles of cable connecting all of them."

---

Every month, that cable was checked from the air. Gray had only been able to pull duty "flying cable" once and that took a lot of juggling and wheedling. The two 'copters at Whiteman were for that specific purpose.

Every month a pilot, copilot, and a missile launch officer were aloft flying the route of every underground communications cable. With several THOUSAND miles connecting each of the missiles to one another and the capsules and the command post, it meant many hours aloft for the pilots, enough to keep them qualified for flight pay. Only six crewmen a month ever pulled "back seat duty" but for four to five hours, it was a fun ride at about five hundred feet over the hills and dales of mid-Missouri.

Flying cable had struck Gray as a lot like snipe hunting. If it hadn't cost so much to fly, he would have been sure the flight crew was pulling his leg. Once they had left the base, heads went out the window scouring the ground. As far as Gray could tell... it was ground.

He'd been at it for two hours before he had the guts to ask, "How will we know if there is a problem? The cable is buried." At almost the same instant the 'copter went into a steep bank and began flying circles around... something.

"What's up?" Gray asked.

"Whiteman Wing Command Post, this is flight Sierra 17 Tango, over."

"Go ahead one–seven, over."

"We are at grid point Golf 195.78. There is a large washout on a creek bed here and our map shows pressurized cable traversing this area at about these coordinates, over."

Gray looked down and saw that there was, indeed, a large area of dirt that had sloughed off a hillside into the depression below, exposing clay and rock. He didn't see any cable though.

"Roger, one–seven, we have no reports of pressure loss on any cable in that zone. We're waiting for a cartographer to confirm. Stand-by in that area, over."

"One–seven on station until further notice, out."

It was just some dirt shifted on a hill. But three officers, a helicopter, two officers on base, and a room of maps had been thrust into action. Gray knew that these cables were the lifeline of the system. If one of the cables was breached, the loss of air pressure in its sleeve would sound immediately in adjacent capsules. If it were severed completely, it no longer would carry its message.

Each missile had three cables carrying the same messages in different directions. Two cables could be lost and the third system could get word in or out. An exposed cable may not show a fault at all, but it would be more vulnerable to penetration or the elements... so they were protected by ensuring that they were three to four feet underground and pressurized at all times.

"One–seven, Whiteman Command Post, over."

"One–seven, go ahead, Whiteman, over."

"Captain Peterman, cartography, here. I don't show a cable junction or crossing within a half-mile radius of your reported grid point. However, that is close to the mapping error tolerance. Do you SEE any exposed cable?" Then, mic open, he seemed to respond to someone near him. "Huh... oh yeah, OVER."

The pilot looked disgusted at the Captain's lack of radio protocol. "Standby one, Captain Peters." Gray knew the pilot had gotten the name wrong on purpose.

The 'copter tipped on its side and began to drop... or fall... or suicide dive... toward the gaping hole in the ground. At what seemed like five feet above the hilltop, the pilot flared the chopper and hovered. When Gray regained his stomach, he realized they were a safe one hundred feet or so over the hole. The pilot circled it carefully, flying backwards and sideways on occasion to get the best view.

"Just dirt from up here, sir. Over."

"Sounds like we're clear then. Continue the mission. Thanks One—Seven. WCP out."

"One–Seven, out."

With that, the adventure ended. There was a lot of that in missiles; a lot of activity that produced no fruit. But the point of a deterrent force was to stay as fruitless as possible. It was vital— and boring.

# CHAPTER 21

*You should never have your best trousers on when you turn out to fight for freedom and truth .*
**Henrik Ibsen**

Highway 50, 12 miles East of Kansas City
2 May 1974
1949 Zulu
1349 Local

**"I WANT TO** see one." It was Donna. "So... when can we go see one? Do I need a pass or something?"

"You want to go down into an LF? They may have on-base tours of the training tube. I'll have to check."

"No. I want to see one of the launch sites—one of the real ones. Didn't you say there was one off of Highway 50 along here somewhere?"

"Yeah. Mike–11 is just up the road a piece. But we can't get in. There are above-ground motion detectors and underground sensors for detecting vibration, tunneling, near-miss explosions..."

"I don't want to raid the site, Gray. Can't we just pull over and walk around the outside of the fence?"

That, they could do.

Mike-01

1949 Zulu

1349 Local

The alarm was going off again. "We have an OZ violation on Mike-11."

The computer spat out another report. The Squadron Party Line was ringing.

The commander and deputy grabbed the handsets together as the deputy moved to the next item on the checklist, "Mike Capsule reporting OZ alert at Mike-11."

"Foxtrot Capsule acknowledges receipt of OZ on Mike-11. Keep us informed."

"Will do." The deputy hung up the party line and began buzzing the FSC (Flight Security Controller) topside.

"FSC, sir."

"Situation 6, OZ on Mike-11. I need you to get the SAT saddled up and out for a report."

"Beautiful day for it, sir."

"No rabbit hunting this time."

"Wouldn't think of it, sir."

It was not unknown, particularly during the spring, for rabbits to make their way across the launcher en route to matters more pressing—like mating season. Picking off these trespassers was unnecessary and definitely outside the regs. So it happened a lot.

"Crap, Sarge, the game's on."

"You aren't out here to watch the game, Airman Henderson, now go do your job."

"Great. Now we gotta haul ass out to Mike-11 to run off a nest-building robin or a rabbit getting a tan. C'mon, Billy."

Highway 50, 16 miles East of Kansas City
1953 Zulu
1353 Local

As Gray and Donna crested the hill, the van was directly in front of them and less than a hundred feet away headed straight for them—in their lane. Donna grabbed the dashboard screaming, "GRAY," as he slammed on the brakes and began steering the Cutlass for the shoulder in a four-wheel skid.

The oncoming van was passing a pickup and for a split second Gray could see the passengers of both vehicles in their two windshields— a clean-cut teenager in the driver's seat of the truck and a topless blonde beside a bearded hippie at the wheel of the van, all of them agape.

With "Age of Aquarius" blasting, the van banged into the side of the pickup and they missed the Cutlass as they passed—but Gray didn't know how.

Skidding to a stop, Gray and Donna took inventory and realized they were alive and uninjured. He jumped out of the car to see the damage. "Were we hit? I didn't feel it. Were we hit?" Donna kept asking.

Not a scratch. They were off the shoulder with the right front wheel over the edge of the roadside drainage ditch. Recent rains had left a stagnant pool in the bottom that smelled of mold. There was nothing but a pair of well defined skid marks that blossomed into four at the point of the turning to note the event.

In the distance, Gray could see the pickup chasing the VW van. As indelibly as the image of the kid was branded on his mind's eye, Gray could not seem to see if there was a gun rack behind his head. The image of the bare-breasted blonde in the front seat kept taking over the memory.

"That idiot was trying to pass on a hill…" Gray exclaimed. "In a VW VAN!"

"With his girlfriend's top in his hand," added Donna.

"I'm gonna chase 'em down."

"No, you're not. That hillbilly in the pickup has a better chance than you do. And he's more likely to extract some real vengeance. The last thing you want is a headline reading, 'Air Force Officer Assaults Pinko Hippie Freaks.' Andy'd have you for breakfast."

She was right. But Gray's adrenaline glands didn't care. He wanted some action.

"Come on. Show me your big strong missile and then let's get home."

Gray had forgotten that he was going to show her Mike-11. "It's just up here a bit."

They climbed back in and Gray carefully backed the car onto firm footing and they turned onto the highway. Westbound traffic was picking up. Though much of Highway 50 was four-lane divided, this stretch was two-lane while the south pair of lanes was being repaved. He realized that Donna was right. Even if he lit out after the van, he'd have to pass eight or ten cars against oncoming traffic. There were dozens of turn-offs—he'd never find them.

"Mike–11 is on the north side of the road right over there," Gray pointed. From where they were, it was a chain link fence and a gravel road about sixty feet north of the highway. They slowed, allowing an oncoming car to get clear, and Gray pulled onto the gravel road. He pulled up to within a few yards of the gate.

"Not much to look at," Donna allowed.

"Nope. Everything is underground."

"What are those blue posts?" Gray explained the three Air Force blue radar stanchions that surrounded the hexagonal launcher enclosure.

"Nothing can pass through that space without setting off an Outer Zone alarm back at Mike Capsule. Foxtrot is their backup so they also get the alarm."

"Do they ever go off? Like when the guy comes to mow the grass and stuff?"

"They go off whenever a bird flies through that space. But if there is no motion for five minutes, it resets."

"And if the motion continues?"

Gray didn't answer right away. "Gray. What happens if something keeps moving longer than five minutes?"

Gray was staring straight forward. Donna followed his eye line. She saw nothing unusual.

"What is it, Gray? Is it against the rules to be on this gravel driveway?"

With an almost dry mouth, Gray said, "The gate's open." His adrenaline rush from the near-miss was now a full fledged, heart-pounder. Blood rushed to his ears and he tried to think what he should do.

Donna looked again and saw a chain hanging loose from one side of the gate. The gate itself was ajar slightly.

"I take it that is unusual."

"Very. These are secure sites, Donna. Very secure."

Gray left the Cutlass and inched forward toward the fence. The gate's security chain was off, and a cut link lay on the ground at the gate entrance. From a standing position, he could see the top of the launcher enclosure. On it was a bright green and orange peace sign.

Donna was beside him now. "Vandals?"

"Yeah. Probably that bunch that ran us off the road. I need to…"

"HANDS IN THE AIR. DO NOT MOVE."

Donna and Gray both turned toward the voice.

"I said FREEZE, ASSHOLES." He was, maybe, nineteen, in cam-ouflage fatigues and armed with an M-16 that was pointed more or less toward Gray's head. He had a twin standing on the other side of the Cutlass with a similar bead on Donna.

"Ohmygod, Gray."

"Hold on a second, fellas," Gray started.

"On the ground, hands behind your heads," it was the second SAT member.

"Someone has breached this site, Airman, and…"

"SHUT UP AND GET ON THE DAMNED GROUND."

The kid was terrified. Gray knew they were in deep trouble. An armed, frightened post-adolescent was the most dangerous creature he could think of. He started down to the ground. Donna reached for him to stabilize herself as she started to kneel in the gravel.

"Hands to yourself. I want you ten feet apart." As the airman swung his weapon to gesture in the direction he wanted Donna to go, it discharged. Donna screamed and hit the ground. Gray grabbed for her, missed, and jumped on top of her covering her body with his.

"Don't shoot, don't shoot, don't shoot," Donna screamed.

"Jesus, Billy," Henderson shouted.

"I'm sorry. It went off. I didn't mean to…"

"Airman Henderson?" Gray shouted.

"What? How do you know my name? SHUT UP AND SEPARATE."

"You okay, Donna?"

"No, I'm scared."

"SHUT UP AND SEPARATE!"

"Take it easy, Henderson. I've got them covered," Billy said.

"Are you hit, Donna?"

"No. I don't think so."

"I'm moving. I'm moving now. I can't do it with my hands up. I'm moving, Airman Henderson."

Gray rose on his hands and toes and spider crawled ten feet away from Donna. He looked back to survey her body for blood. There was a wide orange stain on her blouse.

"My wife is hit. She's bleeding. Get her medical attention."

"I'm hit?" Donna shouted.

"Oh, Jesus, Jesus, Jesus," Billy repeated as he dropped his M-16 and rushed to her. Rolling her over, he saw that she was in a small pool of orange paint. "She ain't bleeding, she's got paint on her," he yelled as he scrambled back to grab his weapon. Standing up, he turned to Gray, "You lying bastard. You knew she wasn't hurt."

"How do you know my NAME?" Henderson screamed.

Two angry young men with guns and too much adrenaline in their systems—Gray was thinking as fast as he could.

"I'm Lieutenant Gray Crawford. You know me, Henderson. We've been on alert at the same times."

Henderson was not ready for this. All officers looked alike to him.

"It's a trick," Billy whispered. "It's a trick, Henderson. He lied about the bitch being hit. Hell, your name's on your CHEST for crying out loud."

Henderson looked at the blue and white name tape on his shirt.

"I'd have to be pretty fast to pick up on that with guns on me. Call the capsule. Who is your commander? He probably knows me. I'm an instructor at Whiteman. This site has been breached by vandals in an orange VW van that is headed west toward Kansas City. They ran us off the road…"

"SHUT UP, Billy. Keep 'em covered. I'm calling the FSC."

"PEACH PIE. PEACH PIE FROM THE BLUE INN, HENDERSON. You've eaten my PIE. C'mon."

"He knows about pie."

"Billy… shut up. It could be a trick."

Gray's mind was running a mile a minute. He had to prove to them that they weren't the bad guys here.

"If this were a Whiteman Scenario attack, I would not be here in a bright green sports car and a woman in a skirt and blouse.

THINK, GUYS. Call the capsule. A spy would not be begging you to call the authorities."

"He knows about the Whiteman Sc…"

"BILLY! You don't talk ANYmore. Got it? You stand here and cover 'em. I'm calling in." Henderson started to hike back to the truck parked near Highway 50.

It was bad. This would get worse before it was over and it might cost Gray his certification and his clearance, but chances of survival would be much higher once an officer was involved.

He hoped.

# CHAPTER 22

*Hell hath no fury, like a woman scorned.*
**William Congreve**

Security Police HQ, Whiteman AFB
2 May 1974
0145 Zulu (3 May)
1945 Local

MAJOR BUCKMAN headed up the security police at Whiteman and was at the end of his rope. "Lieutenant Crawford, you need to control your wife."

Andy stepped in before Gray could respond, "Major, I know of no man married to any woman worth being married to who can, or would wish to control her. She is justifiably upset, and allowances should be made."

"No one—particularly no civilian woman—calls me a 'stupid son-of-a-bitch' and gets away with it, Captain. She was in a restricted zone covered in the same paint as the vandalism to the launcher and she will sit down and shut up until we get to the bottom of this."

"As for COVERED, I can get this piddlin' paint smudge off without visiting the Base Cleaners, you…bachelor. And I wouldn't have THIS stain if Wyatt Earp and Marshall Dillon here hadn't panicked. The hippie freaks who actually DID THIS are in an orange van heading for CALI-DAMN-FORNIA right now. While you hold my husband and me *talking us to death*, they are getting AWAY."

"Mrs. Crawford…" the Major started.

Andy waved his hand in compliance and turned to her. With a softness Gray had never heard, he looked her in the eye and said, "Donna. I know you are fit to be tied. I would be, too. But you have to dial the rhetoric down so we can clean this up."

"That's right, Mrs. Crawford and…"

This time it was Gray who cut him off, "Major, is the access road restricted? It isn't posted as such?"

"What?"

"The access road, sir. The driveway. I had taken Donna up the driveway to show her an LF. The 'restricted area' sign is on the fence. I thought it referred to the area INSIDE the fence."

"It does. That is where the vandalism was—along with the gate chain!"

"Yes, sir. But…"

At this point, the squadron commander, Colonel Price, arrived. "Alright, what is this bullshit I hear about arresting one of my junior officers? Crawford, did you vandalize Mike-11?"

It was shaping up to be a turf war. Price was not only a light colonel but a squadron commander. Major Buckman's oak leaves were not even dry yet, but he WAS the head of security, and had worked his way up through the enlisted ranks. He knew, and had done, every job the security police had to offer. He'd also been chewed out by higher-ranking officers than Price. What galled him was the corner these two kids had painted him into. Buckman had been a sky cop since his first assignment. As with most jobs involving guns, the security police were plagued with a spectrum of personnel. At one end were officers and enlisted men (and women) of deep loyalty and devotion committed to a mission that was a critical part of not only Air Force but, by extension, national security. On the other end were kids like Henderson who might

make exceptional leaders one day but who currently were loose
cannons with more ammo than judgment. The kid had made a call
in the field and had operated by the book. How could Buckman
*not* back them up without undermining procedure and the authority needed to maintain security? If sixteen years in the Air Force
had taught Buckman nothing else it had made clear that the best
defense was a good offense.

"I'm conducting this interrogation, Colonel."

"INTERROGATION? I'm sure you meant to say investigation?
Or, have you already decided the Lieutenant and his wife are inter-
national spies?"

Sarcasm dripped off the last two words. The contempt Price
had for Buckman had to have had deeper roots than this episode.
Gray feared that he and Donna were about to become fuel for a
long smoldering fire between these two men.

"I'm asking questions, and I'm getting answers," Buckman
snapped.

Price shot right back, "We'll do this together, or I'll have JAG in
here so fast you won't have time to write a parking ticket."

For the next half hour they unpacked the story—again. At one
point, the Colonel looked Airman Henderson in the face and said,
"Let me understand this, Airman. You have worked with Lieutenant
Crawford for over six months. You knew him PERSONALLY. He
explained to you that he KNEW who had done this, and you chose
to cuff him and his wife, and bring them to the base without putting ANYONE on the trail of these actual vandals? Is that right?"

Henderson was 19. Had he been brighter, by any measure, he
would have been in college somewhere. His draft number had
been 95. He had been sure that the instant he flunked out of his
freshman year he would be drafted, then be lying dead in a rice
paddy in Vietnam a month later. He had enlisted in the Air Force
in an attempt to control some tiny corner of his future. It was
that spark of native intelligence that whispered to him that telling

this angry Colonel that "All officers look alike to me," was not a response that would be accepted graciously. So, what he did say was, "Yes, sir. I'm afraid so, sir."

"What weapons did you find in the lieutenant's car?"

"None, sir."

"None. I see. So there were other suspicious items, I suppose."

"Lingerie, sir."

"You went through my lingerie, you perverted little shit!"

"Lingerie. Your examination turned up—lingerie. Well, I can certainly see how that would support your supposition that America was under attack from two very dangerous villains. Major. Your office."

Price followed Buckman to his office. The volume was inescapable. Of the actual words spoken, the phrase "head out of your ass" and "real subversives" were the only distinguishable comments that could be attributed to the Colonel. None of Buckman's responses were audible. The gaps in the outrage indicated that there were responses... but what they were was anybody's guess.

At some length, they emerged. Buckman turned to Gray, "Lieutenant, you and your wife are released on your own recognizance. In future, please do not give tours of LFs without proper clearance."

The Major's tone was not contrite. Gray knew he had made an enemy. He hadn't meant to do that. Donna hadn't helped.

"What record will there be of this on the lieutenant's file, Major?"

Andy's concern was real. Instructors didn't stay instructors with "incident reports" in their files. Even getting driven home drunk from the "O Club" could get you busted back to crew duty.

"His file shows that he and his wife were... instrumental witnesses and..." the Major was having trouble gagging this down, "... and major contributors to clarifying the issues in this case."

Colonel Price got in Gray's face, "Lieutenant, I want to believe this was a case of wrong-place-wrong-time."

"It was, sir."

"Good. Mrs. Crawford, while I admire your passion, courage, and vocabulary... and while I would love to have you beside me in a fight, your discretion and judgment could use a moment to count to ten. Don't you think?"

Donna gave thought to a response but he beat her to it.

"Mrs. Crawford, your husband is an exemplary officer in a challenging and boring, and difficult job. If he is to have a career outside the Air Force, your independence probably won't damage his military career—but it won't help him, either. Here or outside. *You* are not my business, but *he* is. Don't BECOME my business again. Understood, ma'am?" It was the ma'am that got her.

"Yes, sir. You've given me a lot to think about. I appreciate it."

Across the room, the Major had handed Airman Henderson a set of orders.

"Thule, Greenland? I'm being shipped to Greenland, sir?" Henderson looked toward Gray and Donna with a desperate and stunned expression—every bit the nineteen-year-old that he was.

"What does that mean?" Donna asked.

Gray whispered, "There's a weather station on an ice field in Greenland at the Arctic Circle. I guess Henderson is being reassigned to guard icebergs."

"He was just doing his job. What if we HAD been spies, Gray?" Donna was heating up again. The Colonel stepped between her and the Major.

"Major, I have no business commenting on your assignment prerogatives, but I would like to suggest a course of action for you to consider with respect to the Airman."

The Major had not expected this. The Colonel was handing him his face back in front of the officers and enlisted men who had heard him ripped apart behind the door.

"I would… welcome the Colonel's input, sir."

"I seem to remember you told me once that experience was the only real teacher; particularly in the delicate, dangerous and complex business of security." The Major's eyebrows wanted to go up but the only movement that he would allow to betray his reaction to this unexpected compliment was an almost imperceptible straightening of an already near perfect spine.

"I seem to remember saying that, yes." In fact, he had said it only two minutes earlier at a point where he didn't think the colonel was receiving anything he said.

"Perhaps, what the airmen could use is double tours for a few months, to ensure he gets that experience."

Double tours were the equivalent of hard time to a sky cop. Twelve days on and 1 off with nothing to do but drive from LF to LF, ensuring domestic tranquility. Henderson was now seeing that as a vacation in paradise versus walking perimeter at twenty below in Greenland.

"I do believe in experience, Colonel. I'll give that idea some thought."

"Your call, of course, Major. I'm sure you know best." The Colonel turned and with a stern look to Andy, he left the building.

"What just happened?" Donna whispered.

"If your reports are complete, Major, I'll drive the lieutenant and his wife over to impound to get their vehicle," Andy suggested.

"Good idea. And, Mrs. Crawford."

"Y-yes, Major?"

"I regret that your… shopping items… were roughly handled. If there is any damage, please advise this office and we will ensure they are replaced."

"I'm sure everything is fine. It was just some panties and a bra that…"

"Thank you, Major," Gray said, as he chopped Donna off, and pointed her to the door.

All the way to impound, there was silence from all three. Once back to their car, Donna began to examine her new lingerie. Andy took a quick leave.

Gray never succeeded in getting it through to her that, the level at which men love lingerie is directly proportional to the discomfort they feel in dealing with it in any but a completely private context. Her argument that, "It is just CLOTHING!" though valid, missed the point at such a level that Gray felt it impossible to explain.

"It's... Donna, it's just clothing to *you*. To a man, it is the reminder of forbidden fruit."

"White cotton *panties*?"

"*You* are the one who screamed about the kid 'rifling through your lingerie,'"

"That was to make a point."

"That point—is MY point."

When he returned from the shower, Donna was on the bed in very different lingerie.

"Now, THIS is about forbidden fruit," she said.

Gray was several minutes into exploring the best means and timing for getting her out of what little there was of it when he wondered aloud, "Did Henderson see THIS?"

Donna brought him back into focus quickly. Danger, it turns out, is an aphrodisiac for women as well.

# CHAPTER 23

*Military glory—that attractive rainbow, that rises in show-ers of blood—that serpent's eye, that charms to destroy...*
**Abraham Lincoln**

509th SMS, Squadron Briefing Room
6 August 1974
0200 Zulu (7 August)
2000 Local

H E HAD seen the footage hundreds of times now. Colonel Sydney James looked across the gathering, watching faces illuminated by the light reflected from the projection screen. Scenes from Hiroshima and Nagasaki played out across the frozen faces of those gathered. His predecessor had briefed him on this unique custom when he took command a few months earlier. For almost thirty years, 509th Squadron commanders had shouldered the duty he was about to perform. It was very atypical for a military gathering. He had been instructed that, though it was a time-honored tradition, he was not required to lead it. He could choose not to participate. James had expected only a tiny handful of officers in attendance. He had been surprised to see a significant number entering fresh off alert to take their seats. While the men had to come through the squadron building to check in, he was gratified to see so many stay and be met by their families. In fact, with the others arriving, it had become standing room only. These were very good men. He was immensely proud of them.

With the footage at an end, the lights began to come on in the room and he noticed the confusion on the faces of some of the children, the sadness on the faces of many wives, and the studied control of the faces of the men. He moved to the briefing podium and opened his notes.

"Thank you for coming," he began.

509th SMS, Kilo-01
6 August 1974
0200 Zulu (7 August)
2000 Local

Gray and Andy had changed over at 1830 local to give the day crew an early departure. The crew commander had wanted to be back at the squadron building in time to meet his wife and son. Tonight, there was to be a short gathering in the squadron briefing room to commemorate the anniversary of the bombing of Hiroshima 29 years earlier.

Though some crew and families from all squadrons attended the somber little gathering, it was always hosted by the 509th— the squadron to which the fateful Enola Gay had been assigned. It had been the 509th that had dropped the first and only atomic weapons ever detonated in combat. The commemoration was a simple exercise in remembrance of the power and responsibility they must shepherd. Last year, Donna had asked Gray why on earth they would celebrate such an event. Gray wasn't sure. It was Andy who had explained that it was not a celebration of a victory, but an acceptance of responsibility for actions and consequences, and a renewal of personal commitment to freedom and duty.

Gray was digging around in his away bag when the squadron com-line buzzed. Andy, seeing he was engaged, waved him off and caught the line himself.

"Kilo."

"Golf on."

"Juliet, here."

"Lima Capsule."

"Gentlemen, this is Hotel. This is a non-mandatory muster for the 509th Commemoration Service. All are welcome to stay on; none are required."

Covering the mouthpiece of the handset, Andy turned. "Gray. You wanted to catch this, I think."

Gray dropped into his deputy's command chair and piled his schoolwork onto the console as he grabbed the handset with one hand and punched into the com-line with the other. He heard the automatic roll call.

"Golf. Commander and deputy on."

"Juliet. Both here."

"Kilo," Andy said, glancing up into his mirror and seeing Gray on the headset, "Both on."

"Lima. Go ahead, Hotel."

"Okay, then. I mark the time as 0200 Zulu in five, four, three, two, one... MARK." The commander at Hotel cleared his throat and began to read, "At this time in the squadron briefing room, Colonel James is running the Hiroshima and Nagasaki footage. I have a copy of his remarks with me. He's asked us to share them with those of you who would like to have made it to the event but are prevented by our duties here.

"Here, then, is the text of Colonel James' remarks. 'Twenty-nine years ago today, the world changed—forever. And the debate will rage on, also forever, over whether or not we did the right thing. Thankfully, that is not for us to decide. We are all wounded by these events. We all bear the scars. What we can be certain of is that the men of the 509th Bomber Squadron were called upon to perform a terrible deed—and they rose up and did their duty that day. The war ended as a direct result. The daily death toll stopped as a direct result of these two horrific days.

'Today, the men of the 509th Strategic Missile Squadron continue to be charged with the custody of the nuclear hammer. We no longer are alone, however. Our brothers here at Whiteman in the 508th and 510th, along with hundreds of others at F. E. Warren, Ellsworth, Minot, Grand Forks, and Malmstrom stand ready to do our duty should the call come again one day. We join crews in B-52s, in Titan silos, and in submarines on station all around the world. All of us are called to stand ready to send this final destruction once again if given orders to do so. No one wants that. No one wanted these two cities to suffer the devastation that was rained on them. Sometimes it is not about what we want. Sometimes—it is about what circumstance dictates must be done.

'By having this commemoration, we remind ourselves that actions have consequences; and warriors have responsibilities. It is my prayer for all of us that readiness alone will suffice.'

"That ends Colonel James' remarks. This is Hotel. This ends the commemoration exercise."

Without a word, each officer in the squadron hung up his com-line phone. Gray listened as one-by-one their lines went silent. As he gently replaced his handset, he watched Andy take out his journal and make a notation.

# THE EVENT

7 August 1974

# CHAPTER 24

*"I see nobody on the road," said Alice.*
*"I only wish I had such eyes," the King remarked in a*
*fretful tone. "To be able to see Nobody! And at that*
*distance, too! Why, it's as much as I can do to see real*
*people, by this light."*
**Lewis Carroll**

In the Looking Glass

G RAY MUST'VE dozed off. He opened his eyes to find his uniform wet with perspiration and bunched and twisted around him. Falling asleep in the deputy's chair was a bad career move, and embarrassing. His scarf was on backwards and trailed over his collar and down his back instead of being tucked neatly into the front. He always took the scarf off the instant he hit the capsule. Why hadn't he this time? He tried to shake off sleep but the lethargy dug in.

The capsule was dark except for equipment lights and the three pairs of emergency spots that illuminated the command console, deputy's console, and the floor just inside the entry. Andy was nowhere to be seen.

Gray sprang up and noticed he had on only one shoe. He dashed over to the command console. Everything was clean and green—no fault lights anywhere. As he turned, he could see that the blast door was open... the access tunnel and alcove beyond it dark except for the one bare bulb on the wall. Even its illumination seemed to soak into the inky blackness around it. From the equipment building beyond the alcove, he heard a deep groan amidst the constant roar.

As he moved toward the blast door he reached up for his gun belt. It was empty. The holster was unsnapped and the .38 was gone. Gray's heart started to pound. He heard a click behind him and whirled to see the last glimmer of light fade as the command console spotlight burned out, leaving the ten columns of green, yellow, and red lights glowing as if suspended in nothing. Another pop behind him and the entry spot burned out. Something blacked out the vestibule light beyond the open blast door for a second... then it was back... then... Something was moving through the blast door tunnel.

"Andy?"

No response except the sound of a boot hitting the metal bridge plate. Gray was trapped, unarmed, and silhouetted against the glow from the missile status lights.

The Inner Zone/Outer Zone alarm went off. He whirled and instinctively jabbed the ALARM OFF button and watched in horror as Missile Away lights began illuminating across the status panels. They were in launch.

Another footfall behind him. Gray spun the command chair around, knocking something to the side, and sprinted for the blast door. In the dark, there was no way to know exactly when he got there, so he ducked early and felt his way to the tunnel, ducked in and ran full into the closed door and its handles. Bleeding from the mouth and eyes now, he was grabbed from behind and flung back into the capsule.

He hit the floor hard but rolled and jumped to his feet. Grabbing the handle of the radio equipment rack, he twisted it clockwise, swung it open, and stepped through the wires and tubes into... the equipment building? But that wasn't possib...

His scarf snagged behind him on a rack and he pulled at the snaps, but they wouldn't release. The scarf stretched and became a billowing cape in 509th SMS blue with a huge 12/HQ logo emblazoned in the center.

A push on his shoulder and he was off again, running through the trainer. The mirrored walls showed the cape was now the yellow with blue thunderbolts of the Instructor Squadron. He dashed through the glass, shards shattering all around him, cutting into his unshod foot.

He burst into the EWO testing room. Fifty launch officers rose and moved toward him, weapons drawn, as the cape——now bright orange with a green peace sign in the center—fluttered over his shoulder.

He turned to find himself in a flaming equipment building again, a roar in his ears and the PAS speakers blaring, "Fifteen minutes to impact. Incoming missiles. Take cover! Crimson/One. Crimson/One. Turn keys for the memory of your families. Prepare to die."

Running from the sound, cape billowing, peace sign growing ever larger, Gray pulled his hands from his eyes and looked around him. The field he found himself in was ablaze. In every direction, missiles were rising. Mushroom clouds obliterated his view of the sun. His skin began to peel away and fall off, revealing bleached bone.

103 North Carswell Circle
Officer Whiteman AFB, Housing
7 Aug 1974
0230 Zulu (8 August)
2030 Local

Gray awoke—heart pounding, sweating, tangled in his uniform. Noggin was on the bed beside him, nudging his shoulder and whimpering. He sat up. He was on his own bed. The roar persisted.

Clapping his hands to his ears, Gray screamed, "THIS IS NOT HAPPENING!"

It had been another of the dreams, the worst of them so far.

He realized he was wearing only his left shoe. The other lay on the floor beside the bed. Clearing the fog a bit, he remembered. He had come in off alert exhausted. The upside down hours and interrupted sleep cycle had screwed up his body clock. He must have started to undress and just fell asleep in the process.

"Donna?"

No answer. But the roar was still there.

It was the B-52s. What time was it? The birds rotated on Monday mornings. Had they changed days or schedules? The disorientation would not clear.

"I just came in off alert… it was… TUESDAY." The kitchen calendar bore him out. It was marked "Gray on alert" across Monday and Tuesday. August 7th was circled and marked "Welcome Home Party."

Had he slept through the night? Had she planned a sexy, let's-try-to-make-a-baby welcoming party and he'd slept through the entire thing?

The clock said 8:31. The sunset confirmed early evening. Nothing said morning. Maybe the planes were rotating a day and a half late?

Gray went to the closet in his study to get the base phone directory. Donna insisted he keep everything AIR FORCE in one room—his study. It was on the shelf exactly where she told him to put it. As he began to close the closet door, he noted that something didn't seem right. Something out of place, perhaps. It took several seconds to realize that it was his Evac Bag. It wasn't out of place. It was gone. And so was Donna.

## Juliet-01

Captain Stu Rutherford was 27, good looking, single, and profoundly cocky. He had made commander as a First Lieutenant, mere days before pinning on his Captain's bars. Missiles was a walk in the park for Stu—routine duty demanding very little of his intellect; no one watching over his shoulder all the time in the capsule. In another year, he planned to make a superb salesman for Procter and Gamble or some other huge multinational.

Just now, he sat with his shoes and scarf off, gun hanging on the equipment rack above and behind his head, his blouse untucked, feet up on the console, and eating a Twinkie as he casually checked off a step in the Green Binder for the drill they were running.

Tucked into his shoulder was the squadron communication line handset.

"Kilo acknowledges."

With his big toe, Rutherford pushed the release button and the line went dead as he tossed the handset onto the Plexiglas-covered console and returned his focus to the Twinkie and reached for his *Playboy*.

"Nice to have this come early in the evening instead of midnight, huh, Davey?"

A movement in the command mirror above his head drew his attention. Twenty-two-year-old Second Lieutenant David Hale, red headed, freckle-faced, fully uniformed, and still armed, was moving toward the documents safe.

With no attempt to disguise the contempt and disgust with which he regarded his green deputy, Rutherford asked, "What the hell are you doing NOW, Davey?"

"Simulating opening the safe and placing the documents and keys at the…"

"There is no one here but us, idiot. A wave in that direction will do. We've acknowledged receipt. There is nothing to do out here in the REAL WORLD now but wait until they back it down and acknowledge THAT. And TAKE OFF THAT FUCKING GUN."

Ring.

It was one of the outside lines.

"Get that, will you, Deputy? Miss August has a prior claim on my attention."

"Well, according to step two of the checklist..."

"Oh, God... It's step two, Davey. Just handle it."

Hale looked at step two of the exercise checklist. He had done this hundreds of times at Vandenberg and in the trainer at Whiteman, but this was the "real world."

The text was identical to the text on the actual war checklists for this step. It did not say "SIMULATE." A quick scan and he decided he'd have to read directly from the text of the checklist.

"Juliet Capsule is accepting only emergency calls at this time. Is this an emergency?"

103 North Carswell Circle
Whiteman AFB Officer Housing

Gray had misdialed.

"Juliet? I thought I had dialed Kilo." Gray did not recognize the crewman's voice.

That wasn't on the checklist. Hale had to think a second. Then, "Is this an emergency, sir?" Gray hung up and quickly referred to the base directory again. Holding his thumbnail firmly on the Kilo-01 phone number, he dialed.

Kilo-01

Instructor Deputy, Lieutenant Dink Dinkins, on alert at Kilo, had his checklist open but on top of it was his Applied Accounting

Principles text. Handset to his ear, he was comparing notes with a classmate at Hotel capsule when the outside line rang.

"Back in a second, Rick." He cleared the squadron com-line and punched the line one button before the second ring. Without glancing at the checklist he said, "At this time Kilo Capsule is handling only emergency calls. Is this an emergency?"

"Maybe so. It's Gray." Dinkins could hear the bombers through the phone. "Dink... What checklist are you on?"

Dinkins hesitated for a second, glanced at his commander, who was looking up through the commander's rear view mirror at him, and said, "I can't talk about your Cutlass right now," and hung up.

Cutlass? Did he misunderstand? Gray wondered aloud why Dink was talking about his Cutlass. Since Vandenberg, Dink had admired its styling and bold emerald green metallic finish. THAT WAS IT.

"He's TELLING me!" Gray shouted out loud. "He's on the green... the EXERCISE checklist. Do the '52s light up on an exercise?" he wondered.

Opening his kitchen door, Gray saw that his green Cutlass wasn't there either. And Noggin, the idiot cocker, dashed out the door.

# CHAPTER 25

*In the fight between you and the world, back the world.*
**Franz Kafka**

"YES, MR. Secretary, that is policy," the briefing officer continued. "Any significant change in security status results in us starting the daily exercise immediately. It brings our forces up in a more routine fashion."

Secretary of Defense Robert Adler was studying the projected world map intensely as a red arcing line crept toward a more vertical line labeled "The Horizon Marker."

"The President is engaged presently and does not wish to be disturbed. I have informed him that an exercise is running. That seems most prudent at this time."

"Has he been told WHY, sir?" General Paxton, the Army Chief of Staff asked.

"He did not ask. He trusts us to handle these... situations."

Paxton was becoming red in the face. "These situations? We've never HAD a situation like this, Mr. Secretary."

"Have we contacted our counterparts in Russia?"

"In sixty seconds, when the bird crosses the horizon line, we can and will. Until then, any sign that we're aware of this will give away our Over-the-Horizon capability."

"OHR costs too much to give it away this soon. That would not be wise," the Secretary said, almost to himself.

The Joint Chiefs were stumped. Adler was so calm. The president wasn't to be disturbed? Would the vaporization of 500,000 people and the crippling of thousands more disturb him?

"So… SAC is at full alert, although in exercise mode. Bombers are not rolled out into position but can be airborne in short order." Adler ticked off the alert readiness list.

"I had the bombers start up," General Blankenship said. "If that blip becomes a threat, they need to be airborne ASAP."

"Very well," Adler agreed. "Subs are already moving to launch positions, Admiral?"

"Of course."

"Okay. So, I guess we challenge the sortie in… what is it now? 48 seconds?"

The man's calm was infuriating.

# CHAPTER 26

*Life is like a log floating down the river with a million*
*ants on it—all of whom think they are steering.*
**Gray Crawford**

Officer's Housing, Whiteman AFB
March Drive at Carswell Circle
0231 Zulu
2031 Local

TIRES SQUEALED. Lt. Matteo swerved right just as a dog ran into the road. Over the curb and into a vacant lot, his sporty red Triumph slid to a halt pointed directly at Gray's back door.

Noggin had felt the left front tire brush his tail on the way by. Idiot that he was, he had the sense to decide that unlimited freedom might not be so hot and he high-tailed it back to the house.

"He came out of nowhere, Gray. Is he okay?"

"Yeah, I think so. Dale, come in the house a minute."

Entering through the carport door into the kitchen, Dale found Gray in a wrinkled crew uniform, wearing one shoe and looking very puzzled.

"How's he doing?"

"Who?"

"WHO? Your idiot dog, Gray."

"Oh. Yeah. Fine I guess… Listen…"

Gray ran through the calls, the responses, the B-52s lit up on a non-rotation day. He left out his missing wife because he didn't have any idea how that could figure into the equation.

"Cutlass. Green. Great clue. Dinkins is sharp. Hell, Gray, he told you it was a fuckin' exercise almost in the clear."

The sound of the B-52s began to change. Checking his watch, Matteo added, "There you go. They're prob'ly out of it by now. Gimme the phone. I'll call Rick at Foxtrot."

The '52s were different. Not louder or softer… just… different. Gray watched as Matteo started to speak and then he stopped abruptly. Glancing at Gray he mouthed, "Emergency calls only."

Turning a new shade of red, Matteo interrupted, "Rick, I have three B-52s lit and turned out. What do you KNOW?"

Startled, Rick broke from the checklist limitations and dumbly asked, "Wh…What?"

Ready to get to the bottom of it all, Matteo thrust the phone out the back door toward the cacophony, then screamed into the phone, "WHAT DO YOU KNOW?"

Lima-01
2030 Local

Rick's commander looked up from his Accounting text, "We're still in exercise lockout status, Rick."

Rick thought a beat and said, "EXERCISE caution. There could be half a dozen reasons for that. Don't call again unless emergency status changes." And he hung up. Then he turned back to his initial message and began to decode it again. Could he have been wrong? Was he in the wrong BOOK?

103 North Carswell Circle
2030 Local

Matteo was staring at a dead handset. Gray broke the silence: "What did he say, Dale?"

"He said EXERCISE caution and some crap about 'half a dozen reasons for this…' "

"Half a dozen. SIX! Dale. EXERCISE caution! Maybe he's trying to tell us Green Slash 6."

"Okay. Maybe. Do you think that means they're in an EXERCISE or that we should haul ass?"

"Okay. Let's work this through. What was his tone?"

"Uhm… nothing out of the ordinary."

"Is he ultra cool?"

"Rick? No. If shit was hitting the fan, he'd be shaking like a leaf in the wind."

"All the steps on Green Slash 6 are the same as for Yellow Slash 6 in the red book, except you don't actually open the safe," Gray mused.

Matteo put his service cap back on. "We aren't gonna sort this out here, Gray. Let's go see what's happening."

"Lemme grab my other shoe."

The pair jumped into the Triumph and headed for the flight line.

Lima-01
0231 Zulu
2031 Local

At Lima capsule, a now very concerned deputy turned to his commander. "So. Do they light the '52s on an exercise?"

"At what, a thousand dollars an hour for fuel? I hardly think so."

"They did tonight."

Considering that for a second, the commander asked, "That did decode green didn't it? Re-decode your message."

# CHAPTER 27

---

*Destiny isn't a predictive map for your life.*
*Destiny is the shape your life takes as a result*
*of your choices.*
**Rick Stevens**

Situation Room-Washington
0232 Zulu ·
2132 Local

I T HAD only been forty seconds but the Joint Chiefs were in a full argument. At issue was, "Should this be a Red Phone conversation by the President?" or "a routine call through regular channels with their counterparts and translators?"

"Under no circumstances can we let Russia know what we know."

"Nixon must be told."

"He doesn't want to be DISTURBED. He's left this to us. That is correct, is it not, Mr. Secretary?"

"If there is a plausible and simple explanation, some oversight, and we reveal too much, we may unwittingly betray the OHR capability, and…"

"Yes. WHAT IF there is a good explanation? We have to get on the horn through regular system channels and ask them what the hell they are up to. 'We see a trajectory rising, Comrade. No idea what's up. Shall we lob one back?' We'll get the bastards scrambling to provide a story."

"They already HAVE a story."

Paxton looked at Adler. "You don't have the balls to push the button. The President does. He isn't afraid to do what is necessary… popular or not."

"The 'button' is not mine to push, General, and you know that," Adler replied coolly. "Neither is it yours."

Paxton wanted to break the man in two. He rose from his chair as Adler remained seated at the head of the table and spoke, "Gentlemen, the President has half of the Republican leadership in his office right now discussing—God only knows exactly what—but, with the future of the American Presidency in the balance, I reassert that this would NOT be a good time to disturb them with news that is not clearly definitive. What is the highest exercise level we have short of the War Message?"

Blankenship had another idea: "Move to Orange/8. Elevated alert status. Roll the bombers into takeoff position."

Saying what others would not, Crewcut asked, "Are you afraid that a war is precisely what he needs tonight, sir?"

# CHAPTER 28

---

*Into the Valley of Death rode the 600.*
**Tennyson**

Juliet-01
0222 Zulu
2022 Local

"SKYBIRD, COPY coded SAC message."

"And now we back it down and I can focus on important things," Rutherford muttered.

But when it decoded, it elevated them from a Green/6 standard exercise to Orange/8.

"What's going on? We weren't briefed on anything that would take us to higher security," the lieutenant whined.

"It is probably AN EXERCISE, Dave. Just one more elaborate EXERCISE. SAC is about practice for nothing. Some department head has to justify his existence every once in a while by spending millions of bucks on gas for us to drive our SAT troops around looking at empty launch sites and beating the bushes for sniper spies with deer rifles."

Kilo-01 LCF
(Launch Control Facility)

Topside at Kilo, the cook and the SAT troops had just finished dinner and were watching the Kansas City Royals. The FSC, charged with security for the site, had decided that standing in the door to the security station and looking down the hall at the TV would serve both of his callings that evening.

After the commercial, the local news station teased the 10 o'clock report. "And tonight the President has gathered his advisors around him for closed door meetings. Though there is no way to know the agenda for the discussions, it is almost certain that impeachment, resignation, and eighteen-minute gaps will come up at some point. Details at 10."

"Get back to the game, man!" exploded Billy, the youngest SAT team member.

"Hey. Cool it, Billy," the cook said. "Your hot head done got you in enough trouble, hadn't it?"

"Shut up, Johnson. I don't need you mouthin' off."

The FSC/Capsule line rang. The FSC jumped for it, feeling guilty that he was not, strictly speaking, "at his post."

"FSC sir. What can I do for you this evening, sir?"

"Security status elevation. Go to Orange Bravo Delta, Sarge," Pratt read from the checklist. "Get the boys out on the road."

"Jeez, they just got in an hour ago, sir."

"I don't recall asking for input or excuses, Sarge. Get 'em in the road," Pratt snapped.

"Sorry, sir. I didn't mean to imply… I'm on it, sir." He hung up, but not before hoping the capsule crew heard him yell out, "SAT. Saddle up, we got work to do."

"WHAT?" Billy groaned. "We just got BACK. Why we gotta go back out and run LFs in the damn rain?"

"We're in Orange Bravo Delta, cowboy. Pack a lunch."

"Aw, SHIT."

Exercise status at this level meant that the SAT team would continually make the rounds of the LFs until called back or returning to gas up the vehicle. Gassing up at local stations was disallowed during an exercise, so the SAT would be running a large figure eight that brought them by the LCF between every five LF checks should they need fuel. Just like during an actual attack, they needed to be on patrol.

Cookie was throwing sandwiches together fast. He dug out some of the pudding he knew Bobby liked and anything he thought would keep for more than a day, and bundled it with water and orange drink boxes into a cooler. Handing it to Henderson, he noticed the clouds moving in.

"Whoa. It's about to come a rippin' storm. Wear your rubbers, boys."

Then, much more intensely, "Think this is the real thang, Henderson?"

"Hell, no."

"Of course it isn't," the Site Manager offered. Walking him through the Ready Room, he pointed out the window to a concrete circle twenty feet from the building.

"See that pad out there with the five round spots on the outer ring. Each one of those is an HF antenna on an explosive charge. We go to war and they pop one of them things – at two thousand dollars a pop – and it stays up until it goes bad, and then they pop another."

"Why would it go bad?" Cookie asked.

A moment passed before it dawned on Cookie that a rolling blast would knock it over. And there were five of them. The war planners were expecting a lot of wind in that immediate area.

The FSC was on the line to the capsule: "I'll keep it clear, sir. Everyone's inside except the SAT and they just departed."

A gunshot-like crack sounded. Cookie and Sarge turned back to the window as a twenty-foot HF antenna emerged from the pad.

"Hope she stays up a long time," Cookie sighed.

"Me, too, kid." Knowing the terror about to overtake the young man, Sarge decided that action was the best cure. "Wonder if you could make me and the FSC some sandwiches. This is hungry work."

Grateful for a job to do, Cookie moved quickly toward the kitchen. "You got it, Sarge. Best in town."

# CHAPTER 29

*Finding needles in haystacks should never become*
*a matter of burning the hay.*
**Farmer Earl**

"OK. I can see the '52s. They're turned out of the parking formation. Hard to stay focused with all this vibration. Damn. Over a mile away, and still those things are loud."

Through the binoculars, Matteo could just make out the ground crew and fuel trucks parked at the edges of the apron a mile and a half to the north.

"Gray… They're pumping fuel into those birds. They're keeping them topped off."

From their vantage point on the roof of the squadron annex building, much of the base spread out to their north and west. To the east was a service hanger and the flight line, with the B-52 station at the northern extremity. To the west of them half a block was Oscar-01. North and west were the Base Exchange, Wing Command Post, administrative buildings, and beyond those the Officer's Club and housing areas.

"Check Oscar. I can't see from here if the HF antenna is up."

Swinging around, Matteo trained the glasses on Oscar-01's Launch Control Facility (LCF) building.

"How tall are they? The pad is on the other side of the building and if they aren't taller than the roof, there's no way to see from here. We could drive by, I guess."

No, they couldn't. Gray pointed to the traffic barriers that had been put up on each end of 12th street, blocking traffic from bypassing Oscar Capsule. Even Vandenberg Avenue, which wrapped around Oscar, had been blocked off with the sawhorse barriers. They heard a crack and seconds later the HF antennae poked up on the far side of Oscar.

"Something's up, Dale."

"Yeah. There's a run at the BX and Commissary. People are smelling trouble."

Turning from his intent examination of this development at Oscar to the parking lot of the Commissary, Gray spotted his Cutlass.

"Get me over there."

# CHAPTER 30

---

*It is easier to fight for one's principles
than to live up to them.*
**Alfred Adler**

Whiteman Base Exchange Parking Lot
0234 Zulu
2034 Local

"OH. HI, Hon. I got some ear plugs. These planes keep this up we'll all go deaf. Jeez, you look a mess." Donna was loading groceries into the back seat of the car as Matteo dropped Gray at the BX. "Hi, Dale."

"Love to chat. Gotta run. Good luck, Gray," and Matteo sped out of the BX parking lot well above the mandatory on-base 25 mph limit. He sailed right by a pair of security police coming the other way. The normally speed-obsessed security troops never gave a hint of slowing or going after him.

"Donna, where is the bag I kept under the daybed?"

Sensing the depth of his concern, Donna said, "Let's go. You drive."

The BX was only blocks from base housing. Gray was going in the back way to stop by the house, grab Noggin and whatever else they could think of before heading west. The goal was to get past the Kansas line as quickly as possible. He explained the real reasoning behind the evac-bag.

"Oh, hell, Gray, I figured what that stuff must be for. I put it in the CAR. If the bag was what I thought it might be—then it needed to be where WE would be if we needed to leave in a hurry," she explained. "You aren't the only one who can keep a secret, you know. But, I gotta tell you, you suck at it. And, Gray! The crap you put in there."

She explained that she had expanded the bag to its fullest dimensions and filled it with layers of warm clothing, dehydrated food, water purification tablets, sewing kits, and medical supplies. He was stunned.

Looking up, Gray saw Andy's house and quickly pulled over. The carport was empty. Both of Andy's cars were gone. The tow-bar for his Morris Minor had rested against the storage shed since he had unhooked it upon arrival at Whiteman. It was not there. As he walked into the carport, Gray's curiosity turned to shock when he saw that the kitchen door was standing slightly ajar.

"ANDY. You in here? Anybody home?"

Donna turned for the car. "Let's go."

# CHAPTER 31

*If a thing can go wrong, it will.*
**Murphy**

"THE BOGIE is on all radars now, sir," a tech reported.

Status spoke up, "We can launch all B-52s except Whiteman and open our contact line to the Kremlin now, sir."

The NORAD floor commander cupped his hand over the phone as he listened to instructions from the Joint Chiefs over the secure line to the Situation Room. "Washington has us holding…"

Every head turned toward him, astonished.

A klaxon horn sounded and the OTH radar tech announced, "We have another bogie rising."

The NORAD commander wheeled to the screen. "What?"

"They've launched another bird sir… from the Cherskiy silos, I think."

"Trajectories?"

"First one looks like… DC, sir. This one we'll have to compute…"

The Floor Commander had had enough. "Get this to the President and get those '52s in the air… NOW. Put SAC in Orange/10."

General Ashcroft turned to him, nose to nose. The FC had given

218

orders to HIS team and he wouldn't let it pass. "JCS says differently, Colonel."

"JCS is wrong, General. The book is crystal clear. We have highly probable incoming. Launch the birds and get us on the Orange/10 checklist. Those documents and keys MUST come out now. We may have less than 15 minutes to LISTEN to the JCS."

"San Francisco," a voice cried out.

"San Francisco, WHAT?" the General demanded.

"That's the other target, sir. D. C. and San Francisco."

Ashcroft opened his mic. It was his team. He would give the orders. "Move to Orange/10. Advise JCS and launch all bombers. Alert the Navy. All ships in San Francisco Bay deploy to sea NOW."

"Whiteman?"

"...no. Hold Whiteman on the apron."

The communications sergeant typed in the flash alert, mumbling, "Thirty minutes flight time... They won't get past the Golden Gate. It's Pearl Harbor all over again."

Ashcroft softly added, "But with just one bomb."

# CHAPTER 32

*Man the lifeboats. Women and children first...*
**Edward John Smith, Captain of the Titanic**

Juliet-01
0239 Zulu
2039 Local

"SKYBIRD, COPY CODED SAC MESSAGE."

Rutherford smiled his smug frat-boy grin, "Okay, Davey, me boy. THIS will back us down out of the exercise and you can quit pissing your pants."

Seconds later, it became apparent that it was not to be. "I have another red book decode... Orange/10 checklist. Jesus."

Silence.

Rutherford looked up into the commander's rearview mirror and saw his deputy staring, open-mouthed at the code sheet. Drool was dripping from his lower lip. He had lost all of his color and was pallid against his orange/red hair.

"Deputy, do you concur."

"Oh, God. Ohgod-ohgod-ohgod-ohgod..."

"Pull it together, Davey. This is NOT a launch order. We're just stepping up. Look. Something's going on, but no need to shit a brick just yet. See? We've done everything already... almost."

Rutherford swung the chair around to face the red safe. In stocking feet, he moved to it and began unlocking his combination.

Opening that box, even at changeover, always gave his stomach a turn. This was much worse.

"You need to get your lock open, Dave,"

"SHUT UP. SHUT THE HELL UP. You smart ass. 'It's only an exercise, Davey. Quit being an idiot, Davey.' Well who's the idiot *now*, CAPTAIN!"

"Pull it together, Lieutenant. We have a job to do."

"My wife. Oh, God, my *wife*. We're trying to have a baby."

"*David*. We have a job to do. OPEN YOUR LOCK and PLACE YOUR DOCUMENTS AND KEYS AT YOUR CONSOLE."

This seemed to snap him out of it. He looked up and said, "Of course. Yes, sir. I'm sorry, I..."

Fumbling with his combination took him several seconds. Had Standboard been there, he would have gotten several minor errors... maybe even a major. But then... this was not a test.

Both locks were removed, Rutherford swung the bales open and dropped the front panel, revealing the two sets of plasti-lock documents and silver launch keys.

Davey was completely frozen. He couldn't touch them. Rutherford decided to pick his battles. He removed both sets, placed Davey's at the Deputy's console right beside the launch key slot, and his own at the command console below his launch key slot.

The Squadron line was buzzing. Rutherford got it and spoke: "Juliet acknowledges receipt and completion of all checklist steps."

Hotel called roll. One by one, each capsule acknowledged... some with quiet resolve... a couple with shaky voices.

"This is Kilo. Gray Crawford just called..."

Dave found his voice, "NO. We can't take calls. It says on the checklist... Only emergency calls. JESUS, WAS IT AN EMERGENCY?"

Rutherford turned his command chair to face his deputy. In

uncharacteristically tender and gentle tones, like to a panicked child, he said, "Davey. Stop. Breathe. Let Dinkins tell us what he knows, okay? Go, Dink."

Dink knew that there were probably more guys than just Rutherford's green deputy who were near panic, but he felt he owed the info to them. "I was reading him the 'only emergency calls' paragraph and he interrupted and shouted that the B-52s were lit. I could hear them over the phone."

"Big deal. This is Jim at Hotel. They're probably rotating out."

"No. They rotate on Mondays. Maybe it's part of their exercise checklist."

"At hundreds of bucks an hour for fuel? No way. This has to be something going down. We have HF antennas up, for crying out loud."

The squadron party line was a secure, five-way connection between all capsules. You might never know WHO was speaking unless you crewed with them regularly and knew their voices.

"What's Gray think?"

"I don't know," Dink responded. "I hung up."

"HUNG UP?"

"It's on the checklist."

"HEY. I say a bunch of B-52s lit and us with our damned safes open qualifies as an emergency. You shoulda stayed on and got the scoop, Dink."

"No. It was before…"

"Wait. It was BEFORE we fully elevated?"

"Yeah… I think so. Hell, it's all mixed together now."

"Okay, listen up. This is C-Major at Hotel. The ALTERNATE COMMAND POST. I'm telling you to quit speculating and hang up until you have squadron business to discuss."

"Golf out."

"…Kilo out.'"

"Lima out."

"Hotel here... Julie? Juliet, you there? Juliet Capsule?"

"Oh, God. Oh God." Davey was losing it.

"Davey. Hang up. I've got this. Juliet, out." Now, Rutherford was starting to worry.

# CHAPTER 33

*Whither thou goest, I will go.*
*Thy people will be my people.*
**Ruth**

103 North Carswell Circle
Officer's Housing, Whiteman AFB
0237 Zulu
2037 Local

"**I** THINK WE should try to find Linda. Dink wouldn't leave you here if the roles were reversed," Gray suggested.

"She's in Arizona. She went to tell her folks in person that she was pregnant."

"She's..."

"Yeah. Yesterday I thought that was good news."

As Donna threw the last unmarked cans of mystery food into the trunk, Gray dumped Noggin into the back seat. Leaving the base front gate, they noted that the line to get INTO the base extended out of sight in both directions. Every vehicle was being thoroughly searched. Rain clouds darkened the late evening sky.

From his T. O. Bag, Gray pulled out a squadron map. It was a much more detailed map of the roads of Missouri than AAA could provide.

"Donna. In the bottom of the bag is a rigid support panel. Under it are acetate sleeves. Get them out."

Once she had found the sleeves, Gray selected one and handed it and the map to her. "Put this map in the first sleeve... this side up."

The acetate was marked with yellow transparent tape. When the map was in the sleeve, it highlighted a specific set of roads— an escape route.

"We're not just heading out Highway 50? That's the straightest route to Kansas City, isn't it?

"We don't want to go to KC. That's likely to get congested quickly, anyway. We want to get to Baldwin City. Right here, see?"

"Why?"

"Please don't challenge me now, Donna, I..."

"Gray. I believe you know what you're doing. I just need to understand it so I can support it...so I can help. Is it a secret that I—don't need to know?"

There was no bitterness, anger, or condemnation in her voice. She was asking for operational data so she could do HER part. Gray knew she was right. He had no reason to feel defensive.

"We are in the middle of a huge target footprint. Whiteman and its 150 missiles make up a LOT of targets. Even if we aren't in a direct hit zone, the blast travels over the land for miles. We want to get past that footprint. Kansas City is probably targeted, too, but not in the first wave, I wouldn't think. If we can get past Baldwin City, we can make our way through a largely untargeted area with the wind in our face."

"Where to? Where are we headed ultimately?"

Gray had struggled with that, too. In a post-apocalyptic world, would there be ANYWHERE to go?

"Right now, I'm trying to get out of the fire zone. We have to get WEST of this target cluster and head for the Rockies. Mountains offer a lot of protection and the potential for water and food."

Donna was putting other maps into sleeves. One route that

descended through west Texas and continued onward further south caught her eye.

"Mexico. That makes some sense. I guess..."

Then it seemed to dawn on her.

"Gray. Our families. How do we warn them? What do we tell them to do? What did those films show you to do when the bombs come?"

Gray had no answer for any of that. She thought he had a complete plan. He didn't; just the first piece of one.

"Listen, I need you to keep alert. We are avoiding a lot of launch facilities but we do drive near a few. You need to keep your eyes open. If there is a near miss anywhere around us, we need to find shelter behind a hill or something until the blast passes."

"But won't the air be radioactive? Do we even have a chance?"

"No. It doesn't work like that. First there is the explosion of the bomb. It is huge and emits a blast wave that travels in all directions outward—outward—but in straight lines. If we're down behind a hill or an underpass, it might just give us a good shaking. With that is heat and radiation. Close in, it is devastating; but, behind something or a few miles away, it dissipates. We'd get a burn—like a bad sunburn."

"And if we're not 'miles away?' If we're close in it..."

"Close in... is total devastation. We probably wouldn't even feel it. But our goal is to thread the needle and get out of those blast and radiation areas. The real ongoing danger is the fallout; tiny particles of radioactive dust that emit gamma rays and kill tissue. It will blow EAST. So we're heading west."

A peal of thunder and a bright crack of lightning startled both of them so much he almost ran off the road.

"Are we hit? Was that a bomb?!" Donna screamed.

"No. That was just the storm."

He hoped.

# CHAPTER 34

*I have good news and I have bad news.*
*Okay... I only have bad news.*
**Dick Martin**

Kilo-11, Hard-line
0239 Zulu
2039 Local

"**K**ILO-11 MAINTENANCE, this is Captain Pratt. I need your crew chief."

"Sergeant Graeff here, sir. Go ahead."

"We have a status change, Sarge. I need you to bring your sortie to full alert and depart."

"No-can-do, sir. We're in the middle of a reseat; we're working in extreme heat conditions. We should have mated these two back at the base and brought out the whole unit in one piece. With the storm coming up, we really should button up and close the van. It's a lightning rod."

"How long?"

"You're serious?"

"How long?"

"Holy, Jesus. Sorry, sir. Uhm. We... I'm not sure. A couple of hours easy. We can't get the missile- away cable to seat right, sir. The warhead takes meticulous positioning, and with the thunder...

We can't work like this. The van and winch are over the open tube with skirts in place, but there is lightning everywhere…"

"Stay on station and complete your assembly as fast as you can. Priority is mating the warhead. Missile- away cable can wait. Report to me every fifteen minutes."

"Excuse me, sir, but if I have to stop what I'm doing and get to this phone every fifteen minutes, we'll never get this job done."

"Okay, but I want to hear from you at EVERY milestone. Got it?"

"I do, sir."

"Get after it, then. Capsule, out."

# CHAPTER 35

*The road to Hell is paved with good intentions.*
**Sixteenth Century Proverb**

509ᵗʰ SMS Squadron Com-Line
Juliet-01
0246 Zulu
2046 Local

STU RUTHERFORD was whispering into his handset, grateful for once that the constant rumble of air over the equipment racks and hum of the powerful motor generator masked what he was saying.

"Yeah. He's losing it completely. Day crew should be out here in a few hours and I'm thinking of having him relieved."

"Rutherford, that is your call. But it will ruin his career. Be certain that he's not just needing some support from you before you sell him up the river like that," Dinkins advised.

"Hey. I don't want to. I don't want to break in ANOTHER deputy. Plus, this might reflect on me somehow. But, he's scared shitless, Dink."

"Okay. Ouch."

"What's wrong, Dink?"

"I pinched my little finger between the arm rest and the butt of my pistol. Damn, that smarts."

"You're wearing your WEAPON? How gung-ho of you."

"It's on the checklist, Rutherford. Where's yours? Hanging on the com-rack behind you?"

Grinning, Rutherford looked up into his rear view mirror and saw his holster hanging, as Dink had described, from the handle of the com rack. But he also saw his deputy – his own gun drawn – watching him, and listening in on the squadron com-line.

"Holy shit."

At that moment, power to Juliet Capsule failed, plunging the capsule into darkness accompanied by the concussive bangs of the battery-powered DC brushes of the motor-generator dropping onto the shaft and blast valves slamming shut.

Never having been on alert during a real power outage, the banging so startled Lt. Hale that he leapt to his feet, discharging his weapon. The bullet traveled straight forward and into the back of Rutherford's command chair.

## Kilo-01

Dinkins, having heard the banging of the motor-generator through the squadron com-line, had then heard a distinctively different sound. Not a capsule sound at all.

"You guys lose power?" Dinkins asked.

Rutherford was looking at a slug impaled in the shattered Plexiglas of his command console right between Kilo-06 and -07's columns of status lights. All around it was a spray of blood. His blood. Looking down at the bloody hole in his shirt, he managed to say, "I'm hit," before sliding out of the chair to the floor.

"What? What did you say, Rutherford?" Dink asked.

"What's going on?" Pratt wanted to know.

"I don't know. But I think... I think Stu Rutherford just got shot at Kilo."

As Rutherford sank to the floor, the handset in his grip hung down over the edge of the console still keyed into the squadron com-line. Davey was screaming.

"INCOMING. INCOMING. WE'RE HIT. OH, GOD, WE'RE HIT."

Dinkins and his commander both could hear the cries. Keying the H, G, and L buttons Dinkins brought the others in the squadron to the phone.

"Hotel."

"Golf."

"Lima."

"HUSH," Dinkins whisper-shouted into the phone, "Get everyone on the line NOW... and listen."

Faintly, they could hear Lt. Hale through his commander's handset, which dangled over the command desk where it had pulled from Rutherford's hand as he slid to the deck of the capsule. Davey was still screaming, "We're hit!" over and over.

"What is going on?" the commander at Hotel demanded.

Dink ran it down.

"Stu said they were 'HIT'? No... I show their computer operating. STU! STU! Lieutenant... What's that new kid's name?"

"David Hale," Dink said. "He's gone over the edge."

"You're saying Stu is SHOT, Dink?"

"I heard a bang... not a motor-gen bang. It was after their DC brush and blast valve bangs..."

"Nothing we can do about it from here. Hotel will report it to the Command Post."

"Dink, we've got a call from Kilo-11. Let them worry about Juliet for a minute," Pratt said.

Dinkins turned his attention to the direct phone line from Kilo-11.

"Capsule, this is Graeff at Kilo-11. It's just one thing after another out here, sir. The booster is seated on the launch ring but no missile away cable is installed. We have the warhead ready to lower onto the guidance system, but with all this vibration from the lightning and thunder around us, lining up all these tiny screws is going to be…"

"YOUR JOB! Line it up and bring it up. Call me when it is ready." Pratt was getting VERY frustrated.

"Sir. With all *due* respect, if lightning hits this solid fuel booster, it will explode. It will take all of us with it along with about a square mile of this chunk of Missouri. That kind of explosion is sure to scatter THIS warhead, making things pretty hot out here, if you get me. Am I to understand that your orders are to proceed, SIR?"

"I'm sorry, Sergeant Graeff, but those are my exact orders. Capsule, out."

# CHAPTER 36

*The mission is too important to allow you to jeopardize it.*
**HAL the Computer**

Soviet Ministry of Space and Defense
0248 Zulu
2048 Local

"LET ME see if I understand," General Gurov began. He was stalling. Just as predicted, the Americans had seen the launch as it crossed their NORAD Distant Early Warning Line (DEW Line) and were now posturing and indignant.

"You are demanding details of what you claim to be an airborne object which you contend that we have launched. You are asking why we did not advise you of such a launch in advance. Is that an accurate understanding of your questions?"

Situation Room-Washington

The American translator was interpreting not only the content, context, syntax, and word choice of the Soviet officer, but was also trying to translate his arrogant tone in the bargain.

"I think we get it pretty well, Henry. Don't strain yourself," said Adler. "Open my mic... That is precisely our question, General. Your actions have put us in a difficult position and we..."

Henry was waving frantically, "This is another voice. He's

233

gone nuts. He's shouting. Pounding. something... on the table...
a shoe??? He is... wait. I can just make out... 'We owe the capitalist dog nothing. Union of Soviet Socialist Republics is sovereign
and owes explanations to no one for any actions it has or might
take." Henry, who on his most manly day was a shrill first tenor,
was trying to duplicate the bombastic basso profundo of this new
General with little success.

Another analyst wrote something on a piece of paper and
handed it to Henry. "This may be General Sadok," Henry reported.
"Dan here says he recognizes the voice. He's saying, 'What proof
do you have this is our vessel? Who told you it flew from our
lands? The Chinese? They would lie to themselves if it suited a
purpose.'

"Uh. Now they seem to be discussing something among themselves. Ah. No. They cut off his mic."

Paxton was pacing. "He's trying to get us to tip our hand on
how we know and how much we know. One in the air less than
fifteen minutes out and another will cross that horizon line in five.
If he's lying, we are all dead men arguing with a madman. We need
ANSWERS. The President needs to be involved."

"We can't reveal our OHR. Open my mic. But watch for my signal to cut off," Adler said.

"General, I think you are bluffing. Perhaps you think that
we are idiots. In any event, you are playing a dangerous game.
Without satisfactory answers from you, we will be forced to take
the most drastic of measures to protect our homeland. This action
of yours could easily be seen as a preemptive strike justifying the
more hawkish among us to retaliate without restraint. Give me
something I can use, General." With a slashing gesture across his
throat, the Secretary cued for his mic to be silenced.

Henry was writing as fast as he could, "He's laughing,
'Preemptive strike? With only one blip on your radar? What fool
would believe that? Do not rattle your saber at me, Mr. Secretary,

rattle it at your impatient dogs of war who…' umm… someone cut his mic off."

Soviet Ministry of Space and Defense

"Sergie, this has gone on long enough. Tell them it is a satellite. Soon they will be willing to believe that; only moments from now. Tell them they are two communications satellites."

"Nyet. I am happy to have them squirm. They will not launch missiles against TWO BLIPS IN THEIR SKY. They will not attack Mother Russia over two lumps of tinfoil in the heavens."

"They don't KNOW what is in their sky. To them, the lump of tinfoil looks like a bomb. Frightened men only ever think the worst, comrade."

The Russian translator was chattering, "They are demanding to know if there are other launches planned that will affect their airspace?"

"Sergie. My friend. General. You must tell them something. They will see the other vessel rising when it crosses their DEW Line and will believe nothing else we tell them."

"Open the sound," General Sadok demanded. "We do not acknowledge that ANY launch has occurred affecting your airspace." With a quick gesture to the technician, his mic was cut off. The General laughed heartily.

"The most effective lie, comrade," Sadok said to the stunned Gurov, "is to tell the absolute truth in a way that cannot be believed, eh?"

# CHAPTER 37

*A coward dies a thousand deaths.*
*A brave man – only one*
**Shakespeare**

Kilo Capsule, Com-Line to Kilo-11
0245 Zulu
2045 Local

"COMMANDER, THERE is no way we can move any faster without risking rain entering the enclosure. These are damned impossible conditions, and..."

"Watch your language, Sergeant,"

"Begging the Captain's pardon, *sir*. This is very delicate stuff. None of us should be out here in this weather. Lives are at stake."

"That may be truer than you know, Sarge. Get that job done. Take any measures that you have to. You know the missile pay-load you have there, do you not?"

Dinkins was stunned to hear this topic come up.

A long pause on the other end was all the answer the Captain needed. "Okay. So maybe you can understand that it is critical, vital, top priority, that THIS missile be on alert as fast as humanly possible and at ANY cost necessary to achieve the objective. EVERYTHING is secondary to this mission. Am I clear."

"Perfectly, sir. If we don't die getting this damned thing ready, we'll die when it is…"

"Graeff!"

"I have a missile to fix, sir. HOLY SHIT"

Immediately, the line crackled and hissed.

"Sergeant! Sergeant Graeff!"

Dinkins heard the tonal shift and picked up immediately.

"What's up, Commander."

"I don't know. Graeff at Kilo-11 was giving me crap about pushing them. And then he shouted and the line went down. OR, or something. I can still hear them."

In the background, there was a great deal of shouting.

"Kilo Capsule to Maintenance Sierra 27. Come in Two Seven."

The phone line picked back up.

"SIR, SOMETHING BLEW UP OVER THE HILL TO OUR EAST! THE SKY IS ALL LIT UP, CAPTAIN! OUR COMMERCIAL POWER WENT DOWN HERE AND WE'RE ON DIESEL NOW! JESUS, SIR. IS THE WAR ON?" Graeff was yelling at the top of his lungs.

"Calm down. I need you to make sense, Sa…"

"We're all half deaf here, sir. I thought it was the warhead until I realized I'm still in one piece. I'm not sure I'm gonna be able to hear you. The explosion was enormous. There is a fireball over there, sir. HUGE. It has the clouds all red."

Dinkins was on the horn to Hotel. "What the hell is going on? Juliet is down, Kilo-11 may have just taken a near miss. We're still on Orange/10? If that was incoming, we need to be launching."

Hotel had little to offer. "We hear what you hear, Dink."

That was when the rolling blackout hit Kilo's commercial power supply and plunged them into darkness.

Pratt became a machine: "Loss of commercial power. Get me cooling air. Graeff, if you can hear me, get that missile up now. Kilo out."

The thud under the floor as the battery-powered D/C brushes

dropped onto the motor-generator shaft was mild, and the EACU started without incident. In the equipment building, the diesel began to cycle. As it came up to revs and the output hit standards, the automatic switching units relayed the new A/C supply to the capsule. The A/C magnets of the motor-generator received fresh power and engaged, drawing the battery-driven brushes up off the shaft.

Just as they did, the diesel power fluctuated for a moment, causing a dip in voltage. The switching unit cut the commercial power, putting the capsule back on batteries, and the brushes dropped again days earlier. Seconds later, the diesel output again normalized, switching the capsule back, once again, to A/C power, and this time when the magnets engaged, the vibration was too much.

Shock isolator number 4 had lost pressure during the overheat condition. The violent shaking of the floor from the DC brushes slamming up and down as the power supplies switched jolted that skin friction loose, and rather than the typical slow slide one would expect as pressure was lost, the shock isolator let go completely. With no support holding the massive weight of that corner, Kilo Capsule tilted violently at a wild angle.

The commander had just returned to the command console and was about to sit when the chair, floor, and everything else dropped out from under him. Grabbing for support, he reached out, hanging one hand around the PAS speaker and another around the capsule clock, ripping both from their moorings as he went down.

Dink had taken a fall as well. Flying binders, coffee pots, and textbooks added to the melee. Shock isolator number one, overburdened from the snap release of its partner, rapidly lost pressure as well. Now the entire right side of the capsule was unsupported.

Stunned, and in a radically tilted capsule, Dink leaned/stood to see his commander sprawled against a communications rack with the PAS speaker shattered all around him and an open wound across his forehead, where he had smashed it into an equipment drawer handle on his way across.

Dinkins immediately moved to administer first aid. The kit had hung on by one screw.

"What the hell," Pratt muttered.

"Easy, Commander. I have to stop this bleeding."

"What happened? Did Kilo-11 get hit? They said there was a fireball…"

If there had been a hit near Kilo-11, maybe the capsule had taken a near-miss as well…

# CHAPTER 38

*Nothing is more dangerous than a man*
*with nothing left to lose.*
**Unknown**

"SO. DO I understand you correctly?" General Sadok demanded. As he spoke, the second blip crossed the horizon line at NORAD. Instantly, the image flashed on the Sit- room screen.

Adler now could play the card. "We now see a second missile rising... with our capital as the apparent target for the first and... the naval base at San Francisco the target for this second weapon."

Henry was waving frantically. His eyes bulged as he translated: "We do not acknowledge that these are weapons of any kind."

Adler was direct. "Don't play games, comrade. We are moving to full retaliatory alert. The next communication will be from our President to your Premier, unless you come clean NOW."

## Soviet Ministry of Space and Defense

At the table in the bunker, deep under Minsk, Gurov went pale. "Brezhnev knows nothing of this idiotic test. This MUST NOT escalate further."

Sadok's bluster was undented. Covering the mic with his hand, he wheeled on Gurov: "THIS IS AN OPPORTUNITY. Nixon is on his knees."

Standing up to his mentor with uncharacteristic venom, Gurov countered, "Nixon IS mad. He will launch against us. His political problems vanish if we are at war! BACK DOWN NOW, GENERAL! TELL THEM WHAT IS HAPPENING. You already have a victory here."

## Situation Room-Washington

Henry had both hands over his headphones, straining to decipher what he thought he might be hearing: "I think there is an argument going on over there."

Paxton slammed his hand on the table, "We have one here, too. Cut off that mic. Mr. Secretary, we must call the President. We must get him to the bunker."

"Nixon is mad!"

Every face in the room turned to Henry in shock. He pointed to the headphones and said, "Mad... Wait! No... I mean... I heard them say... Oh, my God. I didn't say that he was mad! THEY did."

"I don't dare call him in just yet," Adler sighed. His face said he might agree with the Soviets on this one.

If Nixon was not going to the bunker, it was a sure bet that none of them were. Adler was betting everything on this one.

Blankenship hesitated a moment and then said, "There may be one more step."

"What? What could we possibly do now? We have to retaliate FULLY," insisted the JCS Chairman, Admiral Wellburton.

Paxton's cynicism cut through the room: "We cannot do anything more without a Presidential order and authorization from the codes he alone can send. Who has the football?"

"Colonel Dalem is on today."

Adler started to say, "This is not the..."

But Paxton was in his element. "Get him in the room with the President. Interrupt whatever precious meeting he is in. NOW!"

"No." Adler was firm. "Step up as far as you can, short of that."

The on-duty intelligence officer was skeptical. "No matter what you send out as a message, we have to include the possibility that the Soviets have some means of monitoring. If we send an escalation in status but no launch command, they will know we are bluffing."

To which Wellburton exploded: "I have 40 ships of the line that will be vaporized steel in less than 20 minutes if we are wrong about this."

"If we are wrong about this, they are vaporized steel in any event," Paxton snapped. "They can't get to sea in time. Our efforts now are to stop further attacks. If they think knocking out Washington and the fleet will stop us..."

"It would," Adler said flatly. "It would stop us because if we're wrong, we're already too late. Our only hope is that this is something else—saber rattling at the highest levels.

"We haven't heard from Brezhnev. WHY would that be? Do you think he wants to give Richard Nixon something else to focus on tonight?"

Turning to the Air Force Chief of Staff, Adler asked, "What was your idea, General Blankenship?"

"A Crimson/One message."

"Now you're talking," Paxton grunted. "Get the President."

"With no launch time," Blankenship added.

"WHAT? What the hell good will that do?" Paxton bellowed.

Blankenship spun it out: "We have to assume the Soviets have a way to monitor our messages. They may be able to know that we have issued an attack message. They believe our President to be mad, and desperate. They have us outgunned; we have them out-aimed. Whatever is supposed to be falling on us right now, if history is any indication, may miss not only this building, but this area code. That's why they put on such enormous payloads – they can't hit anything accurately. Our missile targeting teams, on the other hand, have picked which WINDOW in the Kremlin the warhead will fall through. And BOTH sides know that."

"You are willing to sacrifice…" Admiral Wellburton began.

"NOTHING. Admiral, I don't think for a minute that they've launched weapons. It makes no sense. Why just two? We can wreak havoc with them. NONE of them seemed aimed at our retaliatory power other than the Navy."

"Are you writing off the ships of our Navy so easily, General?" the Admiral demanded.

"No, Admiral, but your real threats to them, your nuclear armed subs, are AT SEA."

"How do you send a go-to-war message without authentication?" Adler asked.

The General went to the board and began writing six block letters side by side with a slash between pairs. "We send a Crimson Slash One message, but instead of authentication we put… this… in the launch time windows." The General circled groups of letters on the board: "Then here again, in the authentication windows."

A strategist chimed in, "There are no options in the code for that…"

"We send this in the clear. And we put THIS in the Document Identifier box." Blankenship scratched letters and numbers on the board. "Our boys can read. It won't decode. It is an unauthorized message. But they will see that we have them on standby. They'll figure it out. The Russians won't."

"We can't send a war message without Presidential authentication."

"It has no authenticator; it won't be a war message."

"No, it isn't. But you see these letters and numbers. So will the Soviets. To them, it will look like the real thing. But every weapons officer knows what these letters stand for."

"He's right," the strategist said. "That's the code we use for all exercise messages in the trainer."

"Go with it," Adler said. "In the next ten seconds if possible. MOVE."

# CHAPTER 39

*A fanatic is one who can't change his mind*
*and won't change the subject.*
**Sir Winston Churchill**

"JULIE'S NOT responding, Major." Hotel's deputy said. "Kilo's taken some kind of a hit and the command enclosure is lying on its side, almost, if what Dink has explained is true. His commander is nursing a severe head wound. They have no PAS speaker but they can hear us on the squadron com-line. Eventually they will get secondary communication system messages, but we can relay to them much faster."

"SKYBIRD COPY CODED SAC MESSAGE."

"Jesus, I hope this is a back-down," C-Major breathed.

Major Lawrence Collins, commander of Hotel Capsule, the Squadron Alternate command post and the Wing Alternate command post, sighed the sigh of all of his 37 years.

But it wasn't. "God above, it's a Crimson Slash One message."

But his deputy was confused. "The time block has alpha characters and not numbers. The authentication block has P E/N D/N G. I don't get it. The document prefix is the thing we get in the trainer with double zeros. We don't have those documents here. Major, how do we decode this?"

"Not sure." C-Major had seen it all, or so he thought. This was baffling. Fortunately, the book was the book.

"Relay this to Kilo exactly as it is. I'll call the Wing Command Post."

## Kilo Capsule

Dinkins and Pratt took the message in an upturned Kilo capsule. Because they could not sit in their command chairs, they propped themselves as best they could against consoles and equipment racks that had once been walls and now were slanted floors. Pratt's head wound was ugly, but he insisted he was just woozy.

The crew "rest" bed had slipped across the aisle way and now was upside down against the computer racks. Fumbling to decode the message in this topsy-turvy capsule, Dinkins dropped his code flimsy. It slid just out of reach under the springs of the bed.

"Deputy, I have a complete message. I think. The numbers and letters are in the wrong places."

"I think I got it all, but the flimsy slipped out of my hands. Help me move this bed and I'll grab it…"

Stretching for the just-out-of-reach acetate, Dinkins's eyes saw the letters—not as paired groupings of numbers and letters, but as words.

| CODE FORMAT FLIMZY | | | | | |
|---|---|---|---|---|---|
| Use grease pencil to enter alphanumeric codes | | | | | |
| B 5 / 0 0 | PE / N D / N G | | | | |
| C R / 0 1 | PE | N D | N G | 0 7 | 0 8 | 7 4 |

"PENDING," Dinkins said.

"What?"

"It's in the clear. It isn't paired code groupings... it's a place holder. Look. It says PENDING."

"And the prefix is Bravo Sierra..."

"Bullshit," Dinkins spat.

"This is a trainer exercise code," he continued. "What the hell is going on? There was no room to fully spell PENDING. Only six blocks in each sector. The time block is three groups of two... the Launch Code is two sets of three... ALL have the same letters and they spell PENDING... without an 'I'."

The commander reached for his squadron com-line. "Hotel, this is Kilo. We have a complete message—with some variations. We do not—repeat—We DO NOT authenticate."

"Kilo, this is Hotel. It isn't formatted to authenticate. We've been trying to sort it out..."

"READ it, Major," said Dinkins.

"What? We are reading it."

"I don't think you are, sir. Look at the lines of code as WRITTEN WORDS not as coded groups."

"Holy, sh..."

"Exactly."

"I'm relaying your interpretation to the WCP."

It checked out. The wing command post agreed that the message was complete EXACTLY as they had received it. Out of format. It was a non-authentic message—with a "message."

Their instructions were to: 'Run the prior authenticated checklist, do everything for prep, and await an authenticated Crimson/One message.'

Keys and docs stayed in positions. And they waited.

The Minutemen, who could put a thousand missiles into the air in well under sixty seconds, hung on the precipice of the end and waited for six numbers and six letters to tell them how to direct the elimination of the species.

The Deputy at Hotel Capsule received a report from Kilo.

"Captain, Lieutenant Dinkins says the last thing he heard from the maintenance crew at Kilo-11 was that there was fire in the sky."

Major Collins felt a turn in his gut that he had not experienced since Vietnam. "Copy that."

# CHAPTER 40

---

*"The horror of that moment," the King went on,
"I shall never, never forget."
"You will though," the Queen said, "if you don't
make a memorandum of it."*
**Lewis Carroll**

West Central Missouri
0325 Zulu
2125 Local

"GRAY... IS that fire up ahead?

"I see it. That glow." The driving rain had slowed their progress considerably.

"We're driving TOWARD IT? Is it a bomb?"

Gray thought feverishly. Missouri 18 was the ONLY way to Kansas for miles. They couldn't be more than twelve miles away from the state line. Doubling back would dramatically increase their chances of being delayed or even getting lost in the unlit back roads. The rain was so heavy that ditches by the roads were filling rapidly.

Wait a minute. RAIN!

"Donna, if there had been a nuclear explosion nearby, it would have blown this rain out of here. The superheat alone would have dried up all of this. That isn't a bomb impact."

As they crested the hill, they could see the hay barn engulfed in flames. The electrical pole at the road by the barn was shattered and in flames, the transformer gone.

"An SS-9 would dig a three-hundred-foot deep crater. An air burst we would have seen and felt. There would be nothing here but fire. This is something else. Lightning must've hit and touched off the barn."

It looked like something out of *Gone With the Wind* as Atlanta burned. The enormous storage barn had been filled with hay bales the size of a truck, stacked high and wide. The hay and this barn would burn for days. The sky was filled with the light from the flames.

"Gray, look out!"

Just ahead, a man in dark clothing was waving frantically. Gray hit the brakes and immediately hydroplaned, barely missing him. They slid to a stop eighty yards past him and pointed back the way they had come. Noggin began barking frantically.

"SHUT UP, NOGGIN!" Gray exploded as he rolled down the window.

As Matteo came running toward them, they could see he was soaked to the skin—a wild-eyed madman.

"Gray! Come quick; I need help. They're trapped. We gotta get 'em out," he blurted, and dashed away.

"What's he talking about, Gray?"

"I don't know. I gotta go see."

"Gray. We're running for our lives here as I understand it. What are we stopping for?"

Matteo had run back to the Cutlass. "The SAT is trapped in their truck, Gray. If we don't get them out, they're gonna drown. COME ON!"

No more discussion. Gray drove the car up to the side of the road where he had seen Dale run into the brush. A bit further up the road he could see Matteo's red Triumph tangled in fence posts and barbed wire. Half of the engine compartment was crushed like a soda can.

Making his way through the rain and high grass, Gray climbed across the roadside embankment. Fifteen yards ahead of him, he could just make out the wheels of the SAT vehicle pointed skyward at an odd angle.

It was a creek bed that ran parallel to Highway 18. The road had been built up and its drainage ditches fed the creek already swollen with runoff from upstream. On the way to Alerts, Gray had noticed it: a lazy little stream about six inches deep meandering through the woods. Now it was almost two feet deep and moving fast. The hood of the SAT vehicle was submerged under it.

Noggin ran chest deep into the creek before Donna called him back. Something about the water triggered the "sane" in the spaniel. Perhaps he could sense the urgency of the situation.

Gray could hear shouts coming from inside the truck. He and Matteo waded into the water, looking for a way to get the truck doors open.

"When the lightning hit the transformer I was at the top of the hill," Matteo explained. "At first I thought it was incoming. It lit up the whole valley. It touched off the barn. The SAT swerved to avoid the explosion but I think parts of the transformer hit them, too. They went over the embankment. They had to be doing sixty. I can't get the doors unjammed."

A frantic SAT trooper inside began shouting, "I think Bobby's hurt real bad. Get us out. I can't get him to talk. His head is all bloody!"

The barn fire had lit up the clouds, giving everything a dull, orange-pink glow. The interior of the truck was lit up by the dome light and one of their field lanterns. It backlit a large bloody area of driver's window and the water that was rising in the cab. The top had caved in, crushing the windshield and pinning the driver's head between the steering wheel and the roof. Gray felt certain he was dead. This would be a recovery operation as much as a rescue.

"We're gonna try to get you out," Gray shouted.

"Lieutenant? Lieutenant Crawford?" The man inside knew Gray. Not surprising. They were in Kilo territory.

"Yes. Who's there?"

"It's me, sir, Airman Henderson. Bobby and I were on rounds and we got hit by something. It's the Whiteman Scenario, sir. You gotta get us out."

Matteo had been trying to find a branch, a lever of any kind, "We have nothing to work with here, Gray. How are we gonna do this?"

"Henderson. Can you get to an M-16?"

"I don't know. Maybe."

"Hand it out through the opening over here behind Bobby's shoulder. Maybe we can use it for leverage."

"NO. You're gonna shoot us! You're pissed 'cuz I arrested you. I'm sorry. I was doing what I wuz supposed to do. Don't let us die, Lieutenant. PLEASE don't kill us!"

Gray was stunned.

"Arrested? What's he talking about, Gray?"

"Later. Listen, Henderson, we have NO TOOLS out here. We need a lever. Hand out the weapon."

"You'll shoot us. You or the Russian infiltrators. They're everywhere by now."

"If I wanted you dead, I would just LEAVE."

"Geez, Gray," Matteo whispered. "Easy."

But it had worked. Henderson became noticeably calmer. "Yeah. Yeah, you're right. Okay. I... I can't move my arms. The gun's jammed behind the seat. I think my arms are broke. Bobby's head is underwater. Oh, God, sir. He's gonna drown."

The water had risen. Gray and Matteo knew that Bobby probably was dead already, but now there seemed no way to get Henderson out.

"Gray, I don't think there's much hope here without heavy equipment."

"I know. Donna, what are you doing?"

Donna had reached through the semi-submerged passenger window and pulled Bobby's head out of the water. She was giving him mouth to mouth resuscitation. Her arm was cut from the window shards but she continued.

Between breaths she hissed, "Go get help. FAST."

Reaching in past her, Matteo pushed the butt of the M-16. It worked free and Gray pulled it out the other side. Using it to break out the last of the window gave her more room.

"Bobby! Breathe, man! Lieutenant, get me out of here, PLEASE!"

"Break out the driver's side, too, Dale. I need to get to their radio."

It was an effort. When at last he could reach through, Gray grabbed the mic from the tilted ceiling of the overturned truck.

"Kilo FSC, this is Lieutenant Gray Crawford. Your SAT is upended in a ditch on Missouri 18 a mile east of K-11. Do you read me?"

"Lieutenant. Crawford? Uhm... I'm going to need the authentication code..."

"Henderson, can you authenticate?"

"Damn it, Sarge. We're gonna die in here. The truck is filling with water. Bobby's already dead!"

"No he's not. And you aren't going to die, either." Donna was in an awkward position and straining to breathe for Bobby. "Do your authorizing and get help out here."

"She's right, Henderson."

"Yes, ma'am. Okay."

Henderson calmed a bit and authenticated but the FSC was way out of his league.

"Sir, we're in a raised state of alert and the capsule won't respond. Command Post called to tell us they are turned over down there... over."

"Turned over? Gray, what's going on?" Matteo was now more than knee deep in the rising water.

"FSC, this is Lieutenant Crawford. I repeat. Your SAT is about to drown in this creek. Send out your backup team with as much gear as you can. We have to drag this truck out of here. Over."

"I sent them when we got the authentication, sir. But they don't have much on board. How will they find you?"

"Look for the burning barn. We're across the road."

"Roger. I'll relay that."

Matteo pulled Gray to the back of the truck. "You told me Kilo-11 has maintenance on site. It can't be more than a mile up the road. You go tell them what's happening and get their crane over here or at least the winch. I'll stay with the truck."

"We don't have that kind of time. If I leave here, he'll think we're leaving him to die."

"That's why I'm staying, Gray." It was Donna. Noggin was beside her, climbing up onto the truck.

"Donna, I'm not leaving you here. Besides. The security guard on that site isn't going to listen to us."

"You got a better idea?"

He didn't.

"Henderson, where are your LF keys?"

"They were on the seat beside me. I was getting them out when..."

Gray reached into the water and felt around the crushed roof of the cab that was filling rapidly with water. Henderson's head started under.

"Hold on, Henderson. Hold on..."

Donna pushed Gray aside just as his hand found the keys to the Launch Facility padlocks.

"Bobby's gone, Gray," she whispered. Then, "Henderson. Turn toward me!"

She reached in and pulled his head to hers, lifting it from the water.

"I'm going to stay with you. I'm going to breathe WITH you. Do you understand?"

Panicked but focused, Henderson looked pleadingly into her eyes, "Yes, Ma'am. Thank you. Bobby's dead, ain't he?" as the water went over him.

Donna began mouth-to-mouth with him, but he was struggling.

Surfacing, she shouted through the water to him, "HENDERSON. Stop. You have to trust me. You have to exhale and let me push air into you. Exhale!"

With broken arms and wedged inverted in the wreckage, he could not surrender the last of his air.

Softly, so that Henderson would not hear and Gray would have to lean close to her, Donna turned to speak, "Gray. Go get help. I can't do this for long."

"Donna, I can't leave you…"

"I can get out. He can't. Noggin won't let anything happen to me. GO. Henderson! Breathe out gently through your mouth. I'll hold your nose closed so no water gets in. DON'T FIGHT ME. It is your only chance."

Henderson had no choice. He let his air go and Donna quickly put her mouth to his, breathing into him as he gulped the air from her lungs.

As Gray began slogging his way out of the creek, he could hear Matteo behind him, "We're going for help, Henderson!"

M-16 slung over his back, Matteo climbed up onto the overturned truck, looking for a way to right it.

"Give it up, Dale. We have to get the five-ton maintenance truck from Kilo-ll. Rain's letting up, so maybe this water will go down..."

"How are you going to get them to help us? We're obviously on a Yellow or Orange checklist. Shit, we may be in RED! They're going to shoot us at the gate."

The two climbed back up the embankment. At the crest of the hill, they stood in the orange glow of the raging barn fire behind them. To the east, the stars shone brightly, and to the north the distant white shine of the lights of Kansas City bathed the broken clouds. A brilliant lightning flash to the southeast revealed a rolling countryside that seemed quiet and at peace after the storm.

"Gray. What is it?" Matteo asked. "What did you see?"

Gray blinked his eyes hard. It was what he was not seeing that drew his attention.

"No missiles are rising."

# CHAPTER 41

*The lady doth protest too much, methinks.*
**Shakespeare**

"THIS IS General Gurov, Soviet Deputy Minister of Space and Defense. What you see on your screens are merely communications satellites. I urge you to relax."

Gurov fought to keep his voice calm. All around him stood the shocked faces of the young men at their consoles as they stared at the gun in his hand. At his feet lay the body of General Sadok.

Situation Room-Washington

"... and his voice is... strange. Nervous?" Henry added as he completed the translation.

"Who is this Gurov?" Adler wanted to know.

Blankenship signaled for his mic to be opened. "General Gurov, we have been dealing with General Sadok, and..."

The speaker crackled to life and in halting English, Gurov said, "General Sadok is not any longer... in control... on this facility. More than that, I am not at liberty to say. What I am telling you is verifiable by your tracking teams. The satellites will enter orbit. You will see it. Please be patient."

The men looked to Henry who said, "His English isn't bad. Never heard a Russian executive or general say 'please' before…"

"Satellites? From operational missile silos? And we're supposed to believe that?" Paxton was near rage as he stared at the blips on the screen.

Then Blankenship spoke up, "We've wanted to do that from Malmstrom for years. Shots from Vandenberg only prove that Vandenberg works. The only way to know the system in the field really works is to launch from the field. But, of course, we can't."

"We can't?" Adler challenged.

"No. None of the states we would over-fly would give us a green light. The Soviets wouldn't ask, though. They'd just launch them. It is… plausible."

"How long until we can we verify that?" Adler wanted to know.

## Space Control – NORAD

The Floor Commander at NORAD keyed his line to the Situation Room. "Gentlemen, the Soviets have never given us a heads-up on a launch. A good many of them end in disaster. They do, however, crow about it quite publicly when they launch something successfully. Their propaganda group at Pravda won't get the word to confirm that for several hours, though."

"We don't have several hours, Colonel!" the squawk box exploded.

"No, sir. But, we do note that the bogies have not started a descent. They do appear to be in an orbit."

### Soviet Ministry of Space and Defense

"This is General Gurov again. Please, I urge you to consider that it has been almost... two hours since launch. Even our slowest missiles are less than half of one hour from their targets. LOOK at where these satellites have settled. I urge you to take no irreversible action. This was a telemetry package launch and a test of our operational silos. Nothing more." And then, after a brief pause, he added, "A timber wolf will not sacrifice himself for nothing, eh."

### Situation Room-Washington

Crew-cut handed Blankenship an update. "What is this?'

"We have a problem at Whiteman, sir. Kilo Capsule has suffered some kind of upset. We don't have complete data that makes sense. We're trying to verify this. Apparently they're upended. The commander has a severe head wound and the capsule is – as near as we can make out – on its side. Additionally, other capsules have heard gunfire at Juliet Capsule through the secure squadron comline. That crew is not responding at all. Two crews in a five crew squadron."

Keying his mic, Blankenship demanded, "NORAD. Are you sure that bogie did not descend?"

The squawk box crackled to life: "We still show it aloft, sir. Settling into orbit altitude."

Blankenship leaned in: "If it had deployed one of multiple warheads, would you have seen it?"

After a long pause, "Possibly, sir. We can see when boosters drop away, even the spacer bands. We don't track them to ground because they burn up in atmosphere... usually."

"USUALLY?" Paxton spat.

"We aren't set up for tracking non-primaries at present. It isn't what the system looks for."

Paxton took a deep breath, "So, either this Gurov is telling the truth or they just launched a space-based platform for multiple reentry vehicles. And the potential exists that one RV—that the system doesn't look for—may have knocked out two of our capsules."

Blankenship turned to Adler. "I have over a thousand nuclear weapons awaiting a proper authentication on a Crimson/1 message. These guys are trained to do their jobs in under a minute. We can depend on them to do that. They are well trained, but the longer we give them to think and worry, the closer we come to someone snapping. If we aren't at war—we need to back them down. If we are at war—we need to KNOW! And ACT!"

# CHAPTER 42

*...you have entertained Angels, unaware.*
**Hebrews 13**

ARL HAD overcome the protests of his wife of 34 years and had left the house in the driving rain to go investigate the red skies in the direction of his hay barn. He had worked for years to design and build that barn. It could hold a full year's supply of hay for his cattle and plenty more to sell to neighbors when their supplies ran low. It was a plan that was supposed to be better than Social Security and would have provided him four years of operating capital.

Now he was parked at the brow of the hill watching it burn. The inferno had not been put out by the raging storm and the local volunteer fire brigade had nothing that would touch it.

Five years of preparation and all of his reserves were black smoke in an even darker sky. Financially, this was going to be the end.

That was when he noticed the car. One of those red sports cars, all bent and wrapped in barbed wire just off the road down by the draw. Just beyond it was a huge hole in the hedge. Broke or not, he was still a man who wouldn't let a neighbor suffer alone.

Donna was nearing exhaustion when she heard the clank of a hook and chain hitting the bumper of the pickup. Turning from her breathing ritual for a second, she saw the back of a man as he moved out of the creek toward a pickup truck, backlit by the fire.

Delivering another gulp of air to Henderson, she lifted her head from the water and said, "Hang on. Someone's here."

# CHAPTER 43

*I am a soldier. I fight where I am told...*
*and I win where I fight.*
**Patton**

Access Road to Kilo-11
0412 Zulu
2212 Local

"I'M HOPING you have some kind of plan, Matteo said, as he and Gray approached Kilo-11.

"Well... surely Kilo's FSC has advised them. I don't want to surprise them though..."

"Definitely not. Surprised, armed 20-year-olds would not be a good idea," Matteo added grimly.

Horn blaring and lights flashing, Gray's green Olds Cutlass screamed up to Kilo-11's entry gate.

The security police trooper charged with safeguarding Kilo-11 emerged from his truck and approached the gate warily.

"Airman!" Gray shouted. "Did the FSC at Kilo-01 advise you that their Security Alert Team has had a wreck over the hill? They are severely injured. We need to get help over there."

"That big ball of fire is the SAT?" he responded.

"No, man," Matteo shot back. "That is the fire that caused their wreck. Quit wasting time and get the Kilo Flight Security

263

Controller. He'll tell you. We need your five-ton to pull them out of the ditch."

"What?" With that, the sky cop ran back to the maintenance van to tell his crew. His timing could not have been worse.

A1C Willie Pace, the winch operator, was starting his fifth attempt to lower the warhead delicately onto the missile. In tenth-of-an-inch increments he jogged the winch to precisely align the dozens of screw holes that secured it to the guidance system atop the booster. With one hand on the winch control and his eyes intently focused on the hand signals of the supervisor down in the launch tube below him, he was taken completely by surprise when the sky cop burst into the van.

"Willie, I have two guys at the gate who want the five-ton. They say the SAT has had a wreck!"

The operator's head snapped around at the sound and, by reflex, his wrist twisted at the same time, rotating the variable speed winch control to full back. The warhead was jerked upward rapidly, ramming it into the winch brace with such force that it cracked the skin of the warhead and snapped the braided steel suspension cable.

The operator watched in horror as the nuclear warhead rotated in what seemed like slow motion and plunged back into the launch tube. In a shower of sparks, the weakened metal housing of the warhead scraped along the metal launcher liner until it slammed into the top of the guidance system atop the missile.

Looking up from his work platform, the Sergeant Graeff could not believe his eyes, "What in bloody hell…"

Above him, he saw the impossible; a nuclear warhead wedged between the launcher tube wall and the booster, the skin of each ripped open.

"Radiation suits on! NOW!"

Gray and Matteo saw the flash and heard the shouts as the sky cop ran from the van, followed by the winch operator who threw open a panel, pulled out a radiation suit, and began scrambling into it.

"Radiation? Radiation? AM I GOING TO DIE?" the sky cop was screaming as he ran from the van.

"What are you doing, Gray?" Mandola asked, as Gray began to open the gate lock with a key from his pocket.

"I'm going in there. They need help and the SAT needs that five-ton. Give me the M-16."

# CHAPTER 44

*"You haven't got a prayer" is*
*always a false statement.*
**Charles Gaby**

Kilo-01
0427 Zulu
2227 Local

THE HARD-LINE from Kilo-11 was buzzing. Dinkins had turned the command chair around so that the back w as toward the "down" side of the capsule. In this orientation, Pratt was reclining comfortably in the chair with a cold rag on his head wound, and he could reach his console controls easily.

Dinkins had managed to lean the deputy chair all the way back, which was now "up," given the severe tilt of the capsule. He was propped with his butt on the front edge of the deputy console and his feet on the equipment racks on either side of his communications panel. His back and head were cradled somewhat by the seat and back of the deputy's chair. Reaching down between his legs, he keyed the Kilo-11 hard line and answered.

"That thing ready, Sarge…"

But he never finished the question.

"Sir, we have a BROKEN ARROW. REPEAT. WE HAVE A BROKEN ARROW. The warhead is damaged and wedged between the launcher wall and the missile. I think it is OPEN. Shielding may be ripped and my team is in radiation suits. URGENTLY request permission to seal this hole and secure the site until another crew with appropriate gear can get this monster out of there."

"Commander, Kilo-11 reports a Broken Arrow status. I'll handle him if you can advise Hotel," Dinkins barked.

"Holy Mother of God! Someone stole the warhead?"

"No. It's not gone. They dropped it into the launcher and they think the skin is breached."

"THAT warhead is breached? They'll cook." Blood ran from the head wound into Pratt's eyes.

"They're in radiation suits now, but I have to get them out. And seal the launcher."

"Radiation suits will keep contamination off, but that warhead... surely there will be gamma rays..."

"I KNOW," Dinkins snapped. "Call Hotel. *Please*, Captain."

While his commander communicated the details to the Alternate Command Post at Hotel, Dinkins turned his attention back to the Kilo-11 hard-line.

"Kilo-11, what is your status now?"

"Dink. This is Gray Crawford."

It wouldn't register. This was a hard-line from the capsule to the launcher. There was no way in the world...

"Dink. Can you hear me?"

"Gray?"

"I'm in the launcher, Dink. I came to get help for your SAT. They are dead or dying in a creek not a mile from here. I left Donna there giving mouth-to-mouth to Henderson to keep him alive. There are major problems here at Kilo-11 but what you most need to know is... THE WAR HAS NOT STARTED."

"What?"

Hearing his deputy say Gray's name, Pratt keyed into the hard-line. After a few sentences, he had heard enough. He shifted to the squadron line and hit the ALL CALL button.

"509th, this is Kilo Capsule. Kilo-11 has been breached. I repeat: Kilo-11 has been breached and we have a Broken Arrow. Unauthorized personnel are in the launch tube and we have no contact with our on-site maintenance crew or security personnel."

Though they could not hear it at Kilo, the PAS speakers across Whiteman crackled to life: "SAC, this is Whiteman Wing Command Post reporting a BROKEN ARROW condition at Kilo-11 and a possible on-site intrusion."

### Juliet-01

At Juliet Capsule, Davey had been in his Deputy's chair trying not to look at the still and bleeding body of his Commander lying by the command chair. Repeated attempts to reach his wife had resulted in "all circuits busy" recordings each time.

"She's dead. They are all dead," he muttered to himself.

The endless waiting with the smell of cordite in the air from his weapon had taken him to the edge of his sanity. So, the message from the PAS speaker was all he needed to hear.

"We're being invaded! They're on the ground taking over our missiles!"

### Kilo-01

On the hard-line from Kilo-11, Gray was still talking. "Dink, do you hear me? I repeat. NO BOMBS ARE FALLING. Whatever the status you've been taken to, there are no incoming at this moment."

And then he said the thing Dink had least expected, "Whatever you do—STAY WITH THE BOOK."

# CHAPTER 45

*Older men declare war. But it is youth
that must fight and die.*
**Herbert Hoover**

Sit Room
0426 Zulu
2226 Local

"SO, CAN you tell me why you called this fairy-tale the WHITEMAN SCENARIO?" Wellburton demanded.

"No particular reason, Admiral. Whiteman is the banana belt of missiles and, as such, lent itself well to the possibilities of walk-in infiltrators as detailed in the scenario," Crew-cut explained. "Excuse me. SAC has messages coming in…"

As he turned to the phone, the Admiral continued, "And now an actual Broken Arrow? My God, what is going on? What has happened to security out there, Hank?"

Paxton remained flummoxed by the audacity of the Whiteman Scenario. "And the payoff of this is that the Soviet's would demand we STAND DOWN? With hundreds of B-52s and sub-launchable nukes at our disposal, we're going to stand DOWN because some Ruskie sharpshooter might get off a lucky SHOT?"

Blankenship interjected, "I never seriously gave credence to the Whiteman Scenario, General. Even if the missile skin is penetrable, the bulk of the idea is too much to swallow. Still, it made for an excellent tool for increasing diligence and focusing on the sensitivity of the mission."

"And now we have a Broken Arrow," Adler summarized. "and a pair of Soviet launches with a declared innocent objective."

"I don't believe in coincidence," Paxton stated.

"Nor I," Blankenship agreed. "But we need to give these men definite direction."

"Don't back it down, yet," Paxton asserted.

"When it was just the 509th squadron at Whiteman, we had some control but every nuclear launch team in the world just heard that Broken Arrow announcement. They are hearing rumors or starting them among themselves. They've been hovering with their fingers over those keys for four hours," Blankenship said.

Paxton turned to his old friend with steel in his expression: "Our boys have held for days against no chance at all. Yours can hold a little longer."

The two old warriors held the gaze for several seconds.

"This is different, General." The voice had come, not from the Blankenship, but from Commandant of the Marines, General Irving F. Briggs. A veteran of Guam, Iwo Jima, and former deputy director of the Central Intelligence Agency, the general had been a completely silent observer up until now.

Paxton's respect for the men in the room fell into three categories: none, which applied to the civilian advisors who had never worn a uniform; high, which applied to veterans and those currently in uniform; and highest, which applied to veterans of infantry level, face-to-face combat. Briggs was in the latter category and, if anything, had seen vastly more personal combat than Paxton.

A man of action and decidedly very few words, Briggs' eyes locked on the status map. He spoke to Paxton as if he were the only man in the room, "In two ways. First: every soldier's decision to use deadly force has always had an understandable limit. There is no understandable limit to the death and destruction we're facing here. Second: in combat, silence from HQ means you act on your last orders and your judgment in the changing situation. Knowing we're here is the only evidence they have that civilization is still intact. We don't want to make them start thinking. Some of them will break."

# CHAPTER 46

*A hard man is good to find.*
**Mae West**

Missouri Highway 18
0433 Zulu
2233 Local

MATTEO AND the now-handcuffed sky cop arrived at the wreck scene in the purloined five-ton to find a tractor stretching a dragline cable across the road. It had run out of room and had nowhere else to go.

Dismounting from the cab, Matteo ran to the brink of the creek and saw the overturned SAT truck on its side, with Donna sprawled across the door, holding an unconscious Henderson's head above water.

"Hold on, Donna. We'll get you out."

Turning toward the five-ton, Matteo saw the old farmer fling open the back of the truck and start hauling come-alongs, chains, and cargo webbing out of the back.

"Don't just stand there, son. Let's pull that thing outta the crick."

Staring through the window of the five-ton, the sky cop was shouting something.

Opening the door, Matteo finally understood him.

272

"Unlock the cuffs. I can help. Lieutenant… I see who you are. C'mon."

---

The sky cop was able to relieve Donna. They braced Henderson for the jolts as the truck was dragged out of the creek bed.

Exhausted and bloody with dozens of cuts on her arms from the broken window glass, Donna turned to ask, "Dale… where's Gray?

"Let's get you up to the road, Donna. These cuts look bad."

"Where is GRAY?"

The woman was an unqualified hero. Heroes deserve straight answers. "He went into the launcher to help get a broken warhead free."

"He WHAT?"

Earl had heard. "Them pads. Something's wrong at them pads, ain't it?"

Matteo helped Donna to the ground and turned in time to see Earl headed west toward Kilo-11 with the tractor dragging the tow line. From the east, the backup SAT from Kilo arrived on the scene in the Chevy Suburban crew vehicle, armed to the teeth and very confused.

# CHAPTER 47

*... not when things go always good for you, but the*
*greatness comes and you are really tested ... when you*
*take some knocks, when sadness comes.*
**Richard Nixon**

**D**INKINS WAS listening on the hard-line to Kilo-11. "The warhead is cracked open. It was an accident," Gray explained. "The hoist cable snapped and it dropped. Dale and I had just arrived to get help for your SAT. Dink, we have to get this tube sealed until heavily shielded equipment can get the thing secured..."

"Gray, you have to get out of there."

"I took this launcher by force, Dink. I stole a radiation suit. I'm covered head to toe, so, at first, they thought I was the winch operator. I made the crew chief and his maintenance team evacuate the launcher at gunpoint."

"Where did you get a gun?"

"Well, Dale and I disarmed the on-site security guard."

"How the hell did you..."

"He was in a panic from the Broken Arrow incident and we had the SAT's M-16, so he was in no position to argue."

"Gray..." Dinkins was totally at a loss.

"I know. That's the point. They all thought we were Russian invaders and I can hardly blame them.

"I had to get to this phone, Dink. I bound the winch operator with his own broken cable after forcing him to seal his radiation suit. There is no question. I'm going to Leavenworth … if I survive the radiation. The only thing I can do now is ensure that more lives are not lost unnecessarily."

"No one will believe you, Gray," Dinkins reasoned. "They won't take my word, either. They think you're a Russian infiltrator. Sergeant Graeff is in charge out there. Try to explain the situation…"

"DEPUTY. Get off the line." Pratt was near unconsciousness from his head injury but was now staring hard at Dinkins.

Dinkins tried reason: "Pratt, this is Gray Crawford. He's an Instructor. He's trying to keep things from getting worse. His wife is keeping one of our Security Alert Team alive…"

"Dink." It was Gray on the Kilo-11 hard-line. "Is C-Major at Hotel?"

"Yeah, Gray."

"Tell him to send a message to SAC-HQ. Ask if Major David Kennison's desk top has been repaired properly or if he's still patching it himself."

"WHAT?"

"They will know I'm someone who has been in the War Room. They'll know I'm not a spy. And there's something else you need to tell them – about the Whiteman Scenario…"

Kilo-11

"We can't leave that guy in there with that bomb, can we?" Airman Parker asked.

The Graeff was at the edge of exploding himself.

"No. And we aren't. That guy pulled a gun on me. The bastard took over my launcher and commandeered my headset. I had no choice then, but... He will be dead in three hours, suit or no suit," Graeff insisted. "And without a winch cable, we aren't getting that bomb out."

He thought for several seconds. Then, "What we do now, is stand guard out here and hope like hell some help is coming with more gear than we have left. Where's the five-ton? Did the sky cop get scared and take it?"

"But if it goes off..."

"It AIN'T GONNA GO OFF, Parker. It isn't armed. It's probably leaking radiation like a mother but it won't explode."

Then they heard gunfire from the launcher.

"What's that, Sarge? Is it exploding?"

"That's gunfire."

"Why? Who's he shooting? Is he trying to detonate the booster? Hell, that'll scatter the warhead for miles..."

"That isn't a pistol. That's semi-automatic rounds." Then Sarge took inventory. "Where is the winch operator?"

"I thought he booked it when he dropped the damned bomb," offered Parker.

Turning to the van Graeff said, "Or he's in the van! With an M-16."

### Hotel-01

"You actually expect me to roll that question up to SAC?" C-Major asked incredulously. "We are not about to start negotiating with a terrorist who has taken over a Minuteman Missile launcher... NO."

"He's not a terrorist, Major. It's Gray Crawford."

Pratt interjected, "Major, I want it clearly on the record that Deputy Dinkins is making this request against my direct orders to the contrary."

Dinkins wasn't backing down, "Major, I went through training with this man. He SHOT ME in the trainer in the line of duty. That story is legend! The man is nothing if not a patriot. I know him. Sir, this is an unprecedented situation. This is the only way for him to prove he is who he says he is."

The squadron line was silent for a moment. Then, "I will convey the question exactly as you relayed it in the spirit of keeping SAC informed of a grave situation. Perhaps their profilers can make something of it. You said he had another statement that SAC needed to know?"

"Yes, sir. He says..." Dink weighed the probability of this sentence blowing all the credibility he was struggling to maintain.

"Get on with it, Lieutenant! He says what?"

"He says to remind them that HE WROTE the Whiteman Scenario."

### Kilo-11

Plastered against the steel hull of the launch tube, Gray was trying to avoid being shot.

"Airman, STOP. You'll hit the booster."

"I don't care, you damned Commie! I know who you are. You're trying to take over this launcher. Well, that ain't gonna happen on my watch."

"Airman, the warhead is breached. We're in a radiation field. Tell Sergeant Graeff quickly. We have to get out of here and seal this hole so the decontamination team can recover it."

"NO WAY, Comrade."

Listening to the exchange from outside the van, the Graeff and Parker thought they were beyond surprises—until they turned to see Earl coming through their gate on his tractor.

"The Air Force boy back at the crick said they's a problem with this pad. I don't like 'em. Don't like these pads. But I'm here to help."

"What the hell?" was all Graeff could manage.

Earl, not having had this much adrenaline in his system for twenty-five years, was not willing to be patient.

"What do you need me to DO, man?"

# CHAPTER 48

*When it becomes necessary, and it will, you must be
prepared to shoot your own dog. Farming it out doesn't
make it nicer. It makes it worse.*
**Lazarus Long**

A T JULIET Capsule, Davey had listened to it all. He had become
convinced that the Whiteman Scenario was in full swing—to the
point that now Kilo-11 was in the hands of an enemy infiltrator.

Misery, loving company, had driven Davey to the squadron com-
line and the sympathetic ear of a now almost delirious Captain
Pratt.

"Don't you see, Captain? They've closed off our communications. We've missed the message. They are taking us almost
without a shot. We have to launch to save our country."

Pratt was listening while watching Dinkins carefully to ensure
he didn't pick up the line. His deputy had been focused again on
the Kilo-11 direct line and had said something about gunfire. Then
he had taken out a rosary. Lieutenant Manuel Dinkins had been
praying for some time now.

Pratt was on the very edge of consciousness. "We can't do
much on our own. It takes two votes."

"Well, I'm not dying without a fight. I'm enabling now. You watch. The heroes will step up and join us." Davey pulled the cover open and turned and locked the Enable Switch into position, setting off a flurry of alarms and reports from the printer.

Then he moved from the deputy's console to the command console, staying as far to the right and away from Rutherford's body as he could manage. He brushed by the com-rack and knocked his commander's holster to the floor. Kicking it away from him, he stepped up to the launch console.

He flipped down the Plexiglas cover and inserted the Commander's key into the Launch Switch. Picking up the com-line handset, he very calmly said, "Turn keys on my mark."

Across the 509th, alarms sounded as an Enable Command entered the system. No missile could launch until the system was "enabled" and, for the first time since the system had been built twelve years earlier, that switch had been thrown.

Now, if any two capsules in the squadron entered launch votes within two seconds of each other, the missiles would initiate launch on War Option Code 83 as entered earlier.

"Commander, we have an unauthorized Enable," Dinkins barked. "Can you reach the Inhibit switch?" The Inhibit Launch switch was identical to and adjacent to the launch switch. The only difference was that the launch switch had a keyhole at its pivot point and the Inhibit switch had a built-in handle to facilitate turning.

Pratt had a handset to his ear. He was reaching for the command console as Dinkins switched to the squadron com-line and heard Lt. David Hale cry out, "Key turn in three, two..."

Dinkins whipped his head to the console as Pratt reached, not for the Inhibit switch, but to put his key into the Launch Switch. He was turning it on Hale's "MARK," when the shots rang out.

In all, there were four.

The one Dinkins heard first was through the squadron com-line at Juliet Capsule. Mortally wounded, Captain Stu Rutherford had retrieved his pistol from the floor where Davey had knocked it. His final act was putting a bullet behind the left ear of his now quite insane deputy.

The second, third, and fourth shots he heard were from his own revolver as he blew off his commander's right hand at the wrist and shattered the Launch Console. The first shot did most of the job. Entering an inch-and-a-half under the commander's right thumb, the bullet immediately hit the bones of the wrist and began to spread, ripping tissue, bones, and tendons apart..

Dinkins didn't remember pulling the trigger on any of the shots—though he had. He certainly had.

# CHAPTER 49

---

*If you find yourself in a fair fight,*
*you didn't plan it properly.*
**Nick Lappos**

O N THE floor of the SAC War Room, the hours of waiting for what was trained to be a thirty-minute war were wearing on the men charged with keeping the peace.

"I knew something like this would happen. You can't mess around with Command Control procedures," Major Kennison was saying. "We're not in the business of sending unauthorized messages, no matter how cryptic the situation."

"I think it was a good idea. Sending an unauthorized message is a legitimate exercise," another argued.

"This isn't an exercise, Don."

---

CINCSAC was having an ass-chewing party and, apparently, his entire senior staff was invited.

"Don't debate justification with me, Colonel! We have the 509th at Whiteman under an Inhibit command because two capsules *turned keys!* Two is all we need to be in the middle of a nuclear

282

war! This damned message is clearly not valid, but two scared, confused men with only a tiny glimmer of information panicked and tried to LAUNCH without a valid presidential order!"

"General…"

"And, if this report is accurate, the Deputy at Kilo has killed his commander in the act of turning keys." Silence fell in the booth. "The ACP at Hotel Capsule reports hearing gunfire from Juliet Capsule through their squadron phone line. Now, we have NO contact with Juliet at all. A nuclear launch control center with no CONTACT! Whiteman is presuming the crew dead or so severely injured as to be unable to communicate."

The General was no stranger to death. Under his command in Vietnam, the death and destruction had been a daily trial. But, this report—this handful of men—seemed more catastrophic.

"Add to that, we have an unauthorized person IN a launcher— a launcher with a Broken Arrow in process! The Joint Chiefs and Secretary of Defense are not talking with the President! There are no justifications for this." CINCSAC was struggling to control his outrage… and fear.

"Both of the capsule votes entered were invalid, General," Eagle-Nose was saying. "In each capsule it was only one key, not both that were turned. The Inhibit was just a routine response to an unauthorized Enable command."

"Routine? Tell that to the dead. Tell that to the patriots who have, apparently, had to kill them," CINCSAC breathed as he watched the B-52 blips on his global screen move to Fail Safe points as the two 'Incoming" blips seemed to become stationary in equatorial orbits over the Indian Ocean and eastern Indonesia. "Why hasn't the President moved us forward or pulled us back?"

A Chief Master Sergeant entered carrying a message flimsy as if it were poison. "Sir, we have a message for Major Kennison."

"A MESSAGE? When did my Command Booth become an answering service for staffers?"

The Chief was unfazed, "It is from the intruder at Kilo-11, sir."

"Let me see that."

Situation Room-Washington

0450 Zulu

2250 Local

"In the launcher?" Blankenship was asking.

"It is classic Whiteman Scenario, sir," Crew-cut asserted. "He not only has entered a site where there is an active Broken Arrow; we cannot be certain that he did not create it."

"To what purpose?" General Paxton wanted to know.

Crew-cut scarcely hid his disdain for the General as he turned to answer him: "I'm sure I don't know, General. Not being a terrorist myself, I don't think like one."

As Paxton rose to put the prissy little Colonel in his place, an aide handed a phone to Adler saying, simply, "The White House, sir."

"Now, we're talking," Paxton shifted. "Colonel, though you are not a terrorist, I do believe you think yourself a competent briefing officer. You were about to summarize status, I believe?"

A bit more contritely and very professionally, Crew-cut continued, "Apart from a failed launch command, we have heard nothing from Juliet Capsule in the 509th. Kilo Capsule's deputy reports that his commander tried to turn keys as well, but the deputy stopped him."

"Stopped him? Talked him out of it?" Wellburton demanded.

"Apparently he had to use his sidearm. The commander may still be alive but, according to this report, he is bleeding profusely from an amputated right hand. Kilo's Security Alert Team is reported missing. There are vague reports of some kind of vehicle accident. The backup SAT is out trying to find them now."

A messenger handed additional message flimsies to the Colonel and General Blankenship.

"This is saying the squadron also reports hearing other gunfire through their com-line, presumably at Juliet. There is no response from that capsule and SAC has declared no lone-zone violations at both Kilo and Juliet."

Grim silence took over the room as the leaders of the American military might waited for the Colonel to finish his report. "Of greatest concern presently is the report of gunfire in one of the launchers and a warhead seems to have been hijacked by—according to this dispatch from CINCSAC—'a guy who knows exactly what furniture is scratched in the SAC war room."

General Blankenship looked up from his flimsies. "A 'guy,' I would remind you, who is on the ground desperately risking his life to get us to go by the book!"

Handing the papers to Paxton, he continued, "Look at the rest of the dispatch. This young man claims to be First Lieutenant Grayson Crawford. According to CINCSAC, he was on the First Team last January. This is the kid that wrote the Whiteman Scenario. His message was an urgent plea to go 'strictly by the book.'"

"Hell of a way to butcher the book to do it, wouldn't you say?" Wellburton approached the marker board as an intelligence aide handed Blankenship another message.

"Timber Wolf," he read.

Paxton looked puzzled, "What's that?"

"On the last transmission, Gurov said something about a timber wolf not sacrificing himself so easily..."

"So?"

"Intelligence just gave me this. Timber Wolf is the code name for a deep cover agent in the Soviet Union. He got a lot of photos out to us a while back. He was the one who broke the launchers camouflaged as logging camps cover."

Paxton's wheels were turning. "You think Gurov is Timber Wolf?"

Wellburton turned from the marker board quickly, "That makes sense. Although, I had no idea the asset was that deep."

A stone-faced Adler was hanging up the phone and returning to the table.

Paxton wanted to know, "Was that the President, Mr. Secretary?"

"A message from him. He intends to make," and here he consulted his notepad, "uhm, 'an historic announcement' tomorrow. Well," he consulted the clock, "I guess it will be today, technically. We're all expected in the Rose Room."

Admiral Wellburton barely hesitated, "You didn't ask to speak to him directly?"

"I was told... that he did not wish to speak to anyone under any circumstances until tomorrow. We are on our own here."

Blankenship continued, "Then, I say we have nothing to lose by following procedure. Mr. Secretary, I urge you to allow me to back this down. I can brief you on details, but in the last few minutes we have received intel from a variety of directions indicating that these ARE satellites and that things in the field are getting out of hand. I say we give the field crews a clear and authorized message to return to a lesser status. We get the keys and docs back into the safes. Get the locks back on, and dial this tension back."

"What's the situation with the Broken Arrow?" Adler asked, resuming his seat at the head of the table.

"A warhead is jammed in a launcher tube," Crew-cut explained. "Two men in launch crew uniforms approached the site with a story about the SAT being in a wreck. They then commandeered the site with an M-16."

"What about the on-site security personnel?"

"That part is fuzzy, but the fact is that one of them gained access to the site and, in the process, the warhead was dropped into the launcher, damaging it, along with the guidance can and possibly the booster."

"The other man?"

"Took the equipment truck and left the site with the security personnel as a hostage. The on-site intruder then commandeered the direct com-line to the capsule, then began insisting that the squadron stick to the book. He then authenticated himself as a missile officer by identifying a key communications officer in the SAC war room. He had intimate knowledge of small scratches or something on that officer's console, knowledge one would only have if they had been physically in that room and at that console."

The Secretary of State was dumfounded. He looked to the Air Force Chief of Staff with eyes full of questions.

"It is a separate issue," Blankenship asserted. "This young officer is trying to prove who he is. He is a dead man. There is no way out for him. If he stays in the launcher with a compromised warhead, the radiation will kill him. If he comes out, the on-site security will gun him down. His only demand is that we do what we are SUPPOSED to do."

Wellburton hesitated as he reviewed the status listed on the board. "The Russians pull a high-risk launch and tell us it is nothing; some crap about satellites. This 'kid' in one of our launchers gets us to blink—to back down. What if we do, and then maybe those 'communication satellites' start raining nukes on all of us before we can respond?"

"Even from an orbiting platform we would have ten to fifteen minutes to act. They are MINUTEman Missiles, Admiral. We can return to full status and launch in seconds… once we KNOW the threat is real."

The Admiral considered his options. "And, Timber Wolf…"

"…may have been compromised!" Paxton snapped. "What if they penetrated his cover? Found out he had smuggled out pictures of their missile disguises? What if SADOK was Timber Wolf and this Gurov is using that information to get us to back down? Where is Sadok now? We don't know. Maybe they are using the code name to bait us deeper into this mess."

The NORAD speaker crackled to life: "Bogies one and two in orbit over the Indian Ocean and South China Sea."

"Where north Asian communication satellites would need to be," Blankenship stated.

Paxton said, "Or MIRV space-based launchers covering China. The one over the South China Sea might be in range for us."

"Or it is what it looks like and what they SAY it is," Wellburton sighed.

Paxton's eyes were fixed on the blips, now locked in orbit on the other side of the world. "I still don't like it."

Blankenship responded, "When have you ever liked what the book said, General? Well, Mr. Secretary?"

Adler, glancing at the notes he had taken on the phone, took a deep breath and nodded wordlessly.

Wellburton turned to an aide, "We'll do both. If they are watching, it will look like we're backing down. However, let's do this slowly and in stages. Polaris subs secure from full alert but maintain course to current launch positions."

"Good plan." Blankenship turned to Crew-cut and said softly, "Return SAC and NORAD to standard alert duty status. Turn the '52s back on a slow track. If this is a trick, I want them to midair refuel and get back on target ."

Crew-cut hesitated, "Whiteman's '52s?"

"Whiteman's birds can stand down."

# CHAPTER 50

---

*Greater love hath no man, than to*
*lay down his life for his friends.*
**Jesus Christ**

0448 Zulu
2248 Local
Kilo-11, Launcher Tube

G RAY BEGAN to see whiffs of smoke.

"Airman! You've hit the missile. It's going to blow! Get that warhead clear any way you can!"

Some of his anger and energy consumed, Willie began to consider the gravity of his present situation.

Kilo-11, Topside

Just inside the gate, Graeff was dealing with Earl: "Sir, I can't have unauthorized civilian personnel or equipment on this site. This is a highly contaminated area right now. We have a nuclear bomb that has been breached and…"

Banks burst out of the van, M-16 in hand, smoke trailing after him. "There's a fire in the booster. That bastard is gonna fry, now."

"He shot the booster?"

"No. He ain't shot nuthin'. One of my rounds must've hit it while he was duckin' and hidin'.'"

"What happens if it the bomb blows up?" Earl asked.

"The bomb won't go off, sir. Even if the missile explodes, the bomb will break apart but won't detonate," Graeff assured him.

"But won't nothing grow here for a few hundred years," Banks added.

"We gotta get it out, then," Earl said, moving to his tractor.

Graeff was out of rope but forty-five years of respecting his elders tempered his tone. "Sir, I can't begin to explain to you the danger..."

"Son. This was my land. Everything around you IS STILL my land. We're getting that thing out. NOW. Before it takes the last of what is mine."

"Sir... Going over there may very well kill you!"

"I'm saving my land. You can kill me or you can help me. Decide."

## Kilo-11, Launcher Tube

The shooting had stopped and Gray had heard the winch operator run out of the van. At least, he THOUGHT he had heard it.

The smoldering smoke from somewhere below was becoming more insistent. He could not see exactly where the smoke was coming from, but it hardly mattered. With fire below him and radiation above him, Gray was in a fix. The only way out was past a bomb leaking radiation into the arms of a crew intent on shooting him on site. The prospect of a sudden explosion and an instant death seemed worth considering.

Then, in a shower of sparks and a cacophony of crushed metal, the van disappeared from the top of the launcher—sideways. Even from below, Gray could see that it was being pushed aside by the glancing blow of a John Deere tractor. Almost immediately, cables were being dropped down beside the warhead. Gray poked his head out onto the service deck and looked up to the radiation-suited faceplate of the Sergeant Wilson Graeff.

"I warn you. We are coming in to secure these cables to the warhead," Graeff barked. "Make a move to stop us and I will shoot you where you stand."

Gray tossed the pistol up and out of the launcher, "I don't want to STOP YOU. I want to HELP YOU. Tell me what to do… but we need to hurry, Sergeant Graeff. This thing is smoking."

Earl's dragline went down one side while the Graeff and Banks stripped cable off the winch and fed it down the other side. Gray wrapped the winch cable several times around the loop in the dragline and hoped it would hold. If it separated, it not only would delay the removal, but they would think Gray had sabotaged the effort.

Graeff and Banks pulled the cable, using it to feed the dragline up from under the warhead and on up through the top of the open launcher. They now had a paired, heavy-duty cable strung under the weapon. These were bound to the hitch on Earl's John Deere.

With the cables firmly secured, Earl inched forward until the doubled dragline pulled snug against the warhead. Then, little by little, he moved forward. The cable stretched taut. The warhead did not move. Slipping and biting, the cable moved up the conical shape of the inverted warhead to the point where the cone flared wider. Then it began to tighten. Metal screeched against metal as the cables stretched to their limits.

Realizing that the booster was balanced on a steel ring suspended from cables near the bottom of the launcher; Gray put his back to the wall and pressed the missile away from the side where the warhead was binding. With the tension relieved somewhat, the bomb began to slide upward, showering Gray with what he knew must be radioactive sparks.

"HOLD IT," Gray cried out.

"The commie's trying to stop us," Banks snarled.

"Hold up, Earl," Graeff shouted.

"Will! Don't stop." It was Parker, "This guy is just trying to take us all with him."

Ignoring him for the moment, Graeff chanced a look down into the hole. Just past the warhead he could see Gray looking up at him. Smoke was starting to billow from somewhere beyond him further down the booster. "What is it?"

Gray assessed the problem and shouted, "We need a broader belly band. Once the warhead rises off the guidance system, it will fall out of these two cables. Think about it, Sergeant Graeff. You know more about the center of gravity of this thing than I do."

He did. And he knew Gray was right. Graeff called for the cargo web but was reminded that it was on the five-ton truck—which was missing.

"What is here that we can use?" Graeff demanded of his men. They just stared back at him. They had no idea.

Gray didn't either. He tried to imagine what he had seen topside that might work.

Then he made a decision.

"I think I can use... my radiation suit. Yeah. That'll work. Give me a chance to secure it."

"You take off that suit and you won't have ten minutes, Lieutenant."

"I know. But, I don't have ten minutes now."

Gray began to work his way up the crew ladder to get himself into position. His plan was to shimmy out of the suit and rig it as a belly band around the warhead. First, though, he had to get to a place where he wouldn't fall into the launcher.

Kilo-11, Topside
Earl's Point of View

Earl was holding the tractor at a precise tension. No simple task given the angle he was on and the proximity of the fence in front of him. To finish this job, he was going to have to go through that fence, pushing what was left of the van. But the Air Force boys had told him to hold for a second.

It then became pretty busy. The five-ton pulled into the site, followed by an Air Force blue Chevy Suburban full of armed men.

The sergeant in charge had jumped up from his position lying face down looking into the hole and ran to the back of the truck. Not finding whatever he was looking for, he dragged one of the men from the hole back toward the gate. At first, Earl thought the sergeant was running away, but then he came running back a few seconds later with something white and bulky in his hands yelling, "Be ready to give it all she's got, Earl."

A golden colored spaniel shot out of the Suburban, followed by a pretty, young woman with bloody arms. Then another Air Force boy in one of the blue suits they wore when they came into the Blue Inn for pie. Earl wondered if any of them ever would eat pie again.

The boy in the Air Force blue outfit stopped the woman before she could get too close. The dog had grabbed her pant leg and was pulling her backward, tugging with all his strength. The man pulled her behind the Suburban as she screamed a word that Earl couldn't make out.

Kilo-11, Launcher Tube

Where the bullets pierced the dime-thin skin of the missile, the solid fuel had become superheated by the friction. As the oxygen-impregnated solid fuel began to heat, it had begun to smolder, and now it approached the threshold of combustion.

As Gray got into the first position, he was fighting issues of balance as well as pretty poor visibility. The smoke rapidly was growing denser.

Fatigue was wearing on Gray as well. So much so that when he got braced into position to remove the radiation suit, he thought he was hearing and seeing things. First he thought he heard his name.

"GRAY!"

It sounded like Donna. Then... he thought he saw a radiation suit floating before him. Perhaps it was like the illusions that he had seen before—of missiles rising where there were none. But when he reached to touch it—it was real. Suspended from a head-set line was an empty radiation suit.

Wasting no time questioning gifts from above, Gray quickly fashioned the sling. August nights in mid-Missouri start off steamy. With no breeze, the booster on fire, and him in an air-tight radiation suit, it was getting unbearably hot.

"Lieutenant, we don't have any more time!" Willie shouted. Though he still wasn't sure he could trust the man below, it was hard to ignore the risk he was taking to save the rest of them.

"What's your name?" Gray shouted.

Surprised and a little confused he responded, "Willie. Willie Pace, Airman First."

"Willie... If this goes badly, don't let my wife near here, okay?"

Willie glanced over his shoulder at the woman being restrained by a lieutenant. "I'll do what I can, sir. But we gotta move, okay?"

"Yeah... But, also, tell her I told you to keep her away. Tell her I said so."

"I got it, sir. You're thinking of her. I got a better idea. Get this done and you tell her yourself."

"Roger that."

Gray knew that looking down was a bad idea, but in order to attach the last leg to the last cable he would have to climb above the warhead and step onto the top of the headless rocket. He had to look down through his foggy, smoke-stained faceplate in order to place his radiation-suited feet carefully on the center of the guidance can atop the missile, and not in the space between it and the launch tube wall. That's when he saw the jet of flame shooting out of the side of the booster where heat had become sufficient to fully ignite the solid fuel.

The burn would increase in size and heat as the wall of the burning pocket inside the solid fuel was consumed. The heat and expanding gases would take the path of least resistance—in this case through the bullet hole as attested to by the jet of flame shooting out of the rocket's side.

Temperature and rate of burn would increase with the increasing surface area burning. As bad as that situation was, if the burn area grew enough to penetrate the wall of the interior star-shaped core of the booster, the entire core wall would ignite in less than a second, building up heat and pressure.

The easiest place for all of that energy to escape was the open funnels at the bottom of the rocket. As designed, the missile would launch upward but with some added spin based on the number and size of the jets of exhaust from the bullet entry points in its side.

Gray figured he had maybe six seconds.

Looping the radiation suit leg around the cable, he grabbed the boots on one side with his gloved hand and the sleeves on the other side. He sat on the warhead and put his back into pushing away from the launcher wall while yelling, "GO, GRAEFF!"

"GO, EARL," echoed Graeff.

Earl gunned the John Deere. For a full second, NOTHING moved. Then many things happened, seemingly all at once.

The skin of the missile began to split open, exposing more of the solid fuel. It, too, ignited.

Flames shot upward out of the launcher.

Donna screamed her husband's name again.

Then the John Deere rocked forward very fast, pushing past the now crushed van into and through the twelve-foot perimeter fence, flattening it.

The warhead swung up out of the launcher, surrounded by flames—and was flung against the east fence.

Gray Crawford, now straddling it and holding the bellyband together by hand, was flung with it—engulfed in flames.

Inches behind him, the missile, its core penetrated and ignited, rose headless out of what was becoming a swirling inferno.

Then the splitting skin and jets of flame from the bullet entry points defeated the integrity of the skin. It exploded, sending flames, steel, and a concussive blast wave straight up and out for half a mile.

In a remarkable irony, the compressed gases shooting up from inside the launcher created a shielding wall of energy from the bottom of the launch tube upward and beyond the surface another twenty feet. This fiery wind directed much of the blast and debris over the heads of everyone on site. Much—but not all.

The crushing concussion swept everyone and everything away from the tube and into the perimeter fence—or, in Earl and the John Deere's case, the field beyond. The five-ton truck's flat surfaces acted as sails catching the bulk of the concussive wave. It flew backward over the Suburban and on through the gate. It came to rest across Missouri 18 in a crushed mass.

Donna and Matteo were partially shielded from the direct force by first the five-ton and then the crew vehicle. Nevertheless, they found themselves showered in glass from the windows and windshield and propelled backward ten feet into what remained of the south fence behind them.

# AFTER THE EVENT

# CHAPTER 51

*All's well that ends well.*
**Shakespeare**

August 8, 1974
1104 Zulu
0504 Local
Juliet-01

WITH NO response from the on-duty crew at Juliet-01 and a no-lone-zone violation in force, the rescue team began to dismantle the exterior panels of the capsule blast door in order to get to the emergency bypass pumps. These would allow them to retract the pins and gain entry. The relief crew stood by to enter the capsule. First they would secure the documents and keys. Then, they would return the capsule to operational status while the paramedics dealt with the carnage they would find.

Kilo-01, LCF

A small army of maintenance personnel stood by in the tunnel junction as the body of Captain William Pratt was removed. Lieutenant Dinkins had insisted that he would not leave the capsule before the body of his commander. Though Dinkins had inflicted the wounds himself, he had fought valiantly, but vainly, to stem the flow of blood.

The relief crew assumed control of a capsule tilted at a ridiculous angle, covered in blood and with a launch console riddled with bullets. It would take ten maintenance crew members two days to make it look like an LCC again.

Sergeant William Maxwell had refused relief and insisted that he, and he alone, would clean up the capsule.

After all, he reasoned, it was "his boys" who had gone through hell in there.

---

August 8, 1974
2514 Zulu
2014 Local
Oval Office, The White House

"… I will resign the office of President of the United States…"

0914 Local
Red Square, Moscow

Loudspeakers echoed through Red Square as the Hero of the Soviet Union Award was bestowed with grandeur upon the coffin of General Emir Sadok, "For service to Mother Russia and the world."

"A parade in Red Square. Emir, you have your fondest wish," General Gurov sighed as his mad friend's flag-draped coffin moved through the throngs of properly adoring mourners, most of whom had no notion of who he might have been. Watching the engineered spectacle unfold below him, Gurov's countenance was appropriately dour as he outwardly completed the picture of grieving comrade while inwardly rehearsing his debrief with the KGB.

"Timber Wolf will be a delicate matter," the old strategist reasoned. He could produce evidence that would convince them of Sadok's treason. It was something they wanted to believe. Convincing them to honor the grand General instead of revealing the vile traitor was a propagandist's dream. "After all," he had argued, "no one cared about the old rooster's place in history. It is the face of the Soviet Union that must be saved in this situation. What is another ribbon, another piece of tin on the chest of a dead man, against that?"

Still, it was a matter of great relief and even greater puzzlement to Gurov that Sadok's insane actions had not been met with nuclear reprisal. Whatever it was that had restrained the Americans, Gurov was deeply grateful for it. It was his fervent need to support that kind of restraint that had provoked him to send the Americans the photos in the first place. Political and military balance was so critical. Each needed to know enough of the other's secrets to be afraid. That had been Sadok's weakness. He had not been wise enough to fear.

To maintain the ruse, Timber Wolf would have to go silent now. The KGB believed he was in a box in Red Square. The CIA would know the asset had been compromised. No matter. Besides, the Americans had enough to maintain the balance at the moment. Silence was the answer, for now. General Emir Sadok had been right about one thing, however. The very best way to lie had been to tell the absolute truth—unconvincingly.

How poetic that "crying wolf" had prevented a holocaust. And the cry had come from the wolf himself.

---

August 9, 1974
1627 Zulu
The White House Lawn
1127 Local

As Nixon stood on the step of the Marine One Helicopter for the short hop to Edwards Air Force Base, SAT troops at Juliet and Kilo LCFs, along with schoolchildren, housewives, and business executives across the country, watched it unfold on television.

Edwards Air Force Base
Air Force One
1645 Zulu
1145 Local

Entering Air Force One for the last time, Richard Millhouse Nixon, 37th President of the United States, turned to his pilot of many years.

"Colonel... I had intended to make you a general. But like so many good things I intended to do, time just got away from me."

"Thank you, sir. I understand." Fighting back his own emotion, the Colonel shook his President's hand and turned to enter the cockpit.

Kilo-11

At the "pad," many crews were at work—all in those damnable suits. A huge crane was removing burned debris from the launcher and depositing it into a shielded container. A heavy-duty wrecker was trying to collect the remains of the five-ton into another such container in an effort to clear Missouri Highway 18.

In every direction there were armies of "suits" collecting every scrap of debris they could find. Around the launcher, a smaller squad of them was busy replacing fence.

For a hundred yards around the launcher, there was a distinctly visible line where vibrant green corn became brown, withered husks. In the days ahead, all of it would be mowed meticulously, every scrap collected and the topsoil removed to a depth of three feet. Then, by the truckload, it all would be carefully replaced and graded.

It had not been flame that had touched the corn. It had been something else—something that would be removed completely.

Earl sat astride his scarred and scorched John Deere three hundred yards upwind and outside the large security perimeter that the Air Force boys had established. He saw movement in the cornfield. Cautiously approaching him was the spaniel. It would not go within fifty feet of the shriveled stalks. Maybe someone would come for him. In the meantime, Earl knew how to keep a dog happy. Noggin would find he liked the man on the big machine. He would go wherever the man went—except for that place. When the man went near that place, Noggin would watch him from a distance.

In the days to come, Earl would tell the Air Force lawyers that he would not sell them any more of his land. Calmly and respectfully, he would say that he would fight them in the courts—and in the press—if they tried to make him. He knew they were sorry for what had happened, but it was his land and he'd take his chances.

He would, however, accept their settlement check for damages and as "...deep thanks for his critical assistance in a weather-related crisis."

The check would replace the lost crop. It would replace the burned hay. It would rebuild the barn.

It would rebuild many barns.

The Oval Office
1701 Zulu
1201 Local

"... I, Gerald Ford, do solemnly swear to faithfully uphold the Constitution of the United States..."

Whiteman AFB Flight Line
1801 Zulu
1201 Local

As taps was played, a small gathering rose from their folding chairs. Slowly, four flag-draped coffins, most with an honor guard of six security police, moved toward a waiting KC-135. Lieutenant Manuel Dinkins was at the front right of Captain Pratt's coffin, with Sergeant William Maxwell at the left rear.

All of the men who had lost their lives were being taken home with full military honors. All of them. No one had questioned it. They each had died serving their country to the very best of their ability.

Somber and resolute, Lieutenant Dale Matteo stood at attention behind the widows and girlfriends. Beside him in a wheelchair, unable to stand and with both arms in casts, Airman First Class Henderson wept silently as Bobby's coffin passed, carried by his fellow SAT members from Kilo.

Next to Henderson, Donna Crawford stood fighting the emotion that clawed at her throat. Beside her, face and hands blistered, her husband, Lieutenant Gray Crawford, ignored the searing pain to stand at crisp attention saluting the men whose bodies were being loaded into the belly of the big plane.

Blinking back tears of his own, Gray's eyes were distracted from the scene for a second. On the horizon to the east, he thought he saw—a missile rising.

Closing his eyes tightly and reopening them, it was still there. But it wasn't a missile. On closer examination, it was the condensation trail of an aircraft headed west. Must be a big one.

Air Force One
30,000 feet over Mid-Missouri
1815 Zulu
1215 Local

"Kansas City Air Traffic Control, this is Air Force One. By prior arrangement, our call sign will now change to Special Air Mission Two Seven Zero Zero Zero."

"Roger SAM 27000. We copy—you no longer bear the President. Call sign changed. Kansas City, out."